I0614510

Searching
for Closure

by

Iona Morrison

A Blue Cove Mystery, Book 9

Searching for Closure

Cover Art by *Debbie Taylor*

The Wild Rose Press, Inc.
PO Box 708
Adams Basin, NY 14410-0708
Visit us at www.thewildrosepress.com

Publishing History
First Fantasy Rose Edition, 2021
Trade Paperback ISBN 978-1-5092-3454-7
Digital ISBN 978-1-5092-3455-4

A Blue Cove Mystery, Book 9
Published in the United States of America

As her foot touched the walkway, Tombstone suddenly became the vibrant, active, living community of yesteryear—a pictorial window in time opened before her. The hot summer day seemed to give most of the people living in the area the same idea. Dusty streets were busy with cowboys riding into town, and buggies were filled with families hoping for a slight breeze to give them a break from the inferno. Not a hint of rain could be felt in the air. At least there was no mud to mar the hem on her new dress.

The long, green calico dress she wore slapped against her sturdy boots as she walked the wooden walkway. She caught a glimpse of her image in the bank window. Her bonnet matched her dress, with her hair tucked neatly out of view.

"You're as pretty as a picture standing there." The man tipped his hat and smiled at her as he walked out of the bank.

Taking a deep breath, excitement coursed through her. She peeked at the handsome man at her side. His holstered gun rode low across his hip, one hand never far from the handle while the other held onto hers. It seemed a tad tighter after the man addressed her. Probably only her imagination. Still, the clink of his spurs against the wood became a melodic reminder she felt safe when he was near.

Praise for *KEY TO THE PAST*

"A suspenseful, romantic fantasy about two detectives named Matt Parker and Jessie Reynolds. The...book opens with Matt and Jessie finding themselves at the center of a murder mystery. The twist? To crack the case, Jessie must travel to a new dimension, while Matt stays in the present to put the rest of the pieces of the case together. With a compelling story line, relatable characters and mind-bending twists and turns, author Iona Morrison has delivered a truly remarkable book...a page turner that will keep you on the edge of your seat from start to finish!"

~The Book Excellence Awards
~*~

"A book I have read and enjoyed. Heavily romantic contemporary for those fans, with intrigue and time travel to broaden interest. I see why this author is popular!"

~R. Anderson

~*~

"Anxiously awaiting your new book! Love them all!"
~Heidi (Canada)
~*~

"I'm so happy this author is continuing to write in this series. Jesse and Matt and all the other characters have become like family and their adventures are real page-turners! Can't wait for the next one!"

~Vickie

~*~

"I really appreciate your writing style. It flows so nicely."

~Rick

Dedication

Dedicated in memory of Blanche Morrison.
Born with Down Syndrome,
she lived a rich and full life.
A loving person who wanted everyone to get along,
Blanche had a knack for making people laugh.
Her smile and her funny comments are missed.

Chapter 1

Peyton Reynolds wilted the minute the blast of stifling, hot air hit her face. The terminal door slid closed, taking the cool air with it and leaving her standing in the sweltering heat of the Arizona sun. Chalk this up as another one of her friend's crazy ideas that she had gotten sucked into. A smile pulled at the corner of Peyton's lips despite her momentary annoyance. No matter how hard she tried, she was an easy mark when it came to her friend. But she could count on Destiny for a fun adventure every time. Pulling her suitcase to a small shaded alcove near the building, she waited for the next bus. At this point, all she cared about was did her rental car have great AC.

"Is it warm enough for you, little lady?" an airport attendant strolling by asked. His eyes twinkled as he stopped to talk with her.

He stood close enough for her to see the sweaty sheen on his neck and the moisture on the collar of his shirt. "Yes, sir." She smiled at him. How anyone could work outside in this heat was beyond her. "Is it always this hot?" she asked. Soggy strands of hair plastered themselves against the back of her neck. She lifted her tresses, fanning the hot skin underneath the heavy waves.

"It's hot all right. You've managed to get here during our first major scorcher of the season. It's unusually hot for this early in the summer. A real sizzler." He leaned his hip against the building.

"Wouldn't you know it, I had to arrive in time for a heatwave." She slapped her hand playfully to her forehead feeling the moisture being sucked out of her face as she talked. Okay, maybe a tad dramatic, but she could imagine freckles were even now vying to see which one would show up first on the bridge of her nose.

"Are you waiting for a taxi or bus?" the man asked.

"A bus to the rental cars." She told him the name of the company while waving her small notebook like a fan in front of her face.

"You won't have long to wait. I can see several of them coming now." His chin lifted, pointing toward where several buses were coming around the curve. "Get on the one with the company's name on it, and they'll drop you at the door."

"Thank you. Do you mind if I ask you a personal question?"

"Fire away." He swiped at the sweat running down his cheek.

"How do you work in this heat?" She was positive that, as she stood there, the glass of water she drank only moments ago was now exiting her underarms in the form of sweat.

"You get used to the heat, reminding yourself it's all worthwhile when everyone else is shoveling snow." He chuckled. "Where are you from?" He shifted his weight.

"I grew up in a small town in Indiana, but I've spent the last several years living and working in the New York City area." She pushed up her purse strap slipping down her arm.

"Lots of heat and humidity in New York. We have dry heat here." He lifted his hat and wiped the moisture from his forehead.

"You sure do. I can tell the difference in my skin." Her skin seemed dry to the touch even as the sweat trickled down her cheek.

"If it's going to be hot, I prefer it dry. In fact, the drier the better. Hot or cold temps with humidity, that's miserable to me." He smiled and reached for her case. "Your bus is here. Let me help you with this." He waited for her to get inside and lifted the suitcase up to her.

"Thank you." She pressed a tip into his hand. "Get yourself something cold to drink."

He nodded. "Have a nice day and enjoy your visit to our fair city. Remember to drink lots of water and use plenty of sunscreen." He grinned and tipped his hat. "Better yet, stay inside." He winked.

Melt outside or stay inside. Hmm, let's see, it's a no-brainer. She sat in an open seat as the bus began to move. Destiny—her best friend—and her cousin Jessie had played her. It might take some creative thinking on her part, but she would get back at them. They would rue the day they messed with her. She wanted to laugh, but she was afraid her face would crack.

At least for a couple of days before Destiny arrived, she would be staying at a resort in Scottsdale. She planned on cranking up the air, and when the sun went down if anyone wanted her, they'd find her poolside until it closed for the night.

Once the paperwork was signed, getting in the car wasn't easy. The handles were hot to the touch, which was nothing compared to the inside of the car. She got in only long enough to start the engine and turn the AC on before she stepped out for a moment. Hades couldn't be much hotter than this.

She smiled remembering the first time she had heard Destiny tell her all about the burning fires of hell. Destiny had embellished a Sunday school teaching she had heard after they had stolen some flowers from the Thompsons' yard. She promised Peyton they were surely headed to that fiery place in a hurry. Then she added with her childish flair, "And we can't pass go or collect any money on the side." Her childhood had been tolerable because of her friend. Not to mention the fun they had together on each one of their crazy escapades. Any time she could sneak out of the house and hang with Destiny was a good day.

Slipping into the slightly cooler rental, she programmed the GPS. Heavy traffic plus new surroundings added up to her missing the exit and having to drive around another time. Only when the airport was in the rearview mirror did the tension in her hands and shoulders subside. "Finally." She sighed. "Maybe this won't be a total disaster after all."

The vistas were surprisingly beautiful with all the palm trees, super blue skies, the mountains to the east of the city, and with cactus standing tall and proud. A tour of the area would be one of the many things on her agenda. She hadn't taken a vacation for a few years and might need to learn how to be a tourist all over again. An education she looked forward to. Her grandma Sadie booked her a room at the Desert Palms Resort as a gift and had spared no expense. Included was a spa day which she planned to take full advantage of.

The leave of absence she recently took to help her grandmother move also gave her a chance to catch up with her cousin. It had been over a year since they last lunched at their favorite place in New York and even longer for one of their crazy road trips together. She missed Jessie living close more than she had thought possible. But the move had turned out to be a great decision on Jessie's part. She seemed different, stronger this time, and more self-assured than Peyton remembered her. Everything Peyton wanted to be but never seemed to arrive at.

Growing up they both were bookworms and honor roll students. At least Peyton became known as a great student after her first and only display of a potent, unbending strong will. Her kindergarten teacher Miss Draper had told her if she couldn't behave herself to put on her coat and go home. To which she promptly replied okay and left the school with the teacher in hot pursuit. Miss Draper got in trouble, but Peyton got more than she bargained for. Had the principal not came to her rescue, she would have been kicked out of class permanently and had to be homeschooled. Not good, not good at all. Her will remained strong but tempered and out of view from that day until the day she left home. She might have been sitting when she was told to, but she was standing in her heart. That strong will helped her survive and protect her sister.

Even now as an adult, she frequently retreated to a well-ordered, disciplined, and semi-boring life of all work and no play. Her safe place. Suffice it to say, she wasn't standoffish like everyone believed, but it was convenient to keep that as her persona for now. Her cousin's life, on the other hand, had gone all the way to strange, new, and exciting when she moved to be near her friend Katie Donovan in Blue Cove.

Older by a year than her cousin, Peyton had always thought of herself as more worldly and wise. Not anymore. "It's past time for you to get a life." Giving herself a pep talk, she turned her signal on and moved into the turn lane. "Arizona adventure, hot weather and all, here I come."

The resort didn't disappoint. Picture perfect like the brochure, it was beautiful. The attendant opened the car door for her. As she stepped out of the car, the blast of hot air reminded her once again of the intense sun and heat. A big, floppy hat was first on her list to buy. She didn't want any more freckles across the bridge of her nose than she already had. Sadie used to tell her they were angel kisses and gave her face character. Her greatest wish as a teen had been that they would all grow together into a glorious tan. No such luck! The word tan couldn't be used in a sentence to describe her. She was whiter than the color white. Thank heavens for self-tanners.

"Welcome to Scottsdale's Desert Palms Resort. Are you here to check in?" the young man asked, closing her car door. He gave her the once over, rushing ahead to hold the next door open.

"I am." She smiled as she brushed past him into the wonderful, cool lobby.

"Enjoy your stay with us." He thanked her when she turned and pressed a tip into his hand.

Check-in took no time. Sadie had handled everything from her end. The staff was welcoming and accommodating. The meticulously manicured Desert Palms was a lovely resort with lots of amenities which she couldn't wait to explore. Slipping the keycard into the lock, she opened the door to a luxurious poolside room with a huge king-size bed. The soft blues and greens of the room gave it a restful feel. The pops of red, orange, and yellow made the suite visually appealing. And best of all the room was comfortably cool.

For now, the absurd idea of spending time on horseback and sleeping under the stars on the trail were completely forgotten and replaced with lavish surroundings. She smiled, stretching out on the bed. She could get used to this. With any luck, Destiny would forget the whole silly idea and choose to stay in the city when she got a load of the heat.

After a leisurely dinner of chicken piccata, Peyton put on her favorite bikini and suit cover to hang out near the pool. She wouldn't go as far as to describe the temperature as cool exactly but maybe less hot. The sunset was gorgeous, awash with colors like an artist's brush against the canvas of the sky. Hues of pinks, purples, and flaming oranges were breathtaking. Her phone camera wasn't doing the sunset justice. But Sadie had to see the photos of the amazing sky. She sent off a quick text with several pictures included.

Stretching out on the chaise lounge, she closed her eyes, shutting out her cares and concerns. Her mind drifted to more pleasant possibilities and eventually sleep. The sound of a woman's piercing scream awakened her a while later. Disoriented, she opened her eyes, staring up into a darkening sky which made the moment seem even more ominous. Jumping to her feet with a racing heart, she searched for the source of the screams. Instead of running away, she rushed toward the screaming woman.

She helped two resort employees lift the limp man out of the water and position him on the ground. Training and instinct kicked in next. She took charge starting CPR on the victim, teaming with one of the employees. Close to a minute later, Peyton realized why they weren't seeing any results and stopped the chest compressions. "It's no use," she told the young man helping her.

"Isn't there something more you can do?" the woman pleaded.

"I'm sorry," Peyton said. "He's not responding." She stood up and moved out of the way as the paramedics arrived. She put her arm around the woman, hugging her trembling body. "Do you know him?"

"No. I saw him when I jumped into the water." The older woman shook her head, wiping the tears gathering her eyes. "I don't want to go back into that pool again. Ever. I wonder how long he was down there on the bottom."

"I don't know." Peyton glanced at the body, not wanting to mention the fact she thought he was dead long before the woman found him. Together they watched the scene play out in front of them. She couldn't help but question why no one had noticed him.

She counted herself fortunate to have made it to this point in life never having to see a dead person. Not good that the first time had to be a murder. She shivered along with the lady who trembled beside her. *Why?* played over and over in her mind. Who would kill such a handsome young man? She wished her eyes could unsee what she had seen.

A man's deep voice cut into the thoughts racing

through her mind. "I have some questions I want to ask you both." A tall man approached them showing the women his badge. "I was told you found the man when you jumped in the pool, is that correct?" He looked at the woman beside her.

"Yes," the tiny woman replied.

"What's your name for the record?" his gruff, intimidating voice asked.

"Alice, Alice Wittman," the woman stammered.

"Tell me what happened." His tone brusque.

"I went for a swim after dinner, and I swam to this end of the pool." She pointed to the spot. "He was just lying there on the bottom not moving when I saw him." Alice shivered, and Peyton handed her a dry towel to put around her shoulders.

"What did you do next?" The man's voice inflection changed little.

"I screamed. I'm sure that's what I did." Her voice softened, and he moved closer to hear her.

"Yes, she did. I heard her." She squeezed the woman's shoulder gently.

"And your name is?" He looked directly at Peyton. One of his brows arched with the question.

"Peyton Reynolds." She glanced into a pair of honey brown eyes that seemed to look straight through her. Those eyes were framed with dark, thick lashes, which hardly seemed fair that a man should have such ridiculously long lashes. They fit somehow with his tanned skin and sun-streaked, sandy-blond hair. Her mind seemed to be as nervous as she felt. *Focus, Peyton, how he looks doesn't matter*.

"Continue." He slipped his badge back in his pocket.

Her body tensed. "When Alice screamed, I jumped up to help. After the man was lifted out of the water, we did CPR. It took me a minute or two to realize it wouldn't help." She frowned at him, her eyes dropping to the gun holstered on his belt.

"What made you think it wouldn't help?" the detective asked her pointedly. "Are you a doctor?"

"No. But I could see the victim had a small caliber bullet hole near his temple. He was already dead. CPR wouldn't help." She wished she had softened the answer seeing the expression of shock on Alice's face.

"How did you know it was a bullet and not a wound from hitting his head?" He shifted his weight but never took his sight off her.

"Let's just say it appeared that way to me." She paused, hiding her shaking hands. "If you're finished, I would like to leave." She turned her back to walk away.

"I'm not finished with you yet," he snapped. "Tell me how you came to your conclusion." His hands fisted at his side as he scrutinized her.

"I work for a large publishing house in the cozy mystery division. Believe me I have to know about guns, the size of wounds they make, and the difference between a hit on the head and a bullet wound." His tough guy attitude was getting on her nerves. Did he even have a name, for heaven's sake? It didn't help they were watching her either. Peyton didn't want to cry or, worse yet, get sick. She could feel the bile rising in her throat and gulped to hold it back.

"Did either of you see anyone acting strange or who looked out of place near the pool?" He folded his arms across his chest as he quickly changed the subject, taking them both by surprise.

"No, no one," Alice told him.

"I didn't see anyone, but I had fallen asleep," she said, blushing. "Are you finished with us, or do you have more questions?" His grim expression summed up the turmoil going on inside her head. Not knowing what he was thinking worried her, but the fear churning up her insides had nothing to do with him.

"Make sure you give the officer your personal information. Then you're free to go." He pointed them in the right direction. "Don't leave town until I tell you that you can leave. We may need to talk to you again."

Peyton wrote her information down for the young officer. Shaken to the core, she needed time to think about what had just happened. She had seen plenty of photos of bullet wounds but never on a real person. Did it make her look guilty that she told him she knew the wound was made by a small caliber gun? She had no idea since the detective's facial expression never changed the entire time. It was impossible to tell what he was thinking. He'd asked for their names but never told them his. She was positive he did that on purpose to intimidate them. See if she helped anyone again. Slowly anger and fear gave way to tears. Wrapping her arms around her middle, she let herself fall apart. Maybe she was more like her cousin Jessie than she realized. She couldn't tell the cop how she knew the young man was dead. It wasn't only the bullet hole she had seen.

Chapter 2

Ghosts were not new to her. Peyton had plenty in her life. But not the variety she had seen at the pool. There were things in her past that she had never told anyone. Oh, she had wanted to confide in her cousin, but she didn't want to dredge up the mess she called family. Questions Sadie had asked her over the years had Peyton speculating whether her grandmother knew more than she let on.

She thought of her so-called wonderful family as a mirage. As soon as she was old enough to leave home, she had. Followed a couple of years later by her sister Madison. How many times had the two sisters huddled in the refuge of the closet while the endless yelling filled most of their nights? Late fear-filled nights were only a small part of their childhood. The rest she chose to push out of her thoughts as often as they rushed into haunt her.

But even with all her family secrets, what she had witnessed at the pool could make her question her sanity. Her grandmother or cousin would have answers—at least she hoped one of them would. She picked up the phone to call and let it ring several times. Finally. "Hi, Grams."

"Hi, Peyton, you called at the perfect time. Jessie and I were sitting here talking," Sadie said as she answered. "How is your adventure going?" She sounded a bit out of breath. "Sorry it took me so long to answer. I had to find my phone. I think I've been around Jessie too long. I'm forever misplacing it."

Peyton chuckled. She could picture several times as Jessie searched for her phone when they were together. "Did you get the photos I texted you?"

"Yes, they were simply stunning. I might have to head that way in the winter. I'm not a fan of the snow and cold anymore. I'll put you on speaker," Sadie said as she swiped the icon.

"The pictures didn't do justice to how beautiful the sky looked," Peyton told them.

"How's the weather, Cous?" Jessie laughed.

"As if you didn't know. I'll get you back for this someday." Peyton took a deep breath to calm her rattled nerves. "In the meantime, I need to talk to someone. Since you're both there, I hope one of you might have answers for me." Peyton curled her legs under her as she sat in the comfy chair. She explained what had happened earlier, leaving out only a few details. "I'm sure the detective thought it was strange that I knew it was a small caliber weapon."

"Oh, Peyton, dear, I'm sorry this had to happen on the first day of your trip. You didn't need the stress of a murder."

"All teasing aside, cousin, I'm sorry too. What aren't you telling us?" Jessie asked.

"I stopped the CPR when I noticed them staring at me." Peyton paused. "Not them exactly, but the young man's ghost and then another spirit that watched from a distance."

"Well, Grams, I guess that answers your question." Jessie's voice came across the line.

"What question?" Peyton asked. She took a sip of water, listening to them talk back and forth.

"I had wondered, dear, if you would exhibit in time the same ability as many women in the Reynolds family have. I know that life hasn't been easy for you and Madison. We'll talk more about it another time. At least now I know."

"Know what, Grandma?" She closed the curtains in her room. The pool area had lots of police presence and noise.

"You also can see," Sadie replied.

"Yeah, well I don't like it. I don't want to see anything else," Peyton emphatically answered. "It's another family trait I can live without and be happy about."

"It doesn't work that way." Sadie sighed. "Just ask Jessie."

"I've had enough craziness in my life. I only want a bit of peace and quiet for the rest of it. If that's possible." Peyton shuddered to even think about any more stress being added right now.

"Oh, dear, don't we all. We can hope this will be all you see. But I have a feeling that your life is about to be turned upside down, or maybe I should say right side up."

"Cous, you can call me anytime. I know how daunting this all can be," Jessie told her.

"I'll hold you to it. I don't suppose you'd want to come to Arizona and spend a little time with me." She crossed her fingers, holding her breath, hoping Jessie would say yes. "Don't make me beg."

"I would if I could, but Katie's bridal shower is coming fast, and I'm planning it. You know the duties of the maid of honor—you've been one often enough. I need to be here for my friend. Katie reminds me of my duties every day." Jessie paused. "As impossible as it seems, you'll do fine. Stay clear of the hunky cop though. Especially if you want to only have this happen one time." Jessie laughed.

"I never said anything about the detective's looks." Peyton scrunched her face.

"It's what you didn't say that told me all I needed to know. I reacted to Matt the same way when I first met him. Here's a word of advice—run and don't get involved. Come back to the Cove. There are plenty of handsome guys here. Otherwise, you might find yourself living in the heat of Arizona for years to come." Jessie and Sadie both laughed. "Grams, I think we may be too late to rescue our girl."

"Jessie, dear, behave yourself," Sadie scolded with the sound of amusement in her voice. "You follow this where it takes you, Peyton, and we'll be here for you all the way."

"That's the problem. You'll be there for me, but I need you here," she whined.

"If you find you need me, I will come, I promise," Sadie told her. "Give it your best and call us any time."

"I will. One more question before I hang up. Jess, how did you deal with it?" Peyton peeked out the curtain when she heard a loud noise at the pool. "I'm still shaking." The chills felt like spiders crawling up and down her arms whenever she pictured those two sad faces.

"It took me a while to come to terms with what I saw until I understood there was a higher purpose in it all. Now I take the down times when I get them and embrace the other when it comes at me. I also told Matt and let him think what he would about me." Silence filled the air for a moment as no one talked. "Peyton, remember you come to terms with it eventually when you see that you're helping people."

"What about in the meantime?" she asked.

"I had Reba and Sadie. You have all three of us," Jessie said.

"One more question. Who is going to tell me what to do next?" Peyton fiddled with the fringe on one of the pillows.

"We all will, dear, but mostly the ghosts will be the ones to tell you. They'll tell you in their own way what they want from you. Chin up, sweetheart, you've got this." Sadie's calm, reassuring voice carried comfort through the line.

"Thanks, I think. Love you both. I'll call you tomorrow." She checked the locks and went into the bathroom to remove her makeup. Seeing that young woman's ghost staring at the body of the young man was hitting too close to home. They were involved somehow. Had her body been found yet? She would love to ask but didn't want to give that rude man the time of day. Pulling out her laptop, she decided there was one way to find out. With the click of a button and her trusty mouse she searched recent murders and missing persons in the area but found nothing.

****

Jaxon Kincaid had followed her retreat until she was out of sight. He had it all under control until her gorgeous hazel-green eyes locked on his. Damn, he couldn't remember his own name for the next ten minutes. She was the total package with her fresh peaches and cream complexion complete with a smattering of freckles across the bridge of her nose. A real looker, and as far as he was concerned a complication he didn't need or want. He had bumbled his interview with the two women and would have to question them all over again. Not something he looked forward to. He had never reacted to a woman as quickly as he had her. Damn. He raked his hand through his hair.

A background check after she left confirmed the information she had given him. She worked in New York—that should cool his jets. Still, she played across his mind often, and he would like to know more. Starting with what she was hiding from him. He could smell her fear and saw it written on her beautiful face.

Reynolds was right about one thing. The man was dead long before she tried to do CPR on him. Why hadn't anyone seen him at the bottom of the pool? He already knew the victim's name the minute he looked at the body. Elliot Dawson Jr., aka E J, a high roller, playboy type who had plenty of enemies. Question was: who pulled the trigger? Dawson was no stranger to trouble in the Valley of the Sun. Jaxon's department knew him all too well. Dawson skirted his way in and out of trouble often enough that his father had a revolving account with the judiciary system. He paid whatever he needed to whenever his son found himself in a bad situation, which was often. Anything to make it go away.

"Guess Elliot won't be able to fix it for his son this time," he muttered under his breath. Jaxon opened the door to his car. He turned the key and cranked up the AC. E J might have been a troublemaker, but Jaxon didn't relish telling his parents their son and only child was dead. Any parent's worst nightmare. Murder was a heck of a way to die, as if there was a good means. His team were on their way to E J's condo with orders to collect any computers and electronics, among other possessions which might shed some light on the whys of his death. A time-consuming process but necessary. Another investigation begins and one more family's lives will change forever.

His car knew the way to Dawson's house. As a police officer, he had driven there on more than one occasion with an arrest warrant. Somehow, he had managed to forge a friendship with Elliot Dawson Sr. despite all the times he had arrested his kid. Now, as one of the newest homicide detectives, the job of telling his friend was dumped in his lap by the captain.

The Dawsons' beautiful home located on Camelback Mountain offered all who entered an incredible view of the city from the floor to ceiling windows on the entire side of the house. The view alone had to be worth a pretty penny, and Elliot had made plenty over the years. E J was more than willing to spend his dad's money while doing little in the way of work. He wasn't a complete wastrel but close to it.

What did all that money do to secure their happiness? He shook his head. They'd lost their son and only heir. Damn, life was a mystery at times. He turned onto the winding road leading to the elite community built on the side of the mountain.

E J was mixed up in something, Jaxon was sure of it. Whatever it was, the younger Dawson couldn't charm his way out of it this time. Damn. His fingers tapped the steering wheel in frustration. Moments like this made him want to reconsider why he stayed. His car came to a stop in the circular drive in front of the sprawling home. Pausing for a moment, he gave a fleeting glance at the panoramic view of the lights of the city. At any other time, it would have captured his attention, but now it only reminded him of the unpleasant task at hand. Taking a deep breath, he rang the doorbell. His mind grasped at how to approach the subject.

"Hey, Jaxon, what did my kid do now?" Elliot Sr. asked as soon as he opened the door and saw him standing there. "He's not here, and we haven't heard from him in a couple of days. Nothing new—he does that often."

"Mr. Dawson, we need to talk." His words sounded grim even to his ears.

"Why so formal? We're friends. Now you've got me worried." Elliot motioned for him to come in.

"I'm afraid I've got some bad news for you." Jaxon went in wishing he could hightail it out of there.

"Lay it on me." Elliot called for his wife. The two of them sat side by side on the couch. He reached for his wife's hand, anxiety written on both their faces.

"There's no easy way to tell you this." Jaxon struggled for the right words, but they evaded him. Instead, he blurted out, "Your son's body was recovered from the pool at the Desert Palms Resort earlier."

"Are you telling me that E J drowned? Impossible! He was a champion swimmer. Had the damn fool kid been drinking?" He swiped at the tears rolling down his cheeks.

"Only an autopsy and toxicology can tell us if there

was anything in his system, but drowning isn't what killed him. Your son also had a bullet wound. I suspect he was murdered." The words hung in the air like a knife between them.

"Murdered. What was E J involved in? Murdered! I can't believe it." Elliot shook his head, holding his sobbing wife in his arms. "Why would someone murder our boy?" Anguish filled his voice.

Jaxon could think of several reasons, which he wouldn't repeat. "It's too early in the case to have many answers, but we intend to find out. I'm sorry, Elliot; I know this has to be a shock to you and your wife. I wish I could've softened the blow." He leaned forward in the chair. "Can I call some friends for you? I don't think you should be alone." No matter how much he had rehearsed the words, they still came out the same—cold and final.

After their neighbors and friends showed up, Jaxon took his leave. His friend was devastated but realistic.

Driving down the mountain back to the station, he had plenty of time to go over their conversation. Elliot had known his son was headed for trouble but couldn't seem to halt his rush toward catastrophe no matter how hard he had tried to stop him. Jaxon committed himself to find the answers for his friend.

Chapter 3

Peyton propped the pillows up behind her back and stretched out her legs. Her mind raced from one thought to another. The colorful brochures of local tourist attractions in her hand had lost some of their appeal. Although, she admitted, Tombstone did sound interesting. More than a few westerns had their setting in the desert town. One of her favorite books was a western mystery complete with a ghost. The idea of a ghost at the time she read the book seemed innocent. At this moment not so much. Surreal was the best word to describe the situation in which she found herself presently.

Reaching for her phone, she called her friend Destiny. Why hadn't she returned any of her calls? Her friend was up to something. Maybe avoiding her because she was going to be a no show. Truth be told Peyton hoped that Destiny would back out of coming. It would come as no surprise, and she no longer felt like being a tourist anyway. All she wanted to do was go home. As soon as the detective no longer needed her in the area, she would be out of here. After several rings, the phone went right to Destiny's voicemail where she left another message. "Hey, girl, this is me again. Call back as soon as you get this message. We need to talk."

Turning on her laptop she scrolled through emails as she waited to hear from her friend. Most of them were from work, colleagues, or her dad, and she had no intention of dealing with any messages now. "No work" was her mantra for the last several weeks, and she planned on keeping it that way. She wanted to enjoy every moment left on her break. Only a few of the long list of emails needed immediate attention anyway.

Peyton pushed speed dial. "Hi, sis, I got your email. What's up?"

"Where are you? I tried calling you at work, and they said you had taken some time off, which doesn't sound like my workaholic sister." Madison sounded worried.

"I'm in Arizona. Remember I told you about my crazy trip with Destiny? Madi, you can't believe how hot it is here. How would you like to join me?" she asked.

"I forgot about your trip. Hot? No, thanks. I'm not into hot or anything outdoors." Madison laughed. "Come to think of it neither are you. Is your skin red and blotchy yet?"

"You know me too well. I'm no outdoor girl, and so far, I'm still the fairest of the fair." She chuckled. "You'll never believe what happened to me today." Peyton told her about the young man found in the pool.

"Geeze, sis, are you kidding me?" Madison's voice registered her disbelief.

"No, I'm telling you the truth. While I was doing CPR, I noticed the bullet wound. He was murdered, and, Madi, he was young. It's all so sad. I want to go home." Peyton scrolled through the rest of her emails as she talked.

"I don't blame you. I'd want to leave too. I'd

already be on the first plane out of there. Leave. What are you waiting for?" Madison's voice went up a notch in her excitement.

"No can do. I have to stay in the area until the authorities are through with me."

"Why? Do they think you murdered the guy? They couldn't possibly. Not you." Madison paused. "I'll tell them. You're the best sister. I can tell them about how you protected me. You couldn't hurt anyone. They can't think that you killed him. Unbelievable." Madison's voice became angrier with each of her statements.

"Of course not! Calm down," Peyton told her. "I'm sure I'll be able to leave soon." She paused and changed the subject. "Why did you want me to call? I bet I can guess, but I'll let you tell me."

"Okay, here goes." Madison expelled a deep breath. "Dad called." She rushed on. "He said you weren't returning his calls, and he wanted me to get in touch with you. I never told him I would. I thought you should know he's promising to go into rehab again."

"One can hope he does, and that it works. What's his reason this time?"

"Well, he was a bit incoherent. The gist I got is that he's lost everything, Mom's leaving him, and he needs us to bail him out. He said he's ready to get help for real."

"How many times have we heard him sing this song over the years?" She rubbed her hand across her forehead. "I'm not giving him another dime, and you shouldn't either, Madison. We've taken care of them most of our lives, and it hasn't helped yet."

"I know you're right, but when he starts crying, I

feel my resolve slipping away. I need you to help me get it back." Madison sighed.

"We have to help each other remain strong. I think Grandma Sadie knows something isn't right with Dad and Mom. I have no idea how much she knows, but I think she will help us confront Dad. It's long overdue. We need reinforcements. Maybe then they can get real help and not just money relief." Peyton crossed her fingers.

"I told him he wouldn't get anything from me, and I doubted that you would help them either. Still he begged me to get in touch with you," Madison explained. "So here I am."

"I'm glad you told him I wouldn't help. I stopped taking his calls because I didn't want to deal with him anymore."

"For the most part, I've stopped taking a lot of his calls too. But it hasn't stopped him from calling and leaving me messages every day." Madison sighed. "I'm done with our lovely parents. Life was hell for me after you left."

"I know, Madi." Her voice was tinged with regret.

"Don't feel bad. I'm glad you got out when you did. And besides, I believe I'm making progress. This was the first time I've ever stood up to him. You know how intimidating he can be."

"I sure do. I determined to never be taken in by him again, but every time he started the crying routine, like a softy, I forgot my decision. The only way I could break the cycle was to not talk to him at all. I'm following my therapist's counsel." Peyton pushed the stray hair that had fallen in her face behind her ear.

"I took your advice and I'm talking to a therapist

too. Still, I don't want to be cold-hearted. They are our parents after all. What are we going to do?" Madison asked.

"We aren't going to do anything, Madi. We've enabled them all these years while they were making victims out of us. This time we are going to let our grandma and Dad's brother handle him. We've carried this long enough. It's someone else's turn. That's the way our love can best help them."

"I'm glad you called me back, sis. I always second-guess my decision when it comes to them. Are you going to ask Grandma for help?"

"I am," Peyton replied. "I'll call you back as soon as I talk to Grams. She'll know what we should do."

"Sounds good. Until you leave Arizona, promise me you'll be careful. You're the only one who cares about me. I'd be lost without you."

"We've managed to make it this far together, and we'll keep looking out for one another. Plus, we have Grams and Jessie. I know they'll do what they can. Don't answer any more of his calls. I'll get back to you soon. Love you, Madi."

"I love you right back."

As soon as she said goodbye to Madison, Peyton began to hatch a plan to tell Sadie about her dad. Surely none of her relatives understood the troubles of their childhood, or they would have intervened years ago. She shook her head to dispel the images surfacing that she had worked hard to bury the past few years. Right now, she could only handle one ghost at a time, and the two she saw at the pool were more than enough.

Shutting off the light, she laid her head back against the pillow. Images raced in and out of her mind.

No ghosts and no men, you hear me, girl. You don't need another complication in your life. She closed her eyes, but she couldn't shut off her mind.

****

He pulled the car into the parking space. This had been one hell of day. Grabbing the files off the back seat, he clicked the locks, setting the security system. Jaxon had promised himself he would buy a more permanent place if he ever got a promotion. He got the promotion, but he never kept the promise to himself. At this point, he was happy he hadn't made the big commitment. Waiting to hear about whether he had got the job he had applied for with the FBI took up most of his leisure time. He searched for condos and houses near his family every chance he got. Not having to worry about selling a place would make a move a lot simpler for him down the road.

Another time and place, possibly he would've pursued the attraction he had for Peyton Reynolds. It seemed to come out of nowhere, and thoughts of her were still hanging around. He was a rational man. He knew a relationship with her couldn't go anywhere. He didn't want it to. Bottom line, the sooner he got the next interview out of the way and satisfied the nagging gut feeling he had that she wasn't being upfront with him, the sooner he could get her out of his life.

She had told him the truth. All her answers and information had checked out. What was the problem? It was the way she looked when she answered those questions that still made him wonder. Hell, it made no sense even now as he tried to rationalize how he felt talking to her. It was as if she saw something no one else could see about the crime—which wasn't possible.

Still, he would question her one more time before moving on.

Opening the file on E J Dawson, he wrote down his observations from the crime scene. The murder investigation was only in the beginning stages. E J's file, on the other hand, was huge. Somewhere buried in all these pages was a clue to what had happened to Dawson today. Starting at the first arrest, Jaxon made his way through one report after another until his stomach growled, reminding him he hadn't eaten since breakfast.

He made his way to the kitchen, grabbing bread and sandwich makings along with a cold beer. After he satisfied his hunger, he got back to work. There seemed to be a trend he saw as he read over the files. Like most criminals, E J started out with petty crimes and worked his way up to more serious offenses over time. Dawson's last arrest was thrown out on a technicality by the judge. If he had been convicted, there would have been some serious jail time. Who knows if it would have helped or made things worse in his life? Always getting off with a slap on the wrist hadn't helped, and now he was dead. Elliot Sr. was a prominent figure in the life of the city. He had friends in high places, including several judges. The system didn't always work the same way for everyone. If E J were like most of the other boys in the city, he would have gone to jail a long time ago. After another hour of poring over files, he set them aside and let his thoughts take over.

Stretching out on the bed in the darkness of the room, he laid his head back on the pile of pillows behind him. The dull ache of an overused shoulder along with his tired body told the story of his early morning workout. Still his mind raced with thoughts that were hard to shut down. Beautiful hazel-green eyes framed with lush dark lashes weren't easy to forget, but he would find a way. Her incredible legs were a different story. He palmed his face. Reason told him this wasn't the time in his career for distraction, no matter what attractive package it came in. Yet here she was, a major distraction, and everything about her appealed to him. Except for maybe the flash of fire in her lovely green eyes. She didn't like him, and he had done that purposely. Ms. Reynolds would forget him, and eventually he'd forget her too.

Chapter 4

Peyton awakened with a start. Struggling to adjust her eyes to the dark room, she turned to glance at the clock. Two a.m. Darn. What had startled her? Silence filled the air, not a sound, yet an unsettled feeling engulfed her. Seeing the young man's lifeless body pulled out of the water played repeatedly through her mind. An image she would never forget, nor his ghost watching her perform CPR. Her life in one strange moment had become complicated. Odd as it seemed to say aloud, the other spirit who watched from a distance wanted her help.

Leave now, her mind screamed. But how could she walk away? Many times over the years, she had dreamed of someone coming to help her and Madi. Never uttering a word to anyone of their plight. No help ever came because no one knew. Madi's call earlier had reminded her of the cost of never speaking up, which is what they both should have done. They were too scared to say a word. Maybe those words could have helped their parents too. Had this girl been too afraid to ask for help? There had to be a reason Peyton could see her and know what she wanted.

Funny how plans could change. Determined to leave on the next flight, she was now ready to stay. Help was what the ghost was looking for, and help was what she would get. Peace came with her decision.

Adventure and a life, wasn't that what she had asked for? It appeared she was about to find one. She would stay for as long as it took.

And the nameless, rude detective who wouldn't want her help would simply have to live with it. She knew his type. He had made his feelings quite clear in his dismissive attitude. She would simply go around him. *If it's a fight he wants, it's a fight he'll get.* His unchanging, grim expression had told her he wouldn't go down easily, but neither would she. Fairly sure she was in for a fight, she had to find a way to take him on. Stubborn wasn't a foreign concept to her. *No more being passive, Peyton Reynolds. You are going to follow through with this. Do it for yourself, for Madi, and the ghost who asked for help.*

She closed her eyes, and the shadowy faces of spirits gathered at a distance. Their whispering voices reminded her of the wind blowing. They flittered through the air, moving ever closer. The nearer they came, the louder their cries swelled, until the hum of their collective voices drowned out all other sounds. "Help." The sorrowful wails increased until she could no longer stand the clamor. Covering her ears, she opened her eyes, trying to escape their presence, but they were there—filling every corner of the room. Each one a tortured soul who had suffered some untold misery in life and was asking her for help. Her help. What could she do? She knew the sad look all too well. She had witnessed it on Madi's face and often on her own. One face stood out among the others. Hovering close—she had seen her earlier at the pool. "I'll help you," Peyton whispered. Maybe she would find peace when the ghost found peace. It was possible this was her ticket to freedom and a new life. She could hope.

As quickly as they came, they were gone. She pulled the blanket up to her chin. The chill in the room had nothing to do with the air conditioner. It was unnatural and cut through her, making her shiver deep inside.

There would be no sleep for her tonight. She turned on the light and reached for her computer. A quick search of the headlines in the local paper told her who the victim at the pool was. The fame of the family made it hard to keep it a secret for long. The girl's identity might be harder to find. Searching through the news archives on missing persons, she scrolled through several photos of young women. Getting tired, she scrolled faster, and then her computer froze. There on her screen was the face of a girl, the exact one she was looking for. The computer stopping on that picture as she searched was no accident—it had been orchestrated.

Starting at the first sentence, she read every piece of information in the missing person's report. Carlee Blair, a beautiful, vibrant seventeen-year-old, went missing ten days before her eighteenth birthday. Calculating the time in her head, she figured it was coming up on three months to the day. *A ghost means she is dead, doesn't it?* Carlee's smiling face stared back at her from the computer screen. In her senior year, a young girl had so many special events to look forward to—the prom, graduation, and college. Tears slipped down Peyton's cheeks as she read. The description of Blair listed limited physical details but enough to let her draw several conclusions. Carlee was five foot five, blue eyes, with blonde hair. A pretty girl, president of the senior class, and a good student. Not a likely candidate for becoming a runaway. She had simply vanished, leaving no clue. Her survival chances diminished with each passing day that she was gone. No body, no suspects, and no witness or trace of her. Something had interrupted her life, and someone knew where Carlee was. The person who killed her did for sure. "I'll help, but you're going to have to point me in the right direction. I've never done this before," she whispered into the silent room. Decision made, she turned off the light and went right to sleep.

Her ringing phone awakened her. A glance at the clock told her she had slept longer than she had intended. "Hello." Her voice sounded groggy to her ears.

"Ms. Reynolds, this is Detective Kincaid."

"Oh, it's you," she mumbled. "You do have a name. I wondered." She slapped her hand to her mouth after the worlds flew out.

"Sorry about that. I simply didn't think to tell you."

"I thought it was more your way of intimidating us. I considered calling the PD to see if they had a detective in the area, but I thought it might be tacky on my part." *Stop antagonizing the man*, she lectured herself, but the sound of his voice made her angry all over again, and her resolve to behave herself faded quickly.

"Touché. I can tell you'd be a worthy opponent. Let's leave it at we don't have to be friends, but I do need to interview you again, and then you're free to go."

"You seem to bring out the worst in me, Detective. You tell me where and when. I'll be there."

"How about we meet in the coffee shop at the

resort around ten?"

He was giving her an hour and half. "I'll be there. I don't have much to add to what I've already told you."

"Now, there's where you're wrong, Ms. Reynolds. I think you're holding back something from me, and I'm determined to find out what it is. I can be persistent."

"You'll find I'm equally tenacious when I need to be. You have the facts, sir." She slid her legs over the side of the bed.

"We'll see. I look forward to the challenge."

"There is no challenge since I've told you the truth. I'm sure you've already checked out my story." She couldn't believe her audacity to argue with the man. He'd never buy her story of a ghost. He was maddening. "I'll see you at ten." She hung up before she dug a deeper hole for herself.

Jumping out of bed, she got busy with her morning routine. With any luck, she would have enough time to call Jessie for a bit of advice before she had to meet Mr. Kincaid.

****

Jaxon couldn't help but smile. The kitten had claws. He purposely baited her and had no idea why. She could give him a run for his money. It was tempting. If nothing else, it made his morning. He walked into the coffee shop still grinning. He sat in a booth where he could watch her come in. Thanking the waitress when she filled his coffee cup, he couldn't wait for this interview to begin. It felt rather like a chess match to him. His wits against hers. He would win, of course, and enjoy each move. Yes, this could prove to be quite interesting. She would be on the first plane out of here when he was through with her, which would work perfectly for him.

****

He had watched from the shadows yesterday and waited to make sure someone found the body. Dawson was baggage and had become a liability. The plan had worked to perfection. Jaxon Kincaid had showed up as the lead detective. Let the contest begin. He had been waiting for this day for a while and would like nothing more than to lead him into a trap. There were plenty of reasons he would like to see a bullet go through the cop's heart. The top one being Kincaid's promotion. The watcher had plenty of others too. Damn man had been a nuisance to his operation long enough. "Pay day is coming, but I feel like playing first." He sipped his coffee. "Yes, indeed, Kincaid, I'll find your weakness. Your days are numbered." Glancing over the top of his paper, he studied the detective. The sense of dread that coursed through his body wiped the grin off his face. Hell, he didn't like the sensation. Gathering his belongings, he waited until Kincaid was distracted, and then he quickly left the coffeeshop.

Chapter 5

Peyton thought about showing up late to bug him. Instead, she walked into the coffee shop right on time. Not a minute too soon or late. He stood as she approached the table. "Good morning, Detective." Her voice had a tinge of coolness to it.

"Please be seated. Let me introduce myself properly. My name is Jaxon Kincaid. I tend to forget the niceties when murder is involved."

"Detective Kincaid," she acknowledged as she sat. "You already know who I am."

"I do, but you can repeat it for the record if you want." He turned on the small recorder and sat when she did. "Tell me again what happened yesterday when you heard Alice Wittman scream."

"As I told you before, I have nothing new to add." She reiterated the story she had told him the day before. Peyton thanked the waitress who filled her coffee cup and topped off her water glass.

"I have one other question I need you to answer before you're free to leave town."

"Fire away, but I'm not leaving for several days. I'll answer it if I can." Her hand fisted at her side.

"I think you're not telling me something. Your information checks out. You've confirmed Alice's story as she has yours. Still, I believe you're holding out on me, and I want to know what you're hiding."

"I believe you have an active imagination, Detective." Panic rose inside her. How could she tell him about what she saw? Weighing it out in her mind, she came to an important conclusion. She would never see him again, and it didn't matter what he thought about her. "Detective, there is something, but I doubt you'll believe me." The heat started at her neck, and she knew the rosy blush wasn't far behind.

"Jaxon is the name. Try me." His scrutiny flustered her.

"The women in my family have an uncanny ability which I've never exhibited until yesterday at the pool." She took a sip of the glass of water. "You can corroborate this part of my story as well." She wrote Sadie's number on a piece of paper. "This is my grandmother, and she can explain it better than I can. My cousin has the same ability and works with the PD back east."

"What kind of ability are you talking about? Are you a psychic?" He sounded disappointed.

"No, absolutely not." She shuddered. "If you must know, and you asked for this: I saw your victim's ghost, spirit, or whatever you want to call it. He was watching me as I did CPR on him. Believe me, it was quite unsettling to me."

"I'm not sure what I expected, Reynolds, but it wasn't a ghost." He frowned. "Are you sure you weren't a bit overwrought? I mean it's not every day you see a dead man, much less do CPR on one."

"I'm positive. His spirit hovered close by the whole time I worked on him and while you interviewed us." She took a large gulp of water. "I know it sounds strange, and believe me when I say it came as a total shock to me. I wasn't expecting him or what happened after that."

"Are you saying there's more?" His chin edged up as he sat back in the chair.

She nodded at him. "You asked. I don't want you to think I'm withholding any information from you." Her voice took on a sarcastic edge. She explained to him about the girl's ghost watching behind the victim's spirit. "I found a picture of her when I did a missing person's search in the area. Her name is Carlee Blair, and she's been missing for three months. In my opinion, because I saw her ghost, I'm thinking you'll eventually find her body."

"I'm speechless. I don't know what to say. You're either a good actress or you believe you saw something. I'm not saying you did. I'll have to think about this for a while." The skepticism on his face was easy for her to read.

"You don't have to say anything. Be my guest and think about it. Take your time. I'm trying to figure it out myself." Her voice softened as she spoke to him.

"At least I can understand your reluctance to talk to me." He shook his head. "I have no words."

"What you saw at the pool wasn't me withholding information, but rather me seeing a ghost for the first time in my life. If you're surprised by it, consider how I felt." She started to stand. "If you are finished, I'd like to go. You can take time to digest my story. I have a few calls to make."

"Not so fast." He motioned for her to sit. "Tell me about this cousin of yours." His tone was terse. Her back straightened. "Please."

Taking a deep breath, she told him about the last

case her cousin Jessie and Matt Parker worked together. "I only know a few details because I happened to be in town at the time. Matt is the chief of police in Blue Cove. You can always call him too. Parker was skeptical at first about my cousin, but he's come to rely on what she tells him. They've solved some high-profile cases."

"I'll consider calling him. I've never heard of anything as preposterous as the story you just fed me. I'll give you the benefit of the doubt until I can prove you wrong."

She stood. "Good luck with that, Detective. It's your word against mine, and I know what I saw. If I were you, the first thing I'd do is find Carlee Blair in your own department's reports. You might want to talk to her family. She is connected to your victim, and you need to find out how." She smiled sweetly at him. "Now if you'll excuse me, I don't want to waste any more of your precious time. You know where to find me when you want to apologize. And believe me you'll need to if you want my help."

He stood. "Don't hold your breath. Stay in town."

"I wouldn't dream of leaving. I told Carlee I would help when she asked me to. Even you can't stop me from keeping my word." She stood and walked away from him, picking up steam as her anger grew. He made her lose her temper again. All he had to do was open his big mouth. Peyton frowned. His arrogance knew no boundaries, but she had overreacted.

****

He enjoyed the gentle sway of her hips as she walked away. Damn, he had mucked it up again. What was it about her that made him lose control of any intelligence he possessed? She brought out the worst in him, and he had no idea why. Was he that fearful of falling under her spell? The idea brought a grin to his face. Ghost. He shook his head. More like a witch perhaps. He wanted to kiss her and yell at her at the same time. Her story was outrageous, but he would check it out. She seemed genuine. "Ghosts. Hell." He ran his hand through his hair. There's no way he could put that in a report.

When Jaxon arrived at the station, he put in a call to the Blue Cove PD. "This is Detective Kincaid with homicide calling from Arizona. Is Chief Parker available?" Waiting for Parker to answer gave him the time he needed to gather his thoughts and write down a few questions he wanted answered.

"This is Chief Parker. How can I help you?" The man's voice sounded in his ear.

Jaxon explained what Peyton had told him. "I know this sounds odd, but she told me I could check her out with you. Explain this crazy story if you can because none of this makes any sense to me."

"My fiancée has the same ability. They were wondering if it would show up in Peyton. I guess that question has been answered."

"Who was wondering?" Jaxon grew more confused by the minute. Parker sounded reasonable—how could he believe this junk.

"Her cousin and grandmother to name a few. Look, I'm sure this sounds farfetched. It did to me too. But now I and every officer in our unit respects her ability, along with a few FBI agents who are constantly trying to recruit her."

"Are you kidding me?" Jaxon shook his head.

"Nope. Don't get me wrong. I still solve a case using logic. But believe me that what they are capable of hearing and seeing will help to solve any case much faster."

"What do I do?" Jaxon glanced at the file on his desk.

"I can't presume to tell you. I don't know Peyton as well as I know Jessie and Sadie. But do yourself a favor and call Sadie and hear her out. If you agree, then listen to Peyton and follow through using the evidence gathered. See if what she tells you holds up. If it does, pursue it and let her help."

"I already may have messed that up." Jaxon clicked the pen in his hand on and off.

"I did too, but an apology can go a long way to fixing things. I've had to apologize more than a few times." Matt chuckled. "I still do, and Jessie is quick to remind me."

Jaxon listened as Parker talked about a couple of their cases. He asked questions and hung up later feeling a tad better than when he had first called. Maybe Reynolds wasn't a complete whack job. He dialed the next number on his list. After he talked to Sadie Reynolds, he knew he had to rethink what he had said to Peyton. Not that he wanted to work with her on this case. He wanted to stay as far away from her as possible. His freedom was at risk the longer she stayed in the area. Although, single was highly overrated.

A quick name search in the missing person's files brought Carlee Blair's face on the screen. Damn. Ms. Reynolds was two for two. She had gotten to this piece of information before him. He would have never linked E J's death to a missing girl. He grabbed his phone and went out the door.

After interviewing Mrs. Blair and two of Carlee's friends, he left with Carlee's laptop. Why hadn't anyone taken this before? They probably saw her as another teen runaway. The department couldn't track down every missing person—there wasn't enough manpower. Still, a popular young girl didn't fit the profile of a runaway. Reynolds might have mentioned that fact. The rest of the afternoon he pored through Blair's email conversations and social media sites. Jaxon finally stumbled on to a link to E J Dawson. Peyton told him to look for one, and he had called her story preposterous. Rubbing his temples, he read the information in front of him. The two had met online, and she had agreed to meet him for a Saturday hike in the Superstitions. He had his first answer and was working through the apology in his head that he needed to make. It would be only fair to take her along. She gave him the heads-up. In a strange kind of way.

****

Still incensed with Kincaid, Peyton plopped down on the edge of the bed. The colorful brochures she had picked up in the lobby when she checked in were waiting on the nightstand for her to read. Picking up the stack, she glanced through one after the other. The one about the Superstition Mountains attracted her attention. The Superstitions were about forty miles east of Phoenix. She could drive there easily, or maybe the concierge knew of a tour that went there.

Opening her computer, she spent the afternoon scanning several articles on a few of the legends regarding the mountains. Included among them were the lost Dutchman Mine and a few on flying saucers.

The one that brought chills to her as she read was all about an urban legend of a haunted hiking trail. With each word she read came a strong sense that Carlee's body would be found in the Superstitions. Somewhere buried among all the others never found—the early prospectors in search of the mine, or hikers who wandered off the trails where park rangers couldn't easily find them. All simply disappeared into the brutal desert, becoming a part of the legend. Blair's body was hidden somewhere in the wasteland of the Superstitions. How could she possibly know that? She had no idea, but she was sure of it. Anger forgotten, Peyton spent the afternoon in the cool of her room.

Now, what should she do with this information? She couldn't simply take on the mountains and desert in this heat on her own. She would be another number added to the list. No doubt about it, Kincaid would have to listen to her. "Good luck. He's a stubborn man," she told herself. But then again, she was stubborn too.

She reached for her ringing phone. "I bet you've wondered where I've been." Destiny's voice was music to her ears.

"I've been worried. Why haven't you called?" Peyton asked.

"Sorry. My mom was rushed to the hospital, and it was touch and go for a few days. Pretty crazy. Finally, she's improving, but there's no way I can come until I know all is okay with her." Destiny paused and rushed on before Peyton could say anything. "My phone's battery went dead, and I had left my charger at home. This is the first break I've had. I'm home only long enough to clean up and go back up to stay with her. Don't worry—you'll be able to get me if you need to.

I've already put my charger in my purse."

"I'm sorry about your mom. I'm glad she's doing better. What happened?" Peyton asked.

"The doctor thought it was a stroke, but thankfully it wasn't. They are still running tests which all seem to be negative to this point. Good news if you ask me. She's out of ICU and in a room now. Her vitals are improving every day."

"That's good to hear. Tell her I hope she gets better really soon." Peyton doodled on the top of the notepad in front of her. "Is there anyone with her now?"

"No. I came home when she went to sleep. The nurse gave her something to help her rest and told me she'd be out for a while. I'm on my way back to the hospital. I will stay until her sister gets here and then we'll trade off."

"Stay with your mom, and please don't worry about coming. You wouldn't want to be here at this time anyway." Peyton sat forward in the chair.

"Why? Are you backing out on me?" She heard Destiny laugh.

"Look who's talking. I'm here, aren't I?" Peyton murmured.

"Yep, sorry." Destiny paused. "I really am."

"I know. All I'm saying, it's as hot as Hades to put it bluntly. There's no way I'm going to do any trail ride. I would be one massive sunburn head to toe before the day was half done. I don't care if I lose money or not."

"I probably didn't think the plan through very well," Destiny mumbled. "I mean, Arizona in the summer is not a good outdoor destination even if the price was great."

"Duh, you think," Peyton said sarcastically. "I'm at

a resort in Scottsdale. No need to worry about me. I'm fine." Peyton told her about the resort.

"Sounds heavenly." Destiny sounded wistful.

"It's divine and cool too." Peyton glanced around the lovely room. "Concentrate on your mom. She is the one who needs you now. I don't intend to leave this air-conditioned room until I'm on a plane headed home."

"Promise me you won't go home yet. I'll get there and we'll do something. The Southwest Adventures Company rep called. Geeze, that was over a week ago. Anyway, the guy told me because of the heat the company has a backup plan for such emergencies."

"Why didn't you tell me that, and I would've stayed in Blue Cove?"

"Because you would have stayed home. I was also a bit preoccupied. Besides, I wanted to have you all to myself. I had no idea how sick my mom would get. Hang tight—we'll still have a great time if I make it. Don't get bored. I'll come if I can. My aunt arrives tonight, and as soon as the doctor says Mom can go home, I'll call and let you know."

"Don't rush, for heaven's sake. Stay with your mom. I'm enjoying the break from work. I can honestly say I'm not bored in the least bit. Get back to your mom and stay until she's all better."

"I will. We'll talk later." Destiny suddenly laughed again. "Did you meet a man? Is that why you're not fuming and angry with me?"

"Sure, that happened in a twenty-four-hour period, and I'm having a torrid affair. Not. Destiny, you're crazy. When you call back, I'll tell you what is taking up my time."

"Tell me now or I'll wonder about it all day."

"No, I'm making sure you have to call me back. Talk to you later." She hung up on Destiny's lengthy protests.

Chapter 6

Jaxon did his best to delay the inevitable. Filling the rest his day with busy work that he normally avoided until pressed by time to get it done, he finally faced what he had to do next. Pulling the notebook with Reynolds' number out of his pocket, he flipped to the page. He dialed the number and got ready to eat crow.

"Ms. Reynolds, I'm sure after our morning you'd like to hang up on me. I hope you'll hear me out," he told her the minute she said hello, giving her no time to react.

"I take it you talked to my grandmother, found the information on Carlee I told you about, and no longer think of me as a total kook." He could hear the frustration in her voice.

"Part of what you said is true. I'm not sure about the kook part. The jury is still out on that one." Shaking his head, he could almost feel her bristle over the phone. He couldn't seem to help himself. He leaned back in his chair, grinning at the ceiling.

"If you called only to continue your insults, then this conversation is over." Her loud sigh registered her irritation even over the phone.

"Please don't hang up. It was my feeble attempt at teasing you. If you'll give me a few more minutes of your time, I'll try to conduct myself as a professional. I do have a legitimate reason for calling. I wanted to ask you to dinner."

"Why? Insulting me over the phone isn't enough so you want to do it in person and in public?" She blew out her breath.

"No. You might not believe this, but I'd like to call a truce to this battle we have going on between us," Jaxon told her.

"Mr. Kincaid, you would make a lousy peace negotiator."

"I can't argue with you there. Are you willing to risk dinner out with me?" he asked.

"Only if you promise to be on your best behavior." Her voice sounded cautious.

Hope surged through his body. "I will if you agree to be nice too." He closed the file on his desk.

"I can keep my temper in check for one dinner, I'm sure."

"I'm certain you can." This was one time he wished he could see her expression. He could almost bet she was rolling her eyes at him. "I'll pick you up at six if that works for you. I know a great place that I think you'll enjoy. I can grovel, and we can talk with a bit of privacy." He grinned, enjoying the conversation much to his surprise.

"I'll meet you out front at six. I'm not sure if you know how to grovel. A simple apology would suffice."

"I'll see you soon." He glanced at his watch. There was enough time for him to get home, shower, and change before he needed to pick her up. Damn, he felt happy, which wasn't a good sign for someone not wanting to get entangled in a relationship. For the moment, he didn't care.

****

Peyton wasn't sure what to expect from Detective Kincaid. Going out to dinner with anyone at this point sounded good. She needed to get out of this room and away from the seriousness of the last twenty-four hours. She pulled the awesome sundress out of the closet. Her cousin Jessie had made her buy it on one of their shopping expeditions. She held it up to herself in front of the mirror. "Buy it," Jessie had told her. "The green makes your eyes pop, and as Grams always says, it shows off your figure without giving away all your secrets. The hunky cowboy will love it." The two of them had laughed. Maybe the hunky cop would. Peyton sighed. What was she thinking? She put the dress back in the closet and walked away. Five minutes later, she pulled it off the hanger. She would wear the dress, but not for him.

Glancing one last time in the mirror, she put on lip gloss, pursing her lips together. Her cousin had been right—the dress looked great and brought out the green in her hazel eyes. Her hand ran over the soft material of the fabric. Perfect. She clasped the chain securing her necklace around her neck. She was ready and confident for the next round in the battle with the detective. He wouldn't give in quietly, and neither would she. No one said she had to play fair. She flipped her hair over her shoulder. Another spray of perfume and she was ready.

She walked across the room and reached for her ringing phone. "Grams wanted me to check on you. Are you doing okay?" Jessie asked.

"I take it she got a call from Detective Kincaid." Peyton twirled a strand of hair around her finger as she talked.

"Yep, and so did Matt. He told me Jaxon sounded a

lot like he had when he didn't know what to think of me, which was all the time." Jessie laughed. "The good detective doesn't know what to make of you."

"I know exactly what the arrogant detective thinks about me. He has let me know already. He thinks I'm a whack job." Peyton sat in the chair, straightening her dress as she did.

"Tell me what's happened so far. I want details, please."

Peyton told her cousin what she knew about Carlee, E J, and the conversation she had with Jaxon. "I'm sure by now he has figured out I'm right about a connection between Carlee and E J. I have to admit I was surprised when I found my ghost in the missing persons' archive."

"Trust me, you're going to be surprised many times over before this is all done," Jessie assured her.

"I have no idea why, but I'm sure her body is in the Superstitions, a mountainous area east of the city where people go to hike. I read about the legends surrounding the site most of the morning, and a strong feeling came over me that she would be found there. Strong!" Peyton emphasized the word, jumping up as she did.

"I'm sure you're right. I'm going to have Jeremy call you. He does research for me, and I know he'll help you too. Ask your detective friend if he wants a bloodhound to track the area for the missing girl. My friend Frank Wagner would do it in a heartbeat. If he says no, but you want to look anyway, Frank will help you." Jessie paused. "It would probably be better to get his permission. You don't want to be arrested for interfering in his case. I'm not sure how a big city cop would take to you telling him what to do."

"I'd appreciate any help I can get. I've never done this before. I'm determined to bring Carlee home to her family."

"Promise me you'll try to work with Detective Kincaid. Ask him," Jessie begged. "I learned the hard way that you catch more flies with honey than vinegar, whatever that means."

"One of Grams' sayings that I know all too well. I've heard her say it many times over the years." Peyton sighed. "Don't worry, Jess, I'll try to behave and make you proud. I'm not completely unreasonable, you know. Although the detective does seem to bring out the worse in me." Peyton reached for her sweater in case the restaurant was cold.

"I know you'll do fine. The main reason the ghost sought you out in the first place is to find peace and closure. And maybe to bring their killer to justice. Whatever the reason, it's a good feeling to do something for someone else. Be open, because if it's anything like what I've experienced, one clue leads to another. Before long, you'll find out more than you bargained for."

"I've already got more from this trip than I expected. Destiny isn't here and may not come at all. I would head home tomorrow, but I told Carlee I would help her." Peyton stopped pacing. "Like Grams said, 'follow it through', and I plan on it," Peyton told her.

"You and I are a lot alike. I'm a feminist in every sense of the word and always bristle when I'm challenged. You're as strong but much quieter in your approach. I can't wait to see where this takes you."

"I doubt Mr. Kincaid thinks I'm quiet." She put the lip gloss and a brush in her purse.

"I'm happy to hear you're coming out of your shell, Cous. A man doesn't know what to do with a strong woman." Jessie laughed. "Matt won't be happy about me telling you this, but it's a need to know. I told him when he said to stay out of his case that I was involved, and he'd have to learn to deal with it."

"I've already told Kincaid. Carlee asked for my help, and I'm going stay here to help." Peyton paused. "He wasn't happy—but he'll get used to it."

"Maybe he will or maybe he won't. Still it would be fun to watch." Jessie laughed again. "Boy, I would love to be there to see what happens."

"You'd be bored."

"Another thing that happened to me in the process, I laid to rest some of the ghosts from my past. I hope you will too."

"One can wish..." Her voice trailed off. Jessie's words hit close to home and what she had been thinking about earlier.

"Keep me in the loop."

"I will. He's taking me to dinner tonight. He wants to apologize. I see it more as an opportunity for him to gloat and lecture me if I know the man." She put a touch of perfume on the inside of her wrist. A case of the nerves, and she needed to stop fussing. At this rate, she would smell like a perfume bottle.

"I hope you're wearing the dress I made you buy," Jessie said.

"I'm wearing it. Thankfully, it's a sundress. It's too hot for anything else that I brought." She automatically fanned her face.

"The way you look in that dress, the good detective might find himself challenged in more ways than one."

Serious conversation was lost to them after Jessie's statement. They both dissolved into laughter as they had done so many times over the years. "Thanks, Cous, I needed to laugh. It's time for me to go. He should be here in a few minutes. I'll let you know how it goes. Tell Grams I'm fine. And as for help from you or your friends, I welcome it. Love you." Peyton disconnected the call and put her phone in her purse. She could do this. With any luck, this would be the last time she had to see Detective Kincaid. Stepping into the hall, she locked the door. To battle. She smiled at the thought. *Jaxon has no idea who he's dealing with. He has met his match.*

****

He pulled in front of the Desert Palms Resort and stepped out of the car. The vision walking out the opening sliding door made him swear under his breath. First impression, she was gorgeous. Red, fiery strands shot through her hair in the sunlight. His mouth went dry. A second glance assured him he was asinine to believe she'd be easy to forget. Damn, this would be one long night.

"Good evening, Detective." She walked to the passenger side. He stood where he had first stepped out of the car and still hadn't said a word. "I hope you've had a productive day."

"Here, let me get that." He walked to her side and opened the door.

"I was beginning to wonder if you were going to talk to me or if I should go back inside and start the evening over again."

"Sorry, my mind was preoccupied. Thanks for having dinner with me tonight." He started the engine once inside the car. Could he be any denser?

"You asked nicely for a truce. I'm willing to give it a try. If you behave, I will too."

Any pretense of conversation ceased. The silence was palpable. She glanced several times at her watch. "Is something bothering you, Detective, or is it the company?"

"You can call me Jaxon. I'm trying to figure you out is all. What's your angle? Everyone seems to have one." He signaled his turn and moved into the left lane.

"That's a bit cynical. I'm not sure what you mean. I have nothing to gain from sharing what I did with you except for a few insults, as you know since you gave them to me. I saw what I saw. Whether you believe me or not is up to you."

"I didn't mean the question negatively. I'm wondering why a girl like you wants to get involved in this. You don't know the victims; you don't live here. What do you get from it?" There were several cars in front of him, and he moved up as each one turned.

"The experience is new for me. My hope is that there'll be closure for Carlee and her family. In the end, I want what you want." She glanced at him.

"What would that be?" He waited when the light turned red.

"Justice to be served. I'm sure Carlee would like to see her killer pay for his crime. I know I want it for her."

"We're not sure if there even is a crime, but if you are right—and that's a big if—I would want justice for her." He turned on the green arrow.

"Giving yourself a little wiggle room in case I'm wrong I see. I'm not! I know what I saw, and she's connected to the Dawson boy. I even think I know where the body is." She fiddled with her purse on her lap.

"We need to talk. Now." He turned into a strip mall parking lot and stopped the car. "I get it after talking to Parker, but honestly I'm struggling to believe it."

"I know it must be confusing. It is for me too. I must follow where this leads me. I'll try to stay out of your way, but I'm going to try and help Carlee."

"First of all, I'm sorry for how I've acted. You have stunned me in more ways than I care to explain. You are right about the connection between E J and Carlee. They met online and had scheduled to meet." He saw her raise her hand to stop him.

"Don't tell me. They were going to meet to hike in the Superstition Mountains. Am I right?"

He nodded. "How did you know?"

"Call it a feeling." She told him about reading the brochures and the sensation that came over her that Carlee was there. "My cousin told me about her friend who has a bloodhound that will come track if you want him to. Even if you don't, I want him to. I want to find her."

"Hold on. I haven't said one way or the other yet whether you can help. I want to think this through. I need more evidence than just your feelings to start another branch in the investigation. For now, we need to do it my way. I'll listen to what you think and take it under advisement. That's the best I can offer you. I'm not sure my captain will be pleased with me agreeing to anything. I'm willing to take the heat if there's any chance what you're telling me is right."

"I realize you don't know me. I also know I came

into the case when I saw their ghosts. I will try hard to stay out of your way, but I won't leave town until they say I'm done."

"How will you know?" Jaxon asked.

"Don't ask me. I have no idea." She shrugged her shoulders. "I guess I'll know when I know."

He put the car in drive. "Dinner is on me." He pulled back into traffic and made his way to the restaurant. "I think you'll like this place."

"I'm sure I will. We're both adults and should be able to have a grown-up conversation for an hour or two." She smiled at him.

"We'll manage." He glanced at her in time to catch her skeptical expression.

****

All through dinner the strain of answering the questions he was throwing at her began to take their toll. The one subject she hated to talk about was her childhood. She had managed up to this point to answer each question without answering them at all. She'd make a great politician—dancing around the issues without ever giving a straight answer. "Have you lived here all your life?" It was her turn to ask him a few.

"About seven years. This was the first position I got when I graduated from the academy."

"Do you like the heat?" She arranged the napkin on her lap.

"I don't think about it. You get used to it over time." He took a drink of his water.

"I find that hard to believe." She scoffed at his answer.

"That's why the snowbirds leave in the summer. They migrate back to cooler weather."

"I'd migrate too. Still, in the winters it must be great." She placed her fork across her plate. "It's beautiful here despite the heat. The sky is amazing, and the sunset last night was spectacular." She sipped her iced tea. "Where did you grow up?"

"In the Boston area. My family still lives there." He leaned back in his chair. "I've applied for a job that will take me back closer to them."

"I hope you get it. It would be nice for you to live nearer to your family. You seem to enjoy them."

"Yeah, my brother Taylor just had his first kid, and I'd like to see her before she's a teenager. I get back at least once a year, and more if I'm lucky. I want to be around for the special stuff in their lives. There are three of us boys and one girl. I'm the one in the middle. My kid sister, Shannon, is getting married in the fall. It'll be a big affair, and all of us are in the wedding."

"Congratulations to her." Her reply sounded a tad wistful.

"I think she's too damn young to know her own mind. I have yet to grill her fiancé to make sure he's worthy of her. Of course, no one would be good enough. Shannon is a pest but deserves only the best. Kevin, my oldest brother, says the guy is okay. Still, I'd like to drill him to make sure for myself."

"You take your big brother status seriously." She laughed, placing her napkin on the table.

"Yeah, I do." He grinned at her. "How about you, any big brothers to look after you?"

"No, only a younger sister who I watched over." She sighed inwardly. It would have been great to have a big brother. Dinner passed quickly enough. They talked about the case a few times, and when he dropped her off at the resort, he told her he would stay in touch. Truthfully, she thought she'd never hear from him again.

Chapter 7

As soon as she entered her room, her phone started ringing. The name on the caller ID made her smile. "Hi, Grams, I was going to call you. We need to talk." She kicked her shoes off and sat in the chair.

"Yes, we do. I didn't want to talk to you in front of Jessie. It's up to you if you want her to know what's going on or not."

"Thank you. I find it hard to talk about my childhood much. I've maintained an image for such a long time it's hard to let people in." She reached for the box of tissues. The tears were already beginning to form in her eyes. "I should've told you years ago what was going on, but we were too ashamed to ask for help."

"I know, dear. Your grandpa and I knew something wasn't right. I wish you had known us well enough to be able to talk to us. Your dad didn't let us have much time with you girls alone. I'm sure you and Madison must have felt forgotten for all the years you were growing up. Things never seemed quite right, but when I questioned your father, he always had an answer. Your mother defended him, and when we tried to intervene, they threatened us we would never see you girls again. Your mom was complicit, did you know that?"

"Mom had her own addiction issues, Grams. We

58

never knew whether Mom or Dad would show up on any given day." Peyton sniffed and wiped the tears from her eyes. "I don't mean to cry. It's just that I've kept this all bottled up inside of me for so long." She told her grandmother about some of the things they had suffered at the hands of the parents. "I don't hate them, Grams, it's not like that. But I can't help them no matter how hard I try."

Sadie's voice trembled with agitation. "I'm done listening to my son's excuses. I'm sorry it took me so long to see this side of him. Your dad has always been a charmer and could lie his way out of anything. No more! Your uncle checked him into rehab this morning. He'll have to face some harsh truths in the days ahead. We can't and won't make it easy for him. He needs to go through the whole process. Your mother does too. You girls will no longer have to deal with the problem alone. You have family to help now. I only wish we had known what was happening years ago. I'll always regret not helping sooner."

"Part of that is my fault. At first, I thought all families were likes ours until I saw my friends' parents. I wasted time blaming myself for a while for the way they were, and I was embarrassed by them for a long time. The few weeks I stayed at Jessie's showed me the difference between the two brothers. I knew something wasn't right but didn't understand until I was older, and the damage was already done."

"I wish I could make it all go away, but it can't be undone. Still, you two girls have turned out amazing. I couldn't be prouder of the two of you than I am. When you are ready, I want you to tell me in an email how you felt growing up. Madison is going to do the same.

The doctors working with your parents want them to face what they have done to you both because of their addictions. Tell me everything, big or small. It's important."

"Did you call Madison? Dad's been calling her."

"I called. We talked for a long time. She told me how you protected her all those years. How you would take the punishment and not let them hit her. She promised not to take any more of his calls, and I want you to do the same. I will let you know when it's okay to talk with them both again. When you do, I'll be with you."

"I won't talk to him alone, believe me. I don't want to. I've spent the last several years trying to forget what they did. I've tried to stay as far away from both them as I could. I haven't taken his calls for several months. My therapist told me not to. She also told me to start a journal and tell my story as a part of my therapy."

"I'm glad. Sound advice, if you ask me." Sadie blew her nose and repeated what she had learned so far, and they cried together. "I love you, Peyton," her grandmother said before she ended the call.

All the pain of those years Peyton had bottled up inside of her started to find their way to the surface. Tears rolled down her cheeks, opening the floodgates. Her grandmother's words of love and regret were breaking through the armor she had encased herself in. When Sadie said "I love you," the light and power of those words poured into her depths, bathing her, freeing her, and she spent herself crying.

When she awakened later, she wasn't alone. She sensed Carlee's presence before she saw her. Suspended at the foot of the bed, the spirit studied her closely. Rubbing her puffy eyes didn't change anything. Peyton could still see Carlee there, and the expression on her face made it seem she understood Peyton's pain. Even the thought of an understanding ghost seemed crazy but real as she watched her. "I wish I knew how to help you, Carlee." At the sound of her name, Carlee flittered about. "You understand, don't you? How can that be? Help me understand you. I want to help." Carlee stared at her, swaying back and forth. The air crackled with something unfamiliar to Peyton. She could sense something significant was about to happen.

Suddenly, a scene began to play out in her mind. It wasn't a dream but more like Carlee's memories playing like a movie for her to see. The terrain looked like a photo from the brochure she studied earlier. The desert landscape awash in the colors of the sunset was beautiful and yet hauntingly spooky. A small lizard scampered across the path, darting behind a rock on the other side of the path. Carlee walked on the dirt trail, her blonde hair pulled back into a ponytail. Her hot pink sneakers moved quickly with almost a skip in her step. Carlee picked up her pace, unaware of the man lurking in the shadows watching her. Darn. Peyton strained but couldn't see his face. Of course she couldn't because Carlee had never seen the man either. The darkness in his heart filled his thoughts with murder. He followed her out of sight. Wanting to warn Carlee and at the same moment realizing she could do nothing to save her, tears filled Peyton's eyes. Death awaited Carlee somewhere on the mountain. The scene continued to roll through her mind.

Carlee Blair met E J Dawson on the path, and they walked together the winding trail through the mountain.

They were connected! She knew it. Hand in hand the two moved in sync, oblivious to their surroundings, chatting as a young couple in love might do. *Love, she hadn't seen that coming.* Carlee bent down to look at the purple opening blooms on the prickly pear cactus and the vibrant orange flower snuggled in the barrel cactus. Dawson watched her movement with adoration in his eyes. The desert, teeming with life and beauty, became the perfect backdrop of the two young people in the early stages of a crush. *Did her parents know?*

The scene changed. As the light faded in the night sky, three men crept from the shadows into plain view in the moonlight. One man still watched from the edge. The largest of the three held Dawson while the other two dragged Carlee into the desert.

"I've done everything you've asked of me, and you promised me no one would get hurt." E J screamed.

"I never promised anything, kid. And all bets were off when you double-crossed me. Let this be your first warning. Keep your mouth shut or join your friend. As far as you're concerned, you didn't see or hear anything." With a few well-placed hits, E J slumped to the ground.

Those must have been the last words Carlee heard Dawson say. Peyton knew she would never forget Carlee's fear as they dragged her away from E J. Carlee wanted justice, and that's what she would have.

Carlee was collateral damage. In the wrong place with the wrong person at the wrong time, and she paid the price. Whatever Dawson had done to the man came back to haunt him too.

****

The evening astounded him. Not easy to do. Rarely

could he be taken by surprise. He was known at the station as the biggest skeptic and a hardnosed detective at his job, an image that suited him and that he worked hard to maintain. He found himself challenged and back on his heels all night.

She answered a few but dodged a lot of his questions which kept him off balance. Yet he had a good time despite her reluctance and his better judgment. Everything about her appealed to him. She held herself in reserve, which he found intriguing. No flirting, not one encouraging signal, and he had searched for them all night. He could get lost in those gorgeous eyes, and her smile disarmed him. The whole ghost thing he found a bit of a turnoff. Still she found the missing Blair girl in the files and connected her to Dawson. What she said she experienced was either real or she was a damn good actress. He found it a challenge to figure it out. Keeping her away from the investigation might be a bit tricky, or maybe he should do what Parker said and take her along. He might find out more quickly if she was genuine or a fraud. But if it turned out the whole ghost thing was real, then hell, he didn't know what to do about that.

Grabbing the remote he turned on the TV. He wanted to catch the last of the Diamondbacks' game. While in Arizona, he watched them. Still his favorite team would always be the Red Sox. He surfed through the scores, happy to see his team had won.

Chapter 8

Peyton closed the door to her room as the sun began to rise in the sky. It wasn't exactly a chilly morning, but the temps were cool enough to get in some exercise before the intense heat of the day settled in. Her cousin Jessie loved to run. She on the other hand could walk for miles and did it as often as time permitted. Because she didn't know the area, she decided to walk around the resort. She calculated how many times she needed to go around the property to get in at least five miles. Her pace was quick—not a jog but not a stroll either. Every mile she walked made her feel alive, and her problems seemed to fade into the background. With the sun fully up, she pulled her sunglasses down off the top of her head where they were perched.

Exercise to her wasn't optional but necessary for her sanity. Half the world's problems could be solved if people would take a walk and think before they talked. By the third time around the resort, she knew she needed to tell Kincaid about what Carlee had showed her. He could think what he wanted. Five times around and she was ready to take on the world to find Carlee's body and bring her home to her family. As she started her final circle around the property, she had a plan in her head how to go about getting the job done. By the time she arrived back at her room, the sun had begun to heat the air and temps to climb, causing beads of sweat to roll down her back. She wanted a cool shower and then food.

Ready to be seen, she closed the door and walked down the hall toward the resort's coffee shop. She stopped at the concierge's desk to arrange a sightseeing tour to the Superstitions for the following day. Writing the information for her planned excursion in her trusty notebook gave her a sense of excitement and trepidation at the same time. Goosebumps covered her arms, and it had nothing to do with the AC. If this didn't take her out of her comfort zone, she had no idea what would.

As soon as she gave the waiter her order, Kincaid walked in. He cut a formidable figure with his sandy-blond hair and bronze skin. Wearing a black shirt and blue jeans, he also had the grim expression she had come to expect. She hoped he wouldn't see her but ducked too late. As he made his way to her table, her body automatically tensed. She expected another match between them. They seemed to bring out the worst in each other. Darn, darn, darn. His nearness rattled her.

"I was hoping to find you here." He stopped at the table. "Do you mind if I join you?"

"Knock yourself out." She smiled sweetly at him, or at least she hoped it looked that way. "I was going to call you later."

"Now that surprises me. I thought you were happy to be rid of me last night." He nodded when the waiter asked if he wanted coffee. "Did I misread your signals?"

And it begins. "There were no signals to misread. I wanted to talk to you about the case. I had a visitor last night, and I thought you might be interesting in hearing about it."

"I'm listening." He poured cream into his coffee.

Be professional, she told herself. Pulling out her notebook, she flipped through the pages and explained to him what she had seen the night before. "Whatever Dawson got involved in eventually led to Carlee's death. His too, most likely. I wish I could give you more details or help with a composite sketch of the three men, or maybe there were four. Three I could see clearly, the other might have been simply a shadow. I never saw any of their faces. I'm not sure Carlee did either. It would seem to me if she had they would be locked in her memory bank." Her fingers tapped quietly on the table.

"How do I know if any of this is true? You could be making it all up." He frowned at her over the coffee cup in his hand.

And the gloves were off. "I could be. But what could I possibly hope to gain? Besides, isn't lying to the police during an investigation considered a crime? I guess you'll either need to arrest me or prove what I've told you. I'm sure in the end everything I've told you will hold up under even your scrutiny. Have it your way, though, and be skeptical." She took a sip of her coffee and scowled right back at him. "If this is your idea of a truce, it lacks any sense of civility. It's doomed to fail. Since I was here first, and this is my table, you're free to leave."

"I didn't say you were telling me a lie, did I? I simply asked a question. Don't fly off the handle."

Her hand fisted in her lap. "Kincaid, I don't fly anywhere." She tried to annoy him on purpose. "I don't care if you believe me or not. I can't even say I care if you want my help or not. I told you what I knew out of politeness and wanting to work with the authorities. I can do it on my own." Her foot tapped under the chair and picked up speed with each word.

He shook his head. "No, you can't."

She thanked the waiter when he placed her breakfast in front of her. "I plan on enjoying my breakfast. This conversation is over as far as I'm concerned."

"Not so fast. We have a few things to settle first." He leaned across the table closer to her. "You aren't involved in this case unless I say you are. You got that." His pointed finger was inches from her face. "I'm pulling rank on you. Two people are dead. I don't want you to be a third. Nor do I want you snooping around and causing trouble."

"Are you going to tell Carlee and E J to stop coming to me? You didn't involve me in this—they did. I'm in. I can work with you or do the research on my own. I'm sure they'll take care of me. Besides, I don't have a choice, do I? Carlee didn't appear to you, did she? You need her help, and in order to get it, you'll either have to see her yourself or trust me."

"Damn. I know I'm going to regret this. I'll listen to you, but I'm not promising anything else. If I involve you at all, you'll have to do what I tell you. I don't want to worry about you every time I turn around."

"You don't have to worry about me. I've taken care of myself for years." She placed her napkin on her lap. "Now if you're finished telling me what do, it's my turn. I want to eat my breakfast before it gets cold. You can growl at me later."

"Fair enough." He threw down the money for his coffee on the table. "I'm not done with you." He stood to leave.

"As enticing as that sounds, I'll pass on hanging out for fun." She glanced at him. "And just so you know, I'm not done with you either, and neither are my friends." She paused and added just to bug him, "I'm headed to the Superstitions in the morning. Have a nice day, Kincaid." She watched him walk away, his hands fisting at his sides. She hit the mark. Having no idea why he irritated her so much, it felt good to have the last word. Her phone chimed the arrival of a text. Victory was short-lived when she saw his name.

She grinned as she read his words.

—Don't push me, Reynolds. You don't want me for an enemy.—

Did she really want to goad him? He could push her out of the investigation and would do it in a minute without a second thought. She took a bite of her toast. Darn. He ruined a perfectly good meal. She shook her head. She had no idea why she let him get under her skin. The man was aggravating. Once again, he got the last word.

****

Jaxon had no intention when he saw her to start a fight. She didn't like him—that was obvious. All the crazy talk of ghosts threw him off his game. He refused to let his mind go there. Peyton seemed like a reasonably intelligent woman. Her reputation was stellar—he had checked. He knew the look he'd seen on her face and could smell the fear the first night. What changed? She wasn't afraid anymore and was ready to go to battle for Carlee Blair. He needed her, but he didn't want her. It was a damn mess. Not wanting her wasn't totally true, either.

****

From the watcher's vantage point, the cop had it bad for the woman. The tension between them could be felt across the room. He wasn't sure about her. He might have to study her for a while. Jaxon he knew well enough to read his every action. The moving scene that played out between the two of them handed him the weapon he had been waiting for. He smiled at the waitress who topped off his coffee. Kincaid's day of reckoning would come soon enough, and he would relish every minute of it. Leaning back in the chair, he wanted to dangle the rope for a while before hanging him. The thrill of the kill didn't excite him as much as the game of strategy to lead them into his web. He got high on it. Collateral damage was part of the game. Yes, sir, this could put a touch of excitement into an otherwise dull summer. He turned the page on the newspaper.

Chapter 9

Jaxon didn't know whether he wanted to walk away and not look back or to pull the maddening woman into his arms and hug her. One thing he knew, she would drive him nuts before this case was solved. He wanted her gone from the area, and today would be perfect. Hell, now he supposed he would have to keep his eye on her and follow the tour to the mountains. Her life could be in danger.

Did she care? Hell no. She'd crash right into trouble with her stubborn attitude. Accept her help or prove what she told him was a lie. How in the hell was he supposed to do that? Starting the car, he cranked up the AC. Another hot day on tap, the heat was already oppressive. He glanced at his watch. Nine-twenty-five was too early to be this warm. Driving out of the resort, he made his way to the station. Accept or prove, she said. That's what he planned to do.

His gut told him she wasn't a liar. He knew people, and she was one of the good ones. If he accepted Peyton's claim that Carlee Blair and E J had met, and that she was murdered, then he needed to find those remains. Almost an impossible task in the Superstitions.

Three unknown men were involved because Dawson owed one of them. Money? Possible. The scenario sounded solid enough except for the ghost telling Reynolds the story. The guys at the station would razz him mercilessly if they ever got wind of it. Still he knew his job, and he'd run down every lead, even the ones from kooks.

He parked the car, grabbed the file off the seat, and walked into the station. Grabbing his coffee mug, he stopped to fill it. He turned when he heard his name.

"Kincaid, the captain wants to see you. He said to tell you the minute you got in," Harper told him. His tall, muscular body filled the area in front of Jaxon's desk. "I wanted say goodbye in case I don't see you again. This is my last day. I've got a new job waiting for me. A big promotion and better pay." He smiled, crossing his arms in front of his chest.

"Congrats on the job, Harper. Tell him I'm on my way, would you? Never mind, I'll go there now." Jaxon threw the file on his desk and headed for Captain Stolberg's office.

He knocked on the open door. "Harper said you wanted to see me." Jaxon saw the bottle of antacids sitting on the desk next to the captain's coffee cup.

"Yes, come in and close the door." He motioned for him to sit. "Here's the deal. I'm concerned. Is it possible we have a mole inside the precinct? Too much information is getting out, and this whole Dawson case feels wrong to me."

"I guess anything is possible, but who? I can't imagine any of these guys being dirty." Jaxon's mind kicked into overdrive going over the officers he knew.

"I trust you, Kincaid. Keep your eyes and ears open. Tell me if you see anything suspicious."

"I will." He couldn't help noticing the stress written on the captain's face. "Are you okay, sir?"

"Hell no." He popped an antacid into his mouth.

"I've got the mayor and governor breathing down my neck on this one. They're pressing hard. They want this murder solved. You know Elliot Dawson is a donor to their campaigns, and there's a lot of political posturing going on. My instincts tell me this case is much bigger than the Dawson kid. Tell me you've got something, anything, please."

Jaxon explained what he had to date, leaving Reynolds out of it. "I learned from the Blairs that E J and their daughter were dating—against her parents' will. They thought he was too old for her. She had gone to meet him the day she disappeared."

"What are you saying?" the captain asked.

"We may have two homicides. I'm following a few leads now," he responded.

"I'm amazed you connected the missing girl to E J. Great work. How did you do it?"

"Luck, and something someone said to me steered me in the right direction." He squirmed inside when he said it. It wasn't a total lie, he reasoned.

"I'm impressed. However you came up with it, you did a damn fine job connecting them. Keep me informed. I'll tell the mayor. Hopefully, it'll stop his calls for a few days."

"Is that all, sir?" Jaxon asked. He didn't want to answer any more questions. He'd be telling the whole story if he stayed much longer.

"Yeah. Before you go, there's a rumor flying around here that you're trying to transfer back east. Is it true?"

"Yes." He nodded.

"Damn. I hate to hear that. You're a good investigator. I hope I can entice you to stay. Have you heard anything yet?"

"No, sir," Jaxon answered

"You'll have to stay on here until this case is solved—you're the lead. Be sure to tell them that if they call or I'll have to." The captain frowned.

"I'll finish the case. You can count on it. I don't like leaving loose ends." Jaxon stood and shook hands with the captain.

"Good to hear, Kincaid. Now get to work solving this case." His voice had a gruff edge to it.

Jaxon wondered what Stolberg would think if he told him the truth. If the case included Ms. Reynolds, he would have to tell him. Damn. What a nuisance. Ghosts. No one would believe him anyway.

****

Peyton finished the last bite of her fluffy omelet when she noticed a stranger watching her. He ducked behind the paper in his hands. Odd. All was forgotten when her phone rang and she saw who was calling. "Hi, cousin, I was going to call you when I got back to my room."

"How's it going? Any more ghost sightings?" Jessie asked her.

"Just a minute." She signed the bill and wrote the room number on it. "I'm back. Yes, is the short answer." She walked the hall back to her room.

"Tell me more. I'm going to put you on speaker so Reba can hear what you tell me. If that's okay?"

She stuck the key card in her door. Wow, the room had already been cleaned. "Fine with me. I can use all the help I can get."

"Peyton dear, this is Reba. I know we only met briefly when you were staying with Sadie, but I wanted

73

you to know Jessie and I are here for you. This must be a perplexing time for you. I remember when it first happened to our Jessie girl. Now she's an old hand at this kind of stuff."

"Have you ever seen a ghost, Reba?" Peyton plopped down in the chair.

"I've seen many things." Reba told her about a few.

"Boy has she ever." Jessie chuckled. "Plus, she'll know stuff about what you're going through that will astound you."

"Don't scare her, dear," Reba told Jessie.

"I'm warning her because I don't want her to be scared," Jessie replied. "Peyton, why don't you tell us what else has happened."

Peyton explained about Carlee's ghost and what she had seen in her mind. "I'm taking a tour to the Superstitions tomorrow to see if I can sense anything being in the area where I think it happened."

"Great idea," Reba said.

"You'll be going with a group, which is a good thing," Jessie added. "It's never good to go alone. If anyone thinks you're on to them, you can become a target fast."

"What did the detective say when you told him? Is he open to your help?" Reba asked.

"He doesn't know what to think. I can understand. It's strange to me too. We're hardly civil to each other." Peyton shook her head, thinking about their earlier conversation.

"Don't let that deter you, sweet girl. You need him on your side. These men are always logical, and they must figure things out their own way. He'll come around when he sees you're right and not sending him on a fool's errand."

"I hope so. I doubt we'll ever be friends, but there are some dangerous men involved. I don't want to tackle this on my own."

"Don't even think about it. Man do I wish I was there with you. I want to help." Jessie's voice rose several decibels.

"Jessie dear, you know she has to learn the same way you did." Reba paused. "Trust your instincts, Peyton, they'll be right. One thing I need to tell you is this case is bigger than it appears. The two homicides are only the tip of the iceberg. There is an additional far-reaching crime underneath. It will take down a few powerful people along the way. The good thing is you'll help a lot of people in the process. Your life will be in jeopardy. They want to use you as bait to get at the one they want to kill."

"Wow." She tried to digest what Reba said to her. Scared, yes. "Cousin, your warning is duly noted." Peyton shook inside.

"I hear you. Our Reba knows a lot. She's a bit of a white tornado when it comes to what she sees, but there's no one better to have in your corner."

"Reba, are you telling me that Detective Kincaid could be a target?" Peyton asked.

"Yes, dear, I guess I am. And if he is then so are you. By working with him, you're also in danger." Reba cleared her throat. "It'll all work out fine. You'll return to us a wiser woman by far with only a few painful bumps and bruises for your adventure."

"Peyton, remember the last part of what Reba said. You'll be fine, and you'll return to us. Those are words you need to play over and over in your mind when the going gets rough. Her words got me through many tough times over the past year, and they'll get you through too. Call us when you want to. I need to run. A customer came in the shop. We're here if you need us. Love you, cousin. Call me anytime."

"I'm sure you'll be hearing from me. I love you too." She shut her phone off.

What should she do with Reba's words? Jessie seemed to take them in stride. Did her cousin ever quake inside like she had when she heard them? For heaven's sake how did Jessie survive? Peyton shook her head. She had no idea how Jessie remained the happy, calm person that she visited with in Blue Cove. She must have been scared many times over the past year. Yet Jessie managed to make it, and she would too.

Changing into her swimsuit, she slipped on her suit cover, happy she had bought the bright-colored sarong. It was perfect. Slathered in sunscreen, she stuck her big hat on her head, glad she had managed to purchase it in the resort's gift shop. Grabbing her book from the nightstand, she went to the pool, found a lounge chair in the shade, and let her cares get lost in a book for the rest of the morning.

Chapter 10

He did it again. Seeing her yesterday made him lose his composure and all common sense. Damn. Someone needed to stick a sock in his mouth whenever she was near. He had no self-control. His professional, no-nonsense reputation was in danger of going up in smoke.

Stopping at the desk before he left the resort yesterday, Jaxon got the skinny on her tour today. Now here he sat waiting in the almost empty parking lot for a tourist group to arrive. The concierge had told him the tour's estimated time of arrival at the museum. He took a sip of his hot coffee followed by a bite of breakfast sandwich. He would keep his distance, but he wanted to be there to make sure nothing happened to her. He owed her at least that much. Several cars entered the parking area. Workers were arriving for the day. He followed each person's movements as they made their way into the building from their cars. As a woman neared the entrance to the museum, Jaxon noticed a man lurking near the front door. His nervous pacing signaled a red flag. He needed to keep an eye on him. Even from where he sat, something about the man seemed vaguely familiar.

The Lost Dutchman Museum seemed a perfect fit in its desert landscape. Situated beneath the west end of the Superstition Mountains with the sun now rising over their tops would make a great photo to send home to his family. He got out of the car for a moment and snapped the picture on his phone. In all his time living in Arizona, he had visited few of the tourist spots. His job kept him busy twenty-four seven and when he did get the time off, he flew home.

He glanced at his watch. The group should be there any time in the next half hour. While he waited, he drank the last of his coffee and reached for the file on the seat to go over the notes he had written last night. The shadowy figure forgotten, he went over every detail in the file, hoping something would jump out at him. He glanced several times to the entrance from the road. Finally, the van from the resort pulled into the parking lot. He automatically began to search for the man, but he was nowhere to be seen. Now what? He knew what he had to do.

****

Peyton stepped out of the van, shielding her eyes from the bright sunlight with one hand while reaching for her shades with the other. She slipped them on. "Detective Kincaid, I didn't expect to see you here. Yesterday's parley wasn't enough for you? Did you have something you left unsaid?"

"Look, if I had my way you would be able to enjoy your tour without me tagging along. I came early and noticed a questionable person lurking about. I feel obligated to make sure nothing happens to you."

"There's no need. I'm sure I'll be fine." She turned to leave.

"Not so fast. I'm afraid we're going to have to endure each other's company for a while if you want to see this place. I'll try to stay behind you unless I see him again, then I'll be right by your side."

"Detective." She nodded and began to walk.

"Jaxon," he stated and fell in step behind her.

She could feel his gaze boring into her back. "Are you going to hang back there and stare at me the whole time?"

"What do you suggest I do?" He sounded perplexed.

"You can walk beside me if you behave yourself, and I'll try to do the same." She stopped until he was standing next to her.

"I'm known among my peers as a no-nonsense kind of guy. I'm sure I can pull it off," he muttered sarcastically and gave her a half smile.

"Kincaid, I think that's the first attempt at a smile I've seen from you." She paused. "It made you look almost pleasant." She held out the last two words to goad him. Turning away from him, she began to read the plaques at one of the displays.

"Jaxon," he said under his breath.

Peyton learned a lot walking through the museum. She wasn't here for that purpose though. Jessie told her about knowing where you need to be for the next step in a case. Although she found facts about the Lost Dutchman Mine interesting, there had to be something more important. The next few things she read sent her mind into overdrive.

She forgot about the detective. Without saying a word to him, she headed for the nearest exit. The Superstitions were among the top five places in the state considered to be haunted. According to what she had just read, several people had gone missing—never to be seen again. Prospectors and hikers alike were random victims. There were many legends surrounding how they vanished. Everything from curses to aliens and rocks that could kill. Hikers had plenty of stories for what took place in the haunted mountains. Carlee was another number she supposed.

She sat on a bench gazing at the mountains surrounding the area. A strange sensation began to creep over her. A dark, foggy mist swirled and twisted around her until she found herself being dragged to the edge of a dark abyss. The hands that had dragged her to the brink forcefully shoved her off the edge. Screams stuck in her throat as she plummeted down into darkness, the walls closing in on her, stealing her breath, suffocating the life out of her. She never hit the ground. There near the bottom in a shaft of light she came face to face with Carlee standing next to her body. The vision left Peyton shaken. She had experienced Carlee's death and knew she was entombed somewhere in those mountains.

"Are you all right, Reynolds?" He shook her lightly. A sheen of perspiration covered her neck and arms. Her face was pale and clammy to his touch.

She tried to focus on his face. "What?"

"Are you okay?" He paused, looking at her with concern. "You seemed lost for a few moments. You left without telling me, and when I saw you here you didn't answer when I called."

"I'm sorry. I needed to come out for air," she stammered. "Carlee is there." She pointed at the mountains. "Somewhere in a cave or a mine shaft you'll find her body." The shivers ran up and down her arms like spiders walking on her skin. Saying the words aloud made what she saw seem even more real.

"Are you sure you're okay?" His voice was still tinged with concern.

She nodded. "You have to find her."

"I'm afraid finding her will take a lot of time, and time is something I don't have a lot of. There are too many places in those mountains where she could be."

"I don't think you need to worry about time. She wants to be found." She folded her hands in her lap to keep them from shaking. "She'll help you."

"You say the strangest things." He covered her trembling hands with his. "You really saw something didn't you? I find it hard to understand, but I know you're telling me the truth. Your body is shaking."

"I'm cold." *The air is way too hot to be cold,* flashed through her mind. Still she shivered.

"Tell me what happened," he said.

"The moment I sat on the bench an odd feeling came over me." Peyton explained everything she saw to him. "She's been waiting for us to come, and now we must find her. It's our greater purpose."

"Tell me what you felt." He squeezed her hand, encouraging her to continue.

"Intensity, fear, as if I were the one falling deeper into the abyss. My body slowly suffocated until I couldn't breathe. Right before I reached the bottom, I saw her standing by her body."

"No wonder you're scared," he mumbled under his breath. "Do you want to leave?" He stood, pulling her to her feet. "I've seen shock, and you're in shock. Let's get you out of the sun." She nodded and let him take charge.

****

"I notified the tour guide that you're riding with

me." He made sure she understood him. "Let's get you in the car and cool you down a bit." Jaxon had parked in the back corner of the lot. What had he been thinking?

Halfway to the car, the first bullet skipped to the side of them, just missing her. "Damn." He pushed her to the ground, protecting her with his body as he searched the area. He pushed her head down with her face in the dirt as another bullet whizzed by. They were sitting ducks out here in the open. It could have been a lot worse on the bench a moment ago.

He called for backup on his phone. Several people came out of the museum in a group and scattered, screaming when they heard the gunfire. A car driving in the parking area made for a good distraction. "Can you run?"

"Yes," she replied. "Tell me when, and I'll move as fast as my legs will carry me. Anything will be better than my face in the dirt." She paused. "Except for getting shot."

"Then move," he yelled. "Run as fast as you can toward my car." He pointed at its location. "Drop the minute I say to." They started running.

"Down!" They both dropped as the next bullet hit a saguaro, sending bits of the cactus flying around them.

"Are we almost there?" She lifted her head to look.

"Here comes another car. Move as fast as you can, and hopefully we'll be out of range." He crossed his fingers, and they took off again.

"Was it my imagination or were we being shot at on purpose?" she asked after they had reached the safety of his car. She turned in her seat when he closed the door and started the engine.

He nodded. "Yeah, you could say that."

"Why?" she asked, a bewildered look on her face.

"Good question. No answer, but I intend to find out. Now, buckle up." He twisted the key in the ignition and put the car in drive.

She latched her seatbelt as he sped out of the lot onto the road, passing several cars along the way. The last one was a patrol car. "Should you tell them we're okay?"

He had the radio in his hand when she asked. He gave dispatch a brief description of the man he had seen earlier. "I don't know if he's our guy, but the suspect is armed and dangerous. I repeat, he's armed." He glanced at her. "Are you okay?"

She nodded. "Shaken but, thanks to you, alive."

"They'll look for the suspect, but I have my doubts if they'll find him." Jaxon responded to a question on the radio.

"I can't imagine why." She leaned her head back against the seat.

"Too many places to hide." He glanced at her again and checked his mirrors to make sure no one was following. "You do know those were real bullets meant to kill you. They seemed to be headed your direction. Who do you know who might want to kill you?"

"No one in this area." Her voice trembled.

"Does that mean someone might have come from another area?" he asked.

"Your guess is as good as mine." She winced at the thought.

"What is that supposed to mean?" Jaxon frowned at her.

"I have no idea who would want me dead, and

that's the truth. I thought people liked me." She swiped at the tears running down her cheeks.

"That narrows our list of suspects," he said, his voice gruff.

"Maybe the same person who killed Carlee wants me gone, or could it be someone wants you out of the way?" She turned her head to look at him. "Kincaid, who wants you dead?"

"Let's leave it at a lot of people and not try to put a number on it." He grimaced.

"That many. I'm not trying to be judgmental or anything, but after the past few days I can almost see why. Kincaid, you might want to try and lighten up a little." She gave him a weak smile.

"Jaxon." He frowned. "I think you do that on purpose."

"Who me?" She feigned a look of surprise. "Before I forget, thanks for saving my life."

Chapter 11

Damn, he missed them. In this instance, anger got in the way of thinking clearly. Call it a calculated risk he hadn't thought through. He failed to consider the possibility of witnesses coming out of the museum in his rush for revenge. Botching several clear shots. Damn, he missed with every one of them. How the hell had he missed? He shook his head. The boss would hear about his failure, and there'd be hell to pay. Those around him hadn't ordered the kill either. This was his own personal vendetta. His supervisors would be mad, all right.

If the cops didn't kill him, one of the other guys would. Damn cops were everywhere. Wiping the sweat rolling down his face with his sleeve, he knew if he didn't get out of the heat soon, they'd be carrying him out on a stretcher, and his worries would be over. No water, no way back to the car but through the line of cops swarming the area. They were questioning every person inside and outside of the museum.

Shielding his eyes from the sun's intensity, he watched the activity below him. He'd let his hatred for Kincaid push him to do something stupid. He picked the pebbles from the soles of his boots. Suddenly, a shadow covered the sun's brightness. He glanced up, expecting to see a cloud. What he saw turned his blood to ice. He reached for his gun, shooting several rounds.

Panicked, he rushed to get away, scurrying across the rocks, slipping and stumbling forward through cactus until he pitched backward and took his last breath. His gun clenched in his hand in a death grip.

****

Jaxon had dropped Miss Reynolds off at the resort, walked her to her room, and made sure she promised to rest before he left her. She still seemed rattled. There was no way he could rationally explain this morning to anyone. He knew what he'd seen, and she was the real deal, as odd as the pronouncement made him feel. The Blair girl's body would be found in the Superstitions. There wasn't a doubt in his mind. How to find her was another question altogether.

Jaxon wrote questions on his notepad as they came to him. Why was E J murdered? He was a pain but mostly dabbled in petty stuff. Did it begin with him or could Carlee's murder hold the key? She fit into the grand scheme of things somewhere.

He was off his game this morning, and they were lucky to still be around, no thanks to him. Perplexed didn't cover his views on how the shooter missed them several times. They were an easy target out in the open. He should have kept his eye on the man. His gut had told him the guy was up to no good, and he let him slip out of his sight.

"Kincaid, do you have a minute?" Amos knocked on the wall of his cubicle.

"Sure, what's up?" There was a strange look on his friend's face.

"We found the suspect." He pulled up a chair and sat down.

"Is he in custody? I'd like to question him."

"No way you'll be doing that. The guy is dead," Amos told him. His forehead furrowed as he ran his hand through his dark hair.

"How?" Jaxon's instinct told him the case was about to become more bizarre.

"It's the strangest thing. We found him dead with his gun in his hand. We thought he was shooting at us, but no bullets came near any of us. Damn. He had the scariest look on his face. His eyes were wide open like he'd seen something." Amos shook his head. "His license said his name was Brice Delaney. Didn't his kid brother go to prison a few years back?"

"Yes, I testified at his trial. He went away for a long time. Brice must have wanted me dead. That answers one of my questions." Jaxon wrote Brice's name in the top of his notepad.

"Do you ever wonder how many enemies you've made on this job?" Amos asked. His blue-gray eyes looked troubled.

"I'm sure there's quite a few. Although, I try not to think about it." Jaxon tapped his pencil on the file.

"I'm telling you, Kincaid, Delaney didn't have a happy ending to his life. Something happened out there. Hell. I guess we'll never know what it was. Makes me wonder about all the rumors you hear about those mountains. I don't scare easily, but a lot of the guys felt the same way I did once they saw that poor guy." Amos pushed up from the chair, his over-six-foot frame unfolding as he did. "I thought you should know we got him, and he won't be shooting at anyone again."

"Thanks, Amos. I'm sure the autopsy will tell us more about how he died, but it can't tell us why." Jaxon shook his head.

"Makes you wonder what Brice has been up to if you know what I mean. Did he have anything to do with Elliot's boy's death?" He stroked his chin. "I'm telling you if the cause of his death isn't cardiac arrest I'll be surprised. He had a look of pure terror on his face." Amos turned to leave. "I'll be seeing that look in my dreams."

Jaxon would say nothing surprised him anymore, but he'd be lying. Everything was uncharted territory right now. Ghosts at the murder scene, Peyton's experience this morning, and now Delaney. What's next? He wasn't sure he wanted to know. He grabbed the file from his desk, stopped by to update the captain, and left the station. He had a few things he needed to check out.

****

Peyton picked up her ringing phone. She had no idea who the caller was. "Hello," she answered tentatively.

"Your cousin Jessie asked me to give you a call. She thought you could use my help. My name is Jeremy, by the way. She said she told you about me."

"Yes, she did. Thanks for calling." She relaxed back in the chair. "What did she tell you about me?" Peyton asked him.

"Only that you saw a murder victim and a few ghosts. Don't worry. I know how this stuff works. I've worked with Jessie long enough. The case you're involved in must seem strange to you. It's bound to get a lot worse before it's over if it goes the way of your cousin's cases." He chuckled. "Tell me what you've got so far."

She told him what she knew including what had

happened to her earlier that day. "I haven't heard if the police got the man who was shooting at us this morning."

"Sounds to me like I need to look into the Dawson boy and his family as well as the Blair girl. I'll call you back as soon as I get something. As Jessie probably told you, I'm a whiz with the computer and with research. Hang in there. I know how hard it was for your cousin when this began happening to her. I helped her where I could, but ultimately Jessie's writing stirred the pot and the spirits showed her what to do."

"What do you mean her writing stirred the pot?" she asked.

"Your cousin always told the victim's story with the belief someone would remember a detail. Writing is her gift. What's yours?"

"I've never thought about it." She pushed her hair behind her ear.

"From what I've observed, a spirit picks a person they believe can help them solve their case. You have something that Carlee and E J see, and you'll need to discover what it is. I'm sure you'll figure it out before long. There are plenty of people who are willing to help you along the way."

"I'm sure I'll need help. So far all I seem to be doing is bungling my way through it." Putting the phone on speaker, she removed the earring from her ear. The hoop was annoying her.

"Everyone has to start somewhere. I can't wait to meet you in person, Peyton. Your family is something." Jeremy reassured her that Jessie and now her were okay in his book. "Jessie singlehandedly has kept me busy with some of the most exciting cases I ever researched.

I have a feeling you'll be no different. Put my contact information in your phone and call me with any details you want me to research. The information I find goes a long way to helping the officers accept the stranger side of the case."

"I'm not sure if Kincaid wants any help or if he'll even accept it. But hey, it's worth a try," she added, sounding optimistic.

"That's my girl. Embrace who you are. I'll call you soon," Jeremy told her.

"Thanks." She disconnected the call. "Whew." Her cousin had kept her promise, and she wasn't in this alone. Peyton had no idea what she could do to stir the pot, as Jeremy mentioned. It would take some inspired thinking on her part. She was more of a creative writer than an investigative reporter. And she had no idea what Carlee thought she could do. Eventually she would figure it out or at least give it her best shot.

****

Kincaid walked right past him with the woman by his side and hadn't noticed him. He left a few minutes later. Standing, he placed the folded paper down on the table beside him. His growling stomach reminded him he was hungry and hadn't eaten since early this morning. The resort café called to him. The smell of food had wafted out to the lobby all morning while he waited. Between him and his buddy, they were keeping tabs on the woman around the clock.

He left the protection of his corner with the huge leafy plant only after the couple was out of sight. This was the perfect spot to watch undetected, and he didn't want to give his location away by being seen. Until the woman checked out, this chair would be called home.

How much did they know? Kincaid had been a thorn in his side for years, but he had no idea who the Reynolds woman was. Talking with staff yesterday and this morning, he learned she was a guest visiting from the east. She was there when E J was pulled out of the water. At least, that's what he had been told. He also learned she was going on a tour to the Superstitions.

If she's not a suspect, why was she still involved with Kincaid? Jaxon worked alone. He knew it wasn't a romantic thing. Kincaid had ice in his veins, and her body language told him she got upset with the detective often. He knew the feeling. The man drove him nuts. But he had to play it cool for now. "Be discreet," they told him, and "don't draw attention to yourself." Damn, he'd like to take Kincaid out and be done with it. *Patience, old boy. The right moment will come.* He talked himself back from the brink.

Delaney felt the same way, but he was a loose cannon. Brice told him this morning he knew how to get rid of Kincaid. Damn. He hoped he didn't go off half-cocked. The number one rule of the organization he worked for was you don't make a move until the order comes down from the top. Damn. He hoped Delaney didn't do anything foolish.

He was tired of dealing with and cleaning up Delaney's messes. For now, he would heed his boss's orders. They were paying the big bucks, and he could use the extra money. A lot of good all the money did him if he couldn't spend a dime of it. They didn't want him drawing attention to that either. At least he could afford a night here and something to eat. There was a time this place was off limits to him. Too high class for his wallet, but not anymore. Yep, he could do what he was told for a while anyway. They were paying for his stay here and rolling his expense account. He was spending plenty. He'd enjoy spending his own money soon enough if he could keep Delaney in line until he had their marching orders.

Chapter 12

Jaxon spent the afternoon talking to some of E J's friends. He found the conversations both interesting as well as enlightening. He speculated that one had called the others to give them a heads-up that they'd be questioned soon. Their answers were similar. Almost exact. Only two of Dawson's closest friends had any idea about Carlee Blair. Their take on her was that she was a bit of nuisance and followed E J around like a lovesick puppy. Of course, those two had watched each other the whole time they answered and played off each other. With their credibility questionable at best, Jaxon knew they were hiding something. According to them, the relationship was a bit one-sided, and Dawson was trying to let her down easy.

One thing all his friends confirmed in one way or another was in the last few weeks before his death Dawson spent money like water. He carried a huge bundle of bills around with him wherever he went. He thought nothing of giving the server at least a hundred-dollar tip. Dawson had told his friends that daddy had given him his inheritance from his grandfather. Each of his friends told him they had benefited from said inheritance.

A quick call to Elliot Dawson later in the day confirmed there was no early inheritance. He had no idea where his son had come up with money to waste.

He gave E J a large monthly income but not enough to throw money around on a whim. He had to pay for car payments and for his condo, which Elliot had purchased. It didn't leave him much to spend other than the money he made from his job.

He checked out where Elliot said his son worked. He had quit months before. Jaxon found himself back where he started. The Dawson kid was involved in something illegal. He needed to track the money. He wondered if Peyton had any tidbits of information for him after her earlier scare.

He still wasn't sure what to do with her. It would be hard to explain what she saw to anyone. Personally, he found it unbelievable himself. His observation of Peyton told him she wasn't a nut job. Her boss had nothing but praise for her and the job she did for his company. Even her story for why she came to Arizona in the first place had panned out. There were no red flags, no skeletons in the closet he could find, and a lot of people willing to vouch for her good character. For now, he would work with her until he found a reason not to. He'd stay close to her, keep his eyes open and his ear to the ground. If she wasn't who she claimed to be, it would show up eventually. With the decision made, he grabbed his phone and headed out of the station.

****

Peyton picked up the room service menu. She wasn't in the mood to eat in public alone. She wished Destiny would get here. How had she let her friend embroil her into an escapade once again? Only this time, Destiny wasn't there to laugh with. According to her latest text, she wouldn't be for a few more days.

Peyton wondered if she would see her at all before she got home.

She reached for her ringing phone. She didn't recognize the number. "Hello," she answered tentatively.

"Is this Peyton Reynolds?" the caller asked.

"Yes, who is this?"

"I'm Jessie's friend Frank Wagner. She told me you might need my help."

Her shoulders relaxed. "Jessie told me she would have you call. I would love for you to come, but you might need to talk to the detective in charge. He seems a bit testy when it comes to my involvement in the case. He tolerates me at best."

Frank's laugh answered her comments.

"I remember Matt felt the same way about Jessie in the beginning. It changed when they solved their first case. Solving that crime made him look good. You have my number. When you see the detective again, have him call me, and I'll talk to him. Tell me about what's happened in the case so far."

Peyton told him everything she had experienced up to this point, including today. "I hope I haven't shocked you." She sat forward in the chair, leaning her head against her hand.

"Not at all. It sounds like a version of the stories your cousin has told me over the past year. Jessie likes to believe she is helping the victims and their families find closure. There is something you can do to help them, or they wouldn't have sought you out." Frank paused. "Always keep the victim in mind, and you'll stay on track. Carlee's family needs to know what happened to their daughter. They need to know how and why so they can put her to rest and grieve."

"A good reminder. It's easy for me to feel sorry for myself and to wonder why this is happening to me." She sighed.

"True, but you need to turn it around a little. The question you need to ask is what happened to them?" Frank told her.

"I'll keep that in mind. As soon as I see Detective Kincaid, I'll tell him about your offer and see where it goes. Thank you for calling me. I appreciate any help you can give me." As soon as she disconnected the phone, it rang again.

"This is Jaxon. Have you had dinner yet?" he asked.

"I was about to order room service."

"If you don't mind the company, I know a great place where we can get the best Navajo taco in town. Are you in?"

"Sounds nice, although I can't say I've ever had one before." She paused. "I'm willing to give it a try."

"Trust me, you'll like it," he promised.

"I can't believe I'm about to say this." She smiled. "I'll trust you in this one instance." She closed her mouth tight to stifle her laugh. "Besides, I have a few things I want to talk to you about."

"I'm in the lobby. I drove here on a whim daring to believe you'd say yes. I hoped you would have something new for me. I've seemed to hit a wall."

"I won't be long." She terminated the call. She took a quick look in the mirror, ran the brush through her hair, applied some lip gloss, and dabbed on a bit of her favorite perfume. Reaching for her purse, she shoved her phone into it and stepped out into the hall, pulling the door closed behind her.

****

Jaxon stood as she approached, reminded once again of the effect she had on him. Pretty as a picture came to mind, followed swift on its heels by the thought his mom would love her. "That was fast."

"I'm hungry, and I admit I'm looking forward to trying something completely new to me." She stopped beside him. "You'd be surprised how hunger can motivate me to get moving."

"Good to know. Let's go." He let her precede him through the doors. She was as stunning from the back as the front. No longer detached, he admitted to himself that his interest in her had moved way beyond the case.

Once in the car, Jaxon talked to her about Brice Delaney. "I put his brother in jail a few years back, and he obviously wanted revenge. I don't believe for a minute I was the only target. He came after both of us, which has me wondering. Why you? You're new to town. I think someone must have watched after E J was found. They think you're involved somehow."

"Do you believe I'm still being watched?" She turned to look at him. "I find the idea of it scary to say the least."

"My gut tells me yes." He moved into the turn lane. "Keep your eyes open and maybe we'll catch the guy in action. Be on guard for someone sitting for a long period in the same place or in the coffee shop every morning while you're there. He'll try to be obscure, hidden behind a paper or magazine."

"I'll do my best." She slapped her hand to her forehead. "Oh my gosh, I forgot."

"What?" He glanced over at her.

"There was a man the other day in the coffee shop. I had the strangest sensation he was watching me."

"Let me know if you see him again."

"I will. All this talk of a possible stalker is making me uncomfortable. Is it okay if we change the subject?" she asked.

"Okay by me. As long as you promise to be smart about keeping your eyes open."

"Are you kidding? I will suspect every man I see now." She touched her earlobe and smiled. Quickly she took off the other earring. One earring wouldn't cut it.

"It could be a woman watching you too," he warned.

"I never thought of that. Of course, it could be. All criminals aren't just men."

"When do you have to go back home?" He turned into the restaurant's parking lot.

"I'm waiting to hear from my friend if she's coming or not. And I promised Carlee I wouldn't leave until we've found her."

"Do you think she'll care? I have no idea how this works." He took the key out of the ignition.

"Yes, I believe she would, and even if she didn't, I gave her my word. I do have to live with me when all is said and done." She opened her door when he got out of his side.

"I would have opened the door for you." He closed it behind her. She impressed the hell out of him. A woman with scruples was rare to his way of thinking.

"This isn't a date. We're two mutual friends out for dinner. I'm capable of opening my own door and not putting you out." She smiled at him. "I appreciate the gesture though."

"Just so you know, my mama trained me to open a door for a woman even if she's only a friend. You wouldn't want to get me in trouble with my mom, now would you?" He opened the door to the restaurant and followed her in.

She glanced over her shoulder at him. "I wouldn't want to be the cause of you disappointing your mama." She winked.

Chapter 13

The ambiance of the restaurant gave the place an inviting quality—pendant lighting, exposed brick with warm, rich tones, and soft music in the background. Together the effect was casual with a modern vibe and atmosphere. The dining area hummed with conversation. Peyton followed the hostess to their table, aware of Jaxon close behind her. Determined to enjoy the evening, she mentally exhorted herself to behave and not pick a fight with the good detective.

Arizona, a safe enough subject, was the first pick of the evening's innocuous topics. She told him about her scheduled tour to Tucson and Tombstone in the next couple of days. She filled Jaxon in on the tourist's sites from what she had read in the brochures.

"Sounds like you have your next few days planned out." His mouth turned up slightly at the corners.

"I figure why not see everything that I can. I won't be in the area long and probably won't be back anytime soon. I'm determined to see as much of the state as possible before I leave." The way he watched her made her wonder if he could see right through her lame attempt to keep conversation on solid ground.

"Good idea. You'll have seen more of the area than I have." He rubbed his hand over his dark stubble. "I might have to play catch up. I can't be outdone by a New Yorker." A smile dangled at the corner of his lips.

"Do you like living here?" she asked. Even a half of a smile transformed his face. She glanced away. That smile made her catch her breath.

"It's okay. As I mentioned before, I came here for my first job interview out of police academy. They hired me, and I've been here since. I want to live closer to my family though. Besides missing the East in general, I miss the green and the trees. Every chance I get I'm on a plane going east." He talked about his family and how much he missed his siblings at holidays.

"I don't know how people handle the heat. I feel like I'm melting when I walk out the door." She fanned her face playfully. "But when I'm inside I need a sweater because the AC is cold. Brrr." She laughed while rubbing her arms.

"It's annoying at times, but the winters are great. Although AC never bothers me." His finger tapped quietly on the table. "My one concern about moving east is I'm not sure I want to shovel snow. But there's something to be said about experiencing all four seasons."

"Snowblower is the one word that could solve your dilemma." She grinned.

"True. How about you? Do you like living in the Big Apple?"

"I love the city, but it's not as fun since my cousin moved. We used to hang out most weekends." She took a sip of water. "Jessie has a nifty red convertible. We took many trips to escape the heat of the summer. We spent quite a few weekends checking out the covered bridges in the area."

"I've seen quite a few myself. They make

wonderful postcard photos in the fall and winter. What will you do now that she's moved?" he asked.

"My sister Madison talks about moving to New York, but honestly after spending time in Blue Cove, I would love to live there. I guess at this point in my life the choices are unlimited." She relaxed as she said the words aloud. True, she really could choose what she wanted to do. Her life wasn't set in stone.

"Wouldn't you like to live closer to your parents?" he asked.

"Not particularly." Her words sounded unkind even to her. Her body tensed.

"The cop in me wants to know why." He studied her.

She felt uncomfortable under his steady gaze. "My parents have issues, and let's just say my childhood was less than stellar. I'd rather not talk about it. It's a private matter."

He reached across the table, his finger brushing the top of her hand. "Look, I don't want to pry, but this seems to be a hard subject for you. Maybe I can help is all I'm saying. Since we'll probably never see each other again once you're done here, I'm a perfect person to confide in."

"I know." His touch unnerved her. "Maybe before I leave, I'll feel free to. We'll see." She moved her hand and fiddled with the napkin on her lap. "I have some other things I want to discuss with you tonight if that's okay?" With a quick glance at his face, she saw his nod. She thanked the waiter as he topped off her water.

After they ordered dinner, she told him about Jeremy and Frank's calls. Writing Frank's phone number on a piece of paper from her purse, she handed it to him. "Frank said he'd be happy to talk to you if you want to call. His dog is quite successful, and Frank's resume is impressive."

"I'll call, but I doubt there's any money in the budget for bringing him all the way here or paying Jeremy for his research."

"Frank said he'd come here to help me because of my cousin Jessie. Jeremy told me he would do the research and get back to me. He's looking into the connection between E J and Carlee. He'll check out E J's financial connections too. I didn't get the idea that either one of them wanted any money for it." She toyed with a lock of hair that had fallen in front of her shoulder.

"Free is good." He gave her a slow, attractive smile.

She looked away from him, but the butterflies were already dancing in her stomach. Dang. She didn't want any complications. Her mind went in search of a new idea to talk about. Hopefully one where he wouldn't smile again. In one single moment, that smile had breached the wall she had spent years building to keep people out.

****

He watched Peyton go from animated and lit from within to quiet and withdrawn in a few minutes. Jaxon had no idea what had happened. Had he said something wrong? Their conversation seemed normal enough. He searched for a different topic.

"Do you like your job?" He steered the conversation away from her family. Talking about jobs usually was nonthreatening.

"It wasn't the position I studied for, but I do like it.

I get to read some great stories and make dreams come true for a few writers." The waiter placed the plate in front of her. "This looks yummy."

"You're in for a taste treat." He spooned salsa on top of the huge taco, and she followed his lead. "The frybread is what makes this great. I like to eat it plain or with honey as a dessert too." He cut a piece of the frybread and all the fixings and took his first bite. Jaxon sat back and watched her follow his lead.

"My, this is good." She licked the corner of her lip to catch the drip in danger of slipping. Her napkin followed quickly. She dabbed at the corners of her mouth.

He found her movements fascinating. To keep from staring at her mouth, he jumped into conversation. "You should watch the Navajo women make their bread. They toss it back and forth with their hands, stretching the dough as they go. The dough gets air along with the right thickness without a rolling pin. It puffs up light and golden in the hot oil. The perfect thickness is important. If it's too thick, it won't be light like this. Think of the history. One mother teaches her daughter and so on." He took another bite.

"I doubt I'll ever find a Navajo taco back home." She took a picture of her plate. "A reminder of food unique to the area," she told him.

"What job did you want?" he paused between bites to ask.

"I did an internship working with special needs children, and that's the position on the top of my wish list. I couldn't find a position in that field when I moved to New York. I appreciate getting the job I have. Still I'm looking at teaching as a career possibility for the future."

"It seems like we've found a topic we both can agree on." He attacked his dinner, scarfing it down quickly.

"I think we have." She gave him a puzzled expression.

"What?"

"I don't believe I've ever seen a full plate empty quite that fast." She looked down at her still mostly full one. "Never having had a brother, do all guys enjoy their food like you seem to?"

"Sorry. I'm used to eating in a hurry and catching a quick bite whenever I can. It's a bad habit. Plus, growing up with siblings I learned to eat fast or not get seconds." He chuckled. "Our dinner table was a fierce competition between us boys to see who could eat the most. Bragging rights, you know. My sister often was overshadowed by our antics."

"Anyone who works knows what it is to polish off a meal in a few minutes. For me, it wasn't your speed as much as your appetite. I believe I've finally found someone who could hold their own with my cousin Jessie." She laughed.

"I'm intrigued. This cousin of yours sounds interesting, even a bit daunting. Beside seeing ghosts, she likes to eat." In his mind, he pictured a big woman wrestler with muscles.

"Don't get the wrong idea. Jessie likes food but not in excessive amounts. She's a runner—at least ten miles a day. She's one of the prettiest and sweetest people I know."

"I'd like to meet her. After talking to Chief Parker, she sounds like a unique person." Their eyes met across the table. It would be hard to top the attractiveness of the woman sitting across from him.

"She is. I'm rather in awe of her these days." She placed her fork down on the plate.

She was serious. He could tell by her expression, but he couldn't imagine her reason. "Why?"

"I don't know if I can explain it. My cousin over the past year has transformed into a strong, confident woman who can meet the challenges life throws at her. She quit an amazing job as an investigative reporter. Offered a great promotion at the news organization where she worked, she opted to move instead to the small town of Blue Cove, where she has flourished. I've seen those changes firsthand. Me, on the other hand, I've been stuck spinning my gears for a while. This is my first venture outside my comfort zone in many years."

"There's a lot to be said about comfort." He leaned back in his chair, intrigued by the emotions playing out quickly across her face. Insecurity, fear, followed by resolution, each one making her seem vulnerable and yet more beautiful than ever.

"I guess comfort is great if you don't mind being described like a fuzzy pair of slippers or an old robe. I would rather try exciting, if only for a while." She thanked the waiter when he took her plate away. "That's why I won't leave here until Carlee is found. This is my moment, and there may never be another quite like it." She told him a few stories about growing up with her friend Destiny and about times in New York with her cousin. "True comfort was hard to come by until I was on my own. But once in a while, I still want to fly."

"I've never met your cousin, and I'm only beginning to get know you, but I consider myself to be fairly observant. Do I have your permission to tell you what I think?"

"Be my guest." She gave him a cautious smile.

"You shouldn't compare your life to your cousin's because you're both different in your own special ways. What I do know about you is that you're quite capable and strong. You hide the real you behind a structured and well-ordered life. Occasionally, when you least expect it, the strong will in you has to exert itself. The whole picture makes you one damn sexy woman and at times hard to figure out." He raked his hand through his hair. "So much for my astute observations."

Jaxon knew the precise moment Peyton realized she had said more than she had intended, and he had too. Not used to trusting anyone—especially a man—she closed off after that, not saying much the rest of the evening. Their conversation became stilted at best. Still, for a few minutes the real Peyton came shining through. She was no one's pushover or shadow. She might hide behind the persona for what she thought was a good reason, but Peyton's real strengths couldn't be stifled for long. Letting her go wouldn't be easy. In fact, it would be darn near impossible. There were many facets to discover about her, and he liked challenges. Tomorrow he would have to rebuild trust all over again. He looked forward to it.

Chapter 14

"What were you thinking?" She wrapped up in a throw and turned on the TV. "Blabber mouth," she mumbled. Mad at herself, she frowned when she thought of all the personal stories she had told the detective tonight. Those areas were hers alone, and rarely had she shared them with anyone except for her sister. The one time her tongue got the best of her, and it had to be with Kincaid. She blew out a loud breath in protest. "One smile and you went all weak in the knees," she scolded herself and continued her rant. "Peyton, I swear you have no sense at all. I'm done talking to you. No more Jaxon Kincaid. He'll break your heart and you know it."

He had tempted her with kindness and the smile that transformed his face. She could have told him a whole lot more and maybe should have. Well, time would tell if he was the real deal or an illusion like everything else in her life. Although, he was the first one to see through her false front and get to the heart of the real person inside. Warring with her awakening feelings for a man she detested and wouldn't see again was sadly unnerving. She flipped through the stations trying hard not to think about him anymore. Channel surfing until she lighted on the perfect show, she settled on mindless entertainment with a few laughs. Resting her head back against the chair, she watched until her eyes became heavy and slowly closed.

Taking a step back in time, she stood alone on a dirt road. Surrounded by old buildings lining both sides of the street. Where was she? The town looked like something out of an old west magazine. The longer she stood there, the more the town came slowly to life. Four men dressed in black from head to toe walked down the wooden walkway, their spurs jingling as they walked. The tallest man tipped his cowboy hat to a woman who scurried past them. His long jacket fell open, revealing the holster riding low across his hips. Mesmerized, Peyton followed their progress until they crossed the road out of her line of vision.

Sensing the excitement, she stood in the crowd watching as a stagecoach raced into town pulled by several horses panting and lathered from their pace. Throwing down a mail bag, an older gray-bearded man riding shotgun jumped off. He opened the door, revealing a beautiful young woman who reached for his hand extended her way, and suddenly the town came alive with people. The walkways were filled with cowboys, prospectors, and businessmen, all coming and going from the buildings which had been empty only moments ago.

The mercantile had a buggy tied to the hitching post in front of the doors, patiently waiting for the man carrying his wife's purchases. The banker opened the shades, soon followed by the door being unlocked and the "Open" sign displayed. The passengers from the stagecoach walked into the Grand Hotel. The plaque beside the door said, "Established in September of 1880". Surreal—was this really happening? As she walked past a large adobe building, Peyton noticed a rendering of the beautiful woman she had just seen getting out of the stagecoach—a singer scheduled to perform the next several nights. She had to be dreaming, or was she?

A little farther down the walkway the Old Bird Cage Theater, complete with a horse watering trough outside the doors, came into view. The closer she got to the building the more she knew that it wasn't a place for her to go. The door swung open and the smell of whiskey filled the air. The piano music was loud, the singing raucous, and the laughter from screeching women caused her to scurry past. The Cage was the destination of many cowboys and prospectors racing to get in. She frowned—men—she shook her head in disgust. Moving to the far side of town, she sat on a bench outside the courthouse. She paused, watching the action with fascination and no idea why she was there. Waiting. The sun blinding and hot. She closed her eyes for a moment and then opened them.

The streets were still filled with people, no longer from the past but the present. In and out of the stores they went buying souvenirs. Ice cream cones were purchased by the dozens, stagecoach rides were filled to capacity, and historical tours kept the tourists spending their money on a hot summer day. Cars moved slowly by the courthouse. People popped out of their cars long enough to take pictures of the hangman's gallows. As quickly as they came, they moved on to watch the next attraction. A man announced over the loudspeaker that the gunfight at the O.K. Corral enactment would be in ten minutes. Still she waited. The sun, high in the sky, beat down on her. She shielded her eyes and continued her watch. Anticipation building, goosebumps filled her arms. It wouldn't be long now. During the sound of gunfire, Peyton saw Carlee. She followed her to the highway sign pointing the way to the southern border only thirty miles away. One ghost after another joined Carlee. Young men, women, and children who must have suffered the same fate through the years. Peyton understood her message.

She awakened in the morning in the same place she had sat the night before. The TV was still on, her body stiff from being upright in the chair. She stretched her legs out, groaning as she did. She had some thinking to do. Peyton was not an investigative reporter by any stretch of the imagination, but she knew a good story when she read one. What had played out in her mind seemed real. Somehow, she'd write Carlee's story. Maybe if she wrote it as fiction, it would make someone think about the plight of murder victims and missing persons in this country.

****

Jaxon had no idea what the day might bring, but his gut told him to keep his eye on Peyton. Whether she wanted him to or not. He needed to talk to Captain Stolberg as soon as he had a clearer picture. After a morning coffee, the next thing on his agenda was to talk to Frank Wagner with Miss Reynolds right beside him when he did. At the moment, he wasn't sure what to think about Peyton's ability. New territory for him, with no other experience similar in his training to gauge it by.

The phone on his desk buzzed. "Kincaid, can you take a call from a Chief Parker of Blue Cove?"

"Sure, put him through." He waited for the call. "This is Detective Kincaid," he answered as the phone rang.

"I thought I should check with you to see how things are going?" Matt asked. "Jessie won't let me rest until she hears from you that all is okay."

"I'm still trying to figure Peyton out. Everything she has told me to this point has panned out. I'm reserving judgment for a while." He leaned back in his chair.

"How's she holding up?"

"She's okay, but all the experiences with the paranormal may be taking a toll on her. I get the feeling it's new territory for her. She's a private person anyway, but when it comes to her family, she's a closed book. Do you have any idea why?"

"From what Jessie told me recently, the family is only beginning to understand what Peyton and her sister went through as kids."

"Makes sense. She doesn't want to talk about her parents. As strange as I find all that she has told me so far, she has been right-on with the case I'm investigating. I've been thinking of bringing my captain in on her ability. I think she needs protecting. Information is leaking out of the department somewhere, and I don't know who is the source. But the Captain is trustworthy—I'd stake my life on it."

Matt explained what had happened in his department in Blue Cove and Jaxon asked him every question he could think of. "How did you figure out that the chief of your town was dirty? Seems like a tough spot for you to be in."

"I almost didn't until it was too late. He kidnapped Jessie and drugged her. He was getting ready to kill her when we got there. A few minutes more and it would've been too late. I couldn't believe the man was a criminal even when my gut told me something was wrong. All I'm saying is, keep your eyes and ears open. You'll know."

"I hope so." Jaxon jotted down a couple of things Parker told him.

"If you feel Peyton's in danger, then she probably is. Even more so if someone is angry with you and has put you two together for any reason."

"I admit I never thought of the angle of hurting her to get at me until the other day. The man who shot at her was angry at me." He explained to Matt what had happened at the Lost Dutchman Museum.

"Stay in touch. Jessie is worried about her cousin, and we are happy to help in any way we can," Matt said.

"I will. You sound like a sane enough guy, and yet you've dealt with similar circumstances with Jessie. You've survived, and I'm thinking I will too." Jaxon shook his head and chuckled inside.

"I kept my sanity by listening to her, then building the case in my methodical, logical way. We managed to solve each case thrown at us by working as partners. I've learned to trust her premonitions, and she trusts my steady approach."

Jaxon ended their conversation a few minutes later. Who should he trust? Before he could bring in Frank and his bloodhound to search for Carlee, he needed the captain's permission, and that meant exposing Peyton. Damn. He needed to think this through. He didn't want her vulnerable to what might follow if the truth got out. On the other hand, she hadn't steered him wrong. She had become a target and her life could be in danger.

Iona Morrison

The thoughts were still racing through his mind when he walked into the captain's office to talk. He had to trust someone, and he knew what he needed to do.

114

Chapter 15

After her morning walk, Peyton got dressed and ready for breakfast. She wanted to go somewhere new this morning. After a quick internet search of local restaurants, she discovered a small gem only a few blocks away from the resort. The reviews were wonderful, and the cafe lived up to all the customers' hype. The atmosphere, friendly and cozy on first inspection, only improved the longer she sat there. A perfect place to read and enjoy her breakfast. She thanked the waitress when she placed her meal in front of her. The first bite of her southwest benedict tantalized her taste buds. A while later, looking at her empty plate, she couldn't believe she ate the whole meal. So good. The hazelnut coffee was brewed to perfection, and she enjoyed several refills. And even though she knew she shouldn't, the fresh baked raspberry-vanilla scone topped her meal off perfectly. Salad and fruit would be on her menu for the rest of the day. Still the scone was worth every salad for the next few days. Each bite reminded her of Molly and Java Joe's Coffee Shop in Blue Cove.

Pulling the brochures from her purse, she planned the itinerary for the next couple of days. Tomorrow, Tombstone was on her agenda. Destiny still hadn't arrived, but Peyton was bound and determined to see the area before she left Arizona. After the dream the other night, she wanted to see the town in person.

"Are you planning on going to Tombstone?" the waitress asked when she noticed the brochure. She topped off her coffee.

"I am. Is it worth the trip?" Peyton reached for the cream.

"Of course, but it's a bit of a tourist trap. There's plenty of history to take in if you're interested in historical facts. I wasn't into all that mumbo jumbo in school. Never paid much attention to the subject, but I liked Tombstone. I think you might like it too."

"I'm sure I will." Peyton smiled at the woman as she walked away.

She spent several minutes texting Destiny and her cousin Jessie. Destiny wasn't ready to come yet, and Jessie wanted to know everything about her dream. Texting was too hard for that much information. Instead, Peyton called to talk to her.

"Tell me all. Your dream sounds amazing."

Peyton told her everything she could remember and was happy to get it off her chest. "What do you think it means?"

She listened to Jessie give her a general overview. "The truth is, cousin, you'll never fully understand what it means until you finish with the case. It will become clear why you were needed and why you saw what you did. There's always a reason for it."

"I'm going there tomorrow. Like everything else, I guess it's best if I adopt a wait and see approach."

"I can't wait to hear your first impressions. Send me pictures and explain your feelings. I'm getting into this case vicariously through you."

Jessie's laugh sounded like music to her ears. "I've

missed all the fun times we had in the city."

"I miss you too, but not the city. I love living at the cove," Jessie told her.

"I know you're happy. And just so you know, I'm rethinking my life right now. I may have to move closer to you and all those handsome guys living around you." Peyton handed the waitress her credit card.

"I'd love to have you around, and Madison too," Jessie added. "But what about the hunky detective you're working with?" Jessie laughed softly.

"You mean the one I fight with every time we are in the same vicinity? There's no danger of him being mine. Besides, if he's even a tad bit serious about me, he could move east to be near me."

"True, or you could move to Arizona to be near him." She heard Jessie cough as she tried to cover her mirth.

"That's not going to happen." Peyton smiled to herself.

"Who knows? He could move closer to his family, which would be closer to Blue Cove."

"How are Katie's plans for the wedding going?" Peyton changed the subject.

"It's all on track. Of course, you are invited. You know what that means."

"No. Tell me."

"This case is about to rev up, and you're in for one heck of a ride. Keep in touch. I want the skinny on it. I might like to write an article around the Tombstone connection."

"Wow, I like how your mind works. I'll call or email you when I have more. See you in a few days." Peyton gathered her brochures and headed back to the resort. The sun beat down on her head. Angling her hat to shade her face, she needed to hurry. It was too hot to be outside for long. If she went anywhere else today, she would drive. Living closer to her cousin would be great. She needed to think about how she could keep doing what she loved while living where she wanted to live.

****

Jaxon knocked on the captain's open office door. "Sir, do you have a minute to talk?"

"Come in and shut the door." When the door was closed, he said, "I'm John to you. You're just the man I wanted to see. Have you got anything new for me?"

The question opened the way for Jaxon to tell the captain about Peyton, and he did. "The thing is, sir, she's not a kook or out to get attention. She's genuinely surprised by what's happening in her life." He went on to tell him about Peyton's cousin Jessie and Chief Parker. He talked about his conversations in the morning with Frank Wagner and Jeremy. "I've talked to them all personally a few times. They've solved some high-profile cases and are highly thought of by the FBI in their area. I even talked to Tom Maxwell, an agent who worked with them on several of those cases." He went on to describe a couple of Parker's and Reynolds' cases. Jaxon handed Stolberg a paper with the phone numbers of all the folks he had talked to about Peyton. "All of them said you could call to check up on anything I've told you."

John folded the paper and slipped it into his pocket. "I've never heard anything quite like this before. I'm willing to trust you on this if it doesn't get too weird. At this point, I'm getting heat from the top to solve this one. Anything that will help us move forward—I'm all for it. I may not want to know all the details I can't explain though."

"Chief Parker told me some things have to be left out of the reports because no one would believe them anyway. I think Peyton would prefer to keep it low-key if you know what I mean." Jaxon stood to leave. "I will keep you up to date on what we learn."

"Before you go, have you been thinking over what we talked about the last time you were in here? Has anyone stood out to you? I know someone is leaking information. I just don't know who at this point." He slammed his fist on his desk. "Damn. There's nothing I hate more than the idea of a dirty cop working among my men." Captain Stolberg stood. "Keep your eyes open. I want to solve the case, but I want to get the dirty cop among us even more."

"I will, sir."

"John," he reminded Jaxon. "Now get out there and solve this one. It'll look good on a resume if you're still thinking about transferring closer to home. I'd rather you didn't. You're a damned fine detective, and I'd hate to lose you."

"Thank you." Jaxon left the station and headed toward his car. If there was someone leaking information, did they know about Peyton? If they did, she could be in grave danger. This upped the stakes another notch.

****

He had followed her from a distance this morning. The small café wouldn't accommodate him without risk of being seen. With the AC in his car running, he waited for her to come out again. Damn. She was taking her own sweet time. Somehow this girl fit into the picture. He just had no idea how yet. Told to watch her and to be sure not to be seen. Here he sat. No one needed to tell him not to let her see him. He was putting his life on the line with this one. It didn't matter anyway. In over his head, he could find no way out of the hole he had dug for himself. His wife would never understand it nor his kids. It was for them that he got in it in the first place. The money enticed him, and his hatred for the boss motivated him. Sick and tired of never having anything and passed over for every promotion and chance to get ahead added more fuel to his anger. Raising kids was an expensive enterprise, and his job paid diddley squat. Hell, he'd probably die before this was over. These guys were ruthless. At least, he would leave his family with something. He was worth more dead to them than alive. What a damned depressing thought.

Chapter 16

Jaxon wouldn't be at peace until he made sure Peyton was okay. He wasn't about to investigate the reason for these strange, protective feelings. Chalking it up as part of the job, he drove to the resort only to find out she wasn't there. "Damn," he muttered under his breath and pulled out his phone.

"Reynolds, where are you?" his terse voice asked her when she answered.

"Kincaid, I'm at the bookstore. What's up?" Her tense tone echoed through the line.

"We need to talk," he threw back at her.

"Right now? At this precise moment?" she asked. "You could have called earlier to let me know. I'm going to finish here, and then I'll head back to the resort." She exhaled. "Will that be soon enough to satisfy you?"

"I'll be waiting." He disconnected the call, shaking his head. How in the hell did that happen? His rush to protect her ended up pushing her farther away. Angry at himself and embarrassed by the way he treated her, he plopped down in the nearest chair in the lobby. What was it about her that drove him to act like a total idiot? He would have to apologize, and she would be in no mood to hear him out. How could he blame her?

****

Peyton took her time looking for a book.

Undecided about her choice, she spent more time than usual at it. Of course, it didn't help that her stubborn side wanted to waste time and make Kincaid wait. With any luck, he would leave before she got back to the resort. Who did he think he was talking to her like he had? The man frustrated her. She had no idea how to handle him. As much as she would love to annoy him, it probably wasn't a good idea to provoke him. The case had to be stressful for him. Decisions made both about books and what to do about the baffling detective, she carried her purchases to the car. If need be, she was quite capable of standing up to the infuriating man. She wouldn't let him walk all over her.

Today wasn't her lucky day. Trouble waited for her in the lobby. Kincaid stood when he saw her walk in the door.

"Detective." She swept past him and looked away from him as she did.

"Please sit. We need to talk," he said.

She sat in the chair across from him. "I'm listening."

"I'll told the captain about you today. He's willing to let me work with you." His hand rubbed his temple as he talked.

She didn't know what she expected to hear, maybe an apology, but not that he told the captain about her. "Is that the reason you treated me to your temper? You didn't want to work with me and you're secretly hoping that being belligerent will make me go away?"

"Sorry. I didn't mean to sound angry." He explained about the captain's concern about one of his officers leaking out information. "His concern was that you could become a victim if they somehow tied you to

122

the case. When I came here and found you gone, I overreacted. Not one of my finest hours. I'm not proud of it."

"Let me see if I have this right. You were concerned about my safety. You have a strange way of showing it, Kincaid."

"In my defense, you're not the easiest female to get on with."

"I see. Now you're blaming your actions on me. If this was meant to be an apology, I would give you an F. You aren't winning any points."

"You're right. I'm making a damned mess of it. I have no idea what it is about you that makes me go nuts."

"I get it. You irritate me to no end. Let's make a pact to finish this case and never have to see or work with each other again." She started to stand.

"Not so fast. We really do need to talk about the case and what you'll be doing the next few days. After talking to your friends today, I'm convinced we need to be on the same page. We don't need any surprises."

"Okay, for the sake of the case I can put my feelings aside. The sooner Carlee is found the sooner I can go home."

"I arranged for us to have a small conference room for a few hours to work out a game plan. At this point it's best if we stay away from the station and other public places where we might be overheard." He led the way to the room the resort staff had shown him earlier.

She sat across from him at the table. "Where do you want to begin?"

"I need to know your schedule the for the next several days. I don't want to be caught unaware again.

I'm concerned for your safety. We're dealing with some nasty people who aren't afraid to attack us out in the open."

She reached for a notepad and pencil on the conference table. Listing her itinerary, she handed it to him. "These are my only plans as of right now. I'm not used to having to tell anyone my whereabouts. Especially since I'm all grown up."

"You won't have to again after you leave town or the case is solved. I'm sorry to have to muck up your vacation like this, but that's how it goes sometimes." He glanced at what was written on the paper. "It looks like I'll be going to Tombstone tomorrow."

"Why? I'm sure I'll be fine. I'll be with a tour group, and no one would be silly enough to try something while I'm in a group."

"That's where you're wrong. None of those things can protect you if someone wants to get at you badly enough," Jaxon emphatically told her. "Remember the museum."

"Well, if that's the case you won't be able to keep it from happening either."

"Let me put it this way. No one else will be looking out for you, but I will do all in my power to keep you safe. Besides, if I'm not with you, there won't be any trip to Tombstone for you." He pointed at her when he said it.

"I see your manners haven't improved in the last few minutes. I'll go along with your demands because I've decided to and not because you've told me I have to. For all your faults, I believe you have my best interests at heart." She scowled at him. "And I will enjoy myself despite the fact you're there."

"Good. With that settled, let's get down to business. I want to know anything you're feeling or seeing regarding this case."

They spent the next hour going over what she had seen and what he knew, trying to work out a tentative plan of action. "Won't this be hard for us to do if we can't even see each other without fighting?" She glanced away when she asked him. "Trust seems important if we are going to work together."

"Why do you think we are instantly at each other's throat every time we're near each other?"

"I have no idea other than we don't like each other." She glanced at him.

"I'd like to venture a guess. I think it's the opposite. We are attracted to each other and don't want to be." Jaxon leaned back in his chair and studied her.

"Even if what you say is true, and I'm not saying that it is, we are both going our separate ways when this is done. There's no reason to start something that can't go anywhere." His scrutiny made her nervous. She stood to leave.

He blocked her exit to the door. "I've been thinking about this for days." He pulled her tight against his chest and kissed her. "Damn," he whispered in her ear then turned and walked out of the room.

She watched him leave. Shaken to the core, Peyton let her anger vent. "Walk away from me you, big jerk. You can't just kiss me like that and leave." The longer she thought about it the madder she got. He may be on the trip with her tomorrow, but she didn't have to like it. She plotted in her mind the perfect revenge befitting his action. *Kincaid, I hope you're ready for the ultimate silent treatment.*

Chapter 17

Jaxon was waiting for Peyton when she stepped out of the tour van. He grabbed her hand, and she slapped at his arm and tried to pull free. He held tight. Silent treatment, he had expected and possibly worse. Side by side they walked beside each other in complete silence. When they reached Allen Street, the historic street of the old west and the tourist part of Tombstone, he noticed a sudden change in her demeanor. Something was up but what? "Are you okay?" he asked.

She didn't respond but seemed to be mesmerized by something around her. He couldn't see anything, but she must be. The atmosphere around her seemed charged. He couldn't put his finger on what was happening, but she held his hand tight. Really tight. In a death grip, almost painfully so. He would take his cue from her because he had no idea what was happening with her. At one point, she ducked, flinched, and seemed to weave back and forth as if moving through a huge crowd. "Peyton, what's up?" She ignored the question. He kept pace with her and waited until she returned from wherever she had gone.

****

As her foot touched the walkway, Tombstone suddenly became the vibrant, active, living community of yesteryear—a pictorial window in time opened before her. The hot summer day seemed to give most of the people living in the area the same idea. Dusty streets were busy with cowboys riding into town, and buggies were filled with families hoping for a slight breeze to give them a break from the inferno. Not a hint of rain could be felt in the air. At least there was no mud to mar the hem on her new dress.

The long, green calico dress she wore slapped against her sturdy boots as she walked the wooden walkway. She caught a glimpse of her image in the bank window. Her bonnet matched her dress, with her hair tucked neatly out of view.

"You're as pretty as a picture standing there." The man tipped his hat and smiled at her as he walked out of the bank.

Taking a deep breath, excitement coursed through her. She peeked at the handsome man at her side. His holstered gun rode low across his hip, one hand never far from the handle while the other held onto hers. It seemed a tad tighter after the man addressed her. Probably only her imagination. Still, the clink of his spurs against the wood became a melodic reminder she felt safe when he was near.

Tombstone could turn rowdy with little warning. He had said he wanted her out of there before it did. They were one of the several couples among the endless parade of cowboys and miners racing back and forth in town. The heat meant drinking, and before long tempers would flare. The sound of gunfire was the first sign there was trouble. People scattered in all directions, and she ran with them. The rancid smell of gunpowder filled the air.

As quickly as it started it was over, but the scene changed. Peyton walked no longer among the living but the dead. With their haunted eyes and sunken, tortured faces, the ghosts of Tombstone strolled by them on both sides of the street. Some rode on horseback or came to town in buggies and wagons. They glanced out of hotel windows and from the saloon doors. Ghostly gunfights took place in the street while a dead undertaker picked up the bodies, and a spirit sheriff led someone off to jail.

Before she had time to adjust to what she was seeing, modern tourists were the ones passing by her. Jaxon still had a grip on her hand. Her mind began analyzing what had just happened. People had come and gone through time, one generation after another. Some rested in peace and some were restless, wandering souls still seeking for the justice denied them in life, and she had stood between them as a link. There obviously seemed to be more to life than someone ceasing to exist after death. This once booming town forgotten by time but now resurrected for tourists to relive a small piece of history was trying to tell her something. She had to figure out the message. Piece of cake. "Do you mind if we sit for a minute?" She spied a bench in front of the Crystal Palace and tugged him along with her.

"Fine with me. I want to know what the hell just happened to you?" He sat beside her, stretching out his legs slightly. "You saw something. Am I right?"

"Yes," she answered, her voice barely audible. "As far as what, I'm still processing it."

"Take your time. I'm in no hurry." His hand tightened around hers as he waited for her to talk.

"Do you think our lives simply end when we die?" She glanced at him.

"One of the big questions of life. I tend to believe there's something more and greater than ourselves."

She stared off into the distance. "If I had to describe what I saw, it seemed to be clouds of witnesses. Something I heard Destiny talk about as a little girl when we looked for forms in the clouds. I didn't understand her at the time. I'm not sure I still do. What I saw makes me wonder though."

"Tell me what you saw." He squeezed her hand in encouragement.

"Families, miners, and cowboys were all going about life on these streets. The whole image looked like a scene from an old west town. Maybe a real image of an actual day in the life of this town at its peak time. For a moment, we were one of them. Later, when I got close enough to the people to see them, that's when I saw they were ghosts. The butcher standing outside of his shop waving at those passing by was a ghost. Some seemed to be at peace, and others were haunted. Are they the witnesses of life on these streets here every day? Like the clouds in the sky that we observe, are they watching us, weighing our actions? Are some still seeking justice?"

"Whoa, that's way above my paygrade. I have no idea. How does this relate to our case? That's the question we need to ask and keep asking until we get an answer."

"I believe it's all tied together. What I saw in my vision the other night and today. There are people who have been treated awfully in this life. They have not known justice and maybe they seek it after death. The crimes against them are forgotten over time. In the end, maybe they get to see the justice that life denied them and find peace. Maybe karma in some form is real."

"Your guess is better than mine." He glanced at her profile. "Are you ready to discuss last night?"

"Nope, not yet." She pulled her hand out of his. Standing, she started to walk away.

"Oh, no you don't." He caught up and grabbed her hand. "Look, Peyton, the tension between us has been thick since we met. If you're looking for me to tell you I'm sorry for kissing you, I'm not. Hell, I want to kiss you again. I walked out of the room because I didn't expect to like it or want to do it again. I thought I was doing you a favor by being a gentleman and walking away."

"Kincaid, thank you for the apology." She turned her face and smiled.

"I didn't apologize." He frowned. "You're putting words in my mouth."

"Of course you would've if you understood how you made me feel." She squeezed his hand and tried to pull hers free. "For now, let's forget about it and concentrate on this case. I want to go home as soon as possible."

"Okay. Tell me where you think we're headed." He focused on the conversation at hand.

Over the next hour, they went in and out of buildings and took a tour ride past the courthouse and up to Boot Hill Cemetery. Peyton got a case of the giggles after reading one of the headstones.

"Listen to this one. 'Here lies Lester Moore, 4 slugs from a .44. No, Les, No, More.' " She pointed at the wooden grave marker by the pile of rocks.

Jaxon pointed at the wooden markers of three graves. "These were the outlaws that went up against

Wyatt Earp in 1881. Wow, I can't tell you how many times I watched movies about the shootout at the O.K. Corral as a kid and still do. I'm glad I came with you today."

"Look at this one." She took a photo of the marker. "It says he was taken from jail and hanged by mistake by a mob from Bisbee, and this man was hanged by mistake too." She shook her head. "Can you see what I talked to you about earlier? Right here we have seen two people, their lives taken unjustly from them. Carlee was murdered too. I need to think about this some more."

"I'm hungry, how about you?" He stood beside her. "I asked the tour guide, and he told me about a couple of places where the locals like to eat."

****

If this went the way he planned it, he would have a successful day and some extra money to go with it. After a search of the area, he landed in the perfect place to wait and watch. His hunger was satisfied after he wolfed down the double burger and fries. He could wait for the right moment—if not today or tomorrow, another day would do. This job he relished and couldn't wait to complete. Orders were to scare them off but not to kill them. He could simply say Kincaid jumped in the way and was hit by accident by a stray bullet. Pulling his hat down to shield his face from the sun, he reached for the shades in his shirt pocket and put them on. Damn, it would feel good to put an end to this guy. It was only a matter of time before he'd figure it out. Kincaid had one of the best track records in the department. It would be an honor to get rid him. He'd be doing the criminals of the world a favor. He wiped the sweat from his brow. The sun felt hot on his neck, reflecting off the dark rooftop. If he didn't see them soon, he would have to try again another day. Sweat trickled down his face. It was too damn hot to wait much longer. He took a huge gulp of water, removed his hat, and poured the rest of the bottle over his head.

Chapter 18

As they left the restaurant, a strange sensation came over her. She scanned the area. Nothing seemed amiss. But the feeling remained as Jaxon talked with one of the character actors standing beside the stagecoach. They were all targets standing there, and someone had them in the crosshairs. She squeezed Jaxon's hand, trying to get his attention. He kept talking and tightened his grip on her hand. She leaned close and whispered in his ear. "We need to get out of here. Something is about to happen. You told me to tell you when I got one of my premonitions."

He nodded. "It was nice talking to you." Jaxon shook the man's hand. "We need to be on our—" Before Jaxon could finish the sentence, the sound of gun fire erupted. His eyes searched the area, looking for anything that would qualify for the hiding place of a shooter. "Let's move." He tugged her beside him

"Don't worry, folks. It's only the reenactment of the shootout down at the corral," one of the actors told them right before a bullet ripped through the post where his hand had just rested. "What the hell!" he said as he dropped to the ground beside the coach for cover.

Chaos ensued near the area where they were standing. People fled in several directions, searching for shelter. Some screamed as they were hit and fell to the ground.

Jaxon pulled her close, weaving around people, making his way toward safety. "Damn, those are real bullets." He took out his weapon. "You saw this, earlier didn't you?"

She nodded. "Someone wants to kill us."

"You think. They're not hiding their intentions well." He dragged her around the side of a building, shoving her against the wall. "You've got to tell me when you have a premonition. You left this small detail out when we talked earlier. A heads up would've been nice. If I hadn't seen the gun pointed at us from the rooftop across the street, we'd already be dead. We aren't safe yet." He saw the gun lift over the rooftop. "We need to get help. People are being shot. Get down!" he yelled to a couple walking past them.

The bullets flew around them, too close for comfort, taking more tourists by surprise. One splintered the railing, sending wood shrapnel into the air and hitting a few people passing by. The next bullet hit a person trying to run away, sending him to the ground writhing in pain. An older gentleman sitting on a bench narrowly escaped when the bullet missed his back. The man fell to all fours and scrambled to safety. Two more people went down. Peyton had no idea what their injuries were. She wanted to help, but Jaxon pushed her through the nearest open door as the bullet lodged in the threshold of the quaint ice cream shop. "Call the police," he shouted before showing the woman behind the counter his badge. "Someone is shooting at people."

"Sir, it's only our actors," she told him calmly.

"No, it's real and several people are injured." Jaxon grabbed the phone from her hand which remained frozen in midair. He called for police and several ambulances.

"We have to help those people." Peyton moved toward the door, grabbing a few T-shirts off the table.

"Stay here, I'll go." He pushed her back into the store.

"Would you stop doing that?" She frowned at him. "You're not going out there without me." Peyton pushed in front of him. Keeping her head down, she ran to where the first woman lay on the ground and knelt beside her and held the shirt tightly against her bleeding leg wound. Trying not to become the next victim, she stayed low as she comforted and soothed the hysterical woman. Too much blood. The woman seemed to be fading in front of her. "Help is on the way. Hang on, sweetie." She squeezed the woman's hand.

"Please don't leave me." The woman held tight to her hand.

"I'm not going anywhere," Peyton assured her. "I'll stay right here until help arrives."

"I don't want to die," the woman told her, her voice growing weak.

"Hold on. Keep talking to me. Help is on the way. Do you have family with you?"

"My husband. I don't know...tell him I said I love him."

"You'll be able to tell him yourself." She squeezed the woman's hand. "I won't leave, but I need to let go of your hand now. This man is going to help you." Peyton moved out of the way and the medic got to work.

****

The shots stopped as suddenly as they had started.

135

Jaxon knew if he didn't move quickly the suspect would escape. He glanced over at Peyton who was surrounded by medics and officers trying to help. She would be fine.

"I need to find the shooter," he told her when their eyes met. She nodded.

He ran up the street to the building where he had seen the shooter on the rooftop. He raced up the stairs and out the door, but the suspect was already gone. Searching the area, Jaxon saw a fire escape down the back of the building. The perfect way to escape undetected with the confusion on the street below. He studied the evidence the suspect left behind, careful not to touch or move anything. No doubt about it—their guy had been there. In his haste to escape the shooter left behind a few items that would lead the police to him eventually. Jaxon went down the fire escape, searched the ground around the building, and went to talk to one of the local police.

"The shooter was on the rooftop of the hotel across the street." Jaxon showed the officer his badge.

"Tell me what you saw." The officer leaned his hip against his open car door.

Jaxon described what had transpired only moments before. "At first, everyone thought it was the gunfight, but when bullets began hitting around them all hell broke loose. As soon as I could safely leave the injured, I hurried over here, but the shooter was already gone." He walked with the officer to the rooftop of the hotel.

"What are you doing in town?" the officer asked.

"I'm here as a tourist. We had just finished lunch and came out of the restaurant when the first shots were fired. My friend is helping with the victims." Jaxon showed him the pile of evidence. "It hasn't been touched."

"Thanks. Damn." The officer ran his hand through his hair. "I never thought I'd see this day. We did have a case not long ago when some nut job in the crowd tried to join in the fight reenactment. Thankfully no one was hurt. The guy had real bullets, not blanks. We no longer let them do street fights. We limit the old west shootout to the theater enactment only. Everything is changing."

"You're right." Jaxon handed him a business card. "If you need any help let me know. I'd be happy to support you in any way I can." Jaxon turned to leave. "I'll leave you to your work and get back to my friend."

Chapter 19

The crowd parted, letting the medics move their patients. Sitting on the bench, a disheveled Peyton looked totally done in. Her usually neat hair was tousled about her face, and her clothing had spots of blood splattered down the front. He needed to act fast on her behalf before shock set in. "Are you ready to leave?" Jaxon asked as he approached Peyton. He sat beside her, reaching for her hand. "You're coming with me." Jaxon's fist clenched. Damn, he hated that someone dragged her into this mess.

"Okay." Her voice sounded flat.

"What, no argument?" He held her hand in his. "I'm worried. You're always good to spar with me."

"I'm sorry. I don't have it in me." She sighed. "Did you see how pale the woman was? So much blood. She begged me not to leave her." She turned to look at him. "I thought she was a goner, Kincaid." Her body shuddered. "How can someone randomly cause so much pain? I don't get it. She was a tourist enjoying the day with her husband. And just like that her life is changed forever." She snapped her fingers. "I hope she makes it."

"I do too." He let her talk and didn't try to answer her question. There wasn't any sound answer anyway. "I think we need to get out of here. I have no idea where the shooter is or if he's waiting to ambush us. I want to get you back to the resort." He stood when she did.

"I'm ready." Hand in hand they walked silently back to the car.

The thought of her being a target made the anger inside him rise. Who knew they were coming here? Someone got hold of their itinerary for the day. Who leaked it? Damn, he wished he knew. He glanced at Peyton. She was too quiet, and he didn't know what to do it about it. Words of comfort didn't come easily for him. His sister told him more than once to tap into his softer side, but his days on the force left him hardened by what he saw of the darker side of life. He doubted there was much soft left in him. His mother would never believe it, and he hated to disappoint her. What would she say to Peyton if she were sitting beside her?

"I'm sorry you were dragged into this mess." He checked his mirrors to make sure he wasn't being followed.

"This is her blood. I wonder if she'll make it. How can I find out?" she asked.

"I'll check for you and keep you up to date," he promised her.

"It's not fair that he shot her. When he missed us, he should have left the others alone." She swiped at the tears forming in her eyes. "I felt so helpless holding her hand. My words seemed empty in comparison to the pain and fear I could see in her face."

He understood empty words all too well. "I will do everything in my power to keep you safe. I hope you know that." He gave her a quick glance. "I'm not sure you should do any more sightseeing though. Somehow our suspect got wind of where we were going today.

I'm not sure how, and until I know I don't want you out in the open." He reached the highway back toward the city and merged into the traffic headed toward Tucson and then on to Phoenix. "Are you going to be okay?"

"Yes. No. I'm angry. I want to find Carlee, but I want to find the shooter too." She looked out the side window. "May I ask you something?"

"Of course. Ask away." He glanced at her quickly.

"How do you keep your anger in check? I mean you have to do things by the books, but some criminals must make it hard for you to do that."

"Sure, they do. But I remind myself if I give way to my feelings it will most likely help them go free. Not something I want to do. I try hard to school my emotions and do my job. I admit it's not always easy, and I often take out my anger in the gym."

"That's why I walk. Not a casual stroll mind you, but as fast as I can move without running. Walking helped me survive more than once." She turned to see him. "You'll find out if you haven't already. My father and mother have addiction issues. When they were drunk or high on some drug, they couldn't remember what they did. My sister and I did. There were days, I'm sorry to say, that I hated them both."

"Have you talked with a therapist about it?" He chose his words carefully. He didn't want to shut her down."

"Yes, that's why I've moved on in my life. I don't hate them now. I feel sorry for them in a way, but I refuse to be a victim anymore. Hate has a way of trapping you inside its web. You're only free when you can let your anger go and not let it drive you. I've forgiven them. I've stopped blaming myself for their actions. They will have to make the decisions for their own lives. My father is a charming schemer and never has had to face or account for his actions. Although my grandmother told me he is about to face it all."

"How do you feel about that?" he asked.

"It's about time, and I hope he'll find the help he needs. What I'm wondering is what makes a person do what we saw today."

"Sometimes there are no answers for why people do what they do. From the sounds of it, your dad had great parents. His choices are his and his alone, but they impacted your mother and you and your sister. None of us live in a world alone. Whatever we do impacts someone for good or for bad. It makes you think, doesn't it?" He saw her nod, lean her head back against the headrest, and close her eyes. She was holding up all right, but he noticed the moist sheen in her eyes before she closed them.

****

Peyton's body and mind were weary. She needed a moment to gather herself. But the minute she closed her eyes, she relived the sound of the shots going off around her, the woman in front of her crumbling to the ground, and the nauseating smell of blood that filled the air. All that blood, crimson, pooling, and staining the wood planks of the walkway. Her eyes stung. She closed them tighter trying to fight off the tears threatening to spill out. How was it even possible one person could lose so much blood and still live? Her own clothes were splattered. Her mind had memorized the fear written on the woman's face. There was nothing she could do but hold her hand and hope the woman wouldn't die. Maybe she would visit the woman if

Jaxon could find out where she was. Yes, she would do that. The mere possibility of seeing her again brought Peyton peace.

Relaxing against the headrest, the gentle rocking motion of the car worked its magic. Her last coherent thought before drifting off was how handsome Jaxon looked as a cowboy. She had met her hot cowboy after all. Jessie was right.

****

When Jaxon glanced at her again, she was smiling and sound asleep. How could she be smiling after the day she had. She was gutsy—he'd give her that. She hadn't stayed put when he told her to but rushed to the injured woman's side. The more he saw of Peyton Reynolds, the more impressed he became. He liked her besides being attracted to her. But he didn't know what to think about it. Life has a way of working things out, and he would have to see how this one ended. One thing he knew: Peyton didn't seem to be swayed by him one way or the other. In fact, she seemed to be annoyed with him more often than not. Part of him was happy about it, but his ego couldn't take much more.

Chapter 20

Jaxon found the hospital where the injured woman was airlifted to. Barbara Newsome's condition was stable and upgraded to serious this morning. Peyton would be happy to put a name to the woman and to hear that her condition was improving. He would take her to see Barbara as soon as he could. Possibly he'd earn a few points with her and maybe get on her good side in the process.

He still had no ID on the shooter. It had to be someone who knew his movements. The captain could be right about a leak in the department. But who? It was too hard for him to imagine much less actually consider. The men and woman he worked with were honest, hard-working folks. The monetary compensation wasn't high, but their dedication was. They were a tight group and did their jobs well. He supposed he'd have to keep his eyes open. Hopefully he could prove the captain wrong. The only possibility as far as he could see would be a recruit who came into department with that purpose in mind. A plant. An angle for him to mull over. No way was it someone who came up through the ranks. His mind couldn't go there.

After several morning phone calls and the captain's okay, Frank Wagner would arrive tomorrow with his dog Radar to help search for Carlee's body. He read the reports on the dog's success ratio and convictions and wanted to see him in action. Chief Parker said he'd be amazed, and Jaxon wanted to be astonished. At this point he would appreciate a logical piece of evidence to give him back his footing among all Peyton's reluctant premonitions. She wasn't comfortable with the place she found herself but made the best out of the strange situation. Her accuracy threw him. He didn't want to believe any of it, but he couldn't dismiss it either. Until he could reason it out, he would listen and go with instinct.

****

Peyton spent the morning talking to her cousin. She explained what had taken place in Tombstone. "I'm trying to find out the condition of the woman. Kincaid told me he would investigate it for me. I hope he remembers. I'm anxious to hear. Jess, it was the scariest thing I've ever seen. I watched her weaken in the few minutes she held my hand. Life is tenuous at best."

"It's tough to see another human suffer. It's hard enough to see a murder victim, but to watch a living person succumb to their injuries is something else altogether. It's a helpless feeling. I'm sorry you've gone through all this, but if not there, it would happen sooner or later. You are another Reynolds family member who must deal with ghosts and all that come with them. Call it fate, kismet, or our destiny it is what it is." Jessie paused. "It's ridiculous and kind of cool at the same time."

"I guess, but I don't want to see anything like it again." Peyton toyed with the fringe on the pillow next to her. "Although I have to admit seeing Detective Kincaid as a cowboy was awesome. You were right when you said I might meet a hot cowboy. Too bad I couldn't keep him that way. The illusion is way better than the reality." Peyton laughed.

"Sheriff Kincaid has a nice ring to it." Jessie chuckled. "Before I forget—Jeremy told me he would be calling you later today. He said he has some financial information for you. He likes to follow money. I have a few more messages from others to give you before we hang up. Reba told me to give you her love and to tell you to remember it may get tougher before it gets better. Before you ask, I have no idea what she means by that other than to say it will probably get worse before you come home. Lastly Grams sends her love and said she'll call you later too." Jessie paused. "At least I'm beginning to understand the whole Tombstone connection. Tell me what you're thinking."

"All the ghosts are people who may have suffered erroneously at the hands of others. You know—falsely accused, mistaken identities, or simply being in the wrong place at the wrong time. Their stories have been forgotten over time. Many of their murders have gone unsolved or no one was convicted for them. Am I right? Only time will tell," Peyton answered her own question.

"Sounds feasible to me."

"First I saw Tombstone during its peak years and then as a tourist. A tad strange if you ask me, but I'm handling it the best that I can. The thing is I think someone is trying to kill me and I have no idea why."

"No one knows you there. It must be your association with the detective. Make that guy watch your back and don't try to be a heroine. I want you to come home to us," Jessie told her.

"I've had training in self-defense but it's no match for a gun when you can't even see the guy shooting at you." Peyton jumped out of the chair and began to pace.

"I wish I was there with you," Jessie said.

"I wish you were too."

"I'm going to do some thinking about what you've told me. If I think of anything, I'll call you. Something tells me you won't need my help at all."

"I'd still love to have you here. We'll talk later. Love you." Peyton disconnected the call.

At least she wasn't alone in her peculiarity. Jessie understood, and she could talk to her. When it happened to her cousin, Jessie had no idea what was going on. Peyton couldn't help but wonder who else alive could see the ghosts walking around them. There had to be more. It would take an army to quiet the unsettled spirits roaming the earth. She smiled at the thought.

Peyton talked to her boss after Jessie. She ran a few ideas by him which he promised to think about. If he agreed to her proposal, she would be making a few changes in her life. For the first time in a while excitement about the future filled her. One thing she had learned in the past few hours, you need to live while you can. Reach for your dreams and hold on. Life can change in a moment, and she didn't want to die never having really lived.

Running the brush through her hair, optimism bubbled up from inside her. Even Kincaid couldn't ruin her good mood. If she were honest, lately he hadn't been so bad. Grabbing her book off the table, she reached for her purse and headed to the coffee shop to read and enjoy a latte and muffin.

****

He watched her walk by him totally unaware that he was there. He had done a hell of job blending into his surroundings the past several days. She had no clue how close he had gotten to her on several occasions. Damn, his plan should have gone off without a hitch yesterday. No such luck. Too many folks got in the way. No one was supposed to have been hurt. Instead he found himself stuck here trying to come up with another plan. Before long the cops would be breathing down his neck. He waited, hoping against hope the boss didn't send someone to kill him before Kincaid figured it out. Either way he was dead. What a mess.

Yesterday he got the concierge to tell him everything he needed to know about the woman's plans. Today the damn man at the desk wouldn't tell him anything. Usually, he could get anyone to talk. But the guy wouldn't give him anything and told him it was against the resort's policy to give out information. Even his badge couldn't convince him. Only a warrant could make him talk. Like he could get that. Hell.

After studying their body language, he was positive she was Kincaid's weakness. The perfect hostage for trading his way out of the country or at the very least revenge. His only chance, and it was a slim one. Past feeling remorse and with his survival at stake, he would do whatever was necessary to get through this. Hell, he already had done enough to put himself on death row. He patted the letter in his pocket to his wife and kids. She would never understand, and he couldn't explain it. Tired of the grind and sucking up to his superiors, he had taken another route. He wasn't proud of himself, but there was no use crying over spilt milk. He had moved years ago to the wrong side of the law in his mind, and it was only a matter of time until his actions followed him there.

All his hard work never got him anywhere. The short cuts worked better and now all he had to do was wait.

Chapter 21

She had the strangest sensation that someone was watching her. No one in the coffeeshop seemed suspicious. That is if you could tell by someone's looks. Everyone seemed pretty much normal to her. Whatever that meant. One of the best-looking guys in high school turned out to be a big jerk. His fists had pummeled more than one of the girls that he dated. She bent her head and began reading again.

"I thought I might find you here. What are you reading?" Jaxon sat across from her.

She showed him the cover of the book. "I haven't done much reading. Let's say I'm attempting to."

"I have some news for you about the woman you helped." He leaned back in the chair.

"How is she?" Her concern evident.

"Her name is Barbara Newsome, and she was airlifted to a hospital in the area. Her condition was upgraded today. I thought, if you wanted, I could take you by to see her when she's out of ICU." Jaxon nodded and pushed his cup toward the waitress when she asked if he wanted coffee.

"That would be great. I would love to see her again. It makes me happy to think she is still with us. Truthfully, I wasn't sure she would be. Barbara, the name suits her." Peyton put her bookmark in the page and closed the book. "Thank you for finding out about her."

"It's the least I could do after the day you had yesterday. Have you seen anyone hanging around?"

"I haven't noticed anyone, but I've had the strangest sensation someone is watching me. I have no idea who I'm looking for though."

"Let's start with the feeling. When did you start to feel it?" Jaxon asked.

"Right before you came, but no one looked familiar to me."

"Did you notice anyone in the lobby?" He studied her face.

His intensity made her nervous. "I wasn't paying attention when I walked through the lobby area. Sorry."

"It's a lot to ask of you. I wouldn't, but your life might depend on it. I'm not sure which one of us the shooter was aiming at. He seemed to shoot at both of us equally. Which makes me wonder if our suspect may use you as bait to get at me. I have no proof, or I'd ask for around-the-clock protection for you."

"I'll try to remember to pay attention to my surroundings. I don't want to add to your concerns with this case."

"Before I forget to tell you, Frank will be here tomorrow. We'll do the track to look for Carlee the next day to give them time to rest from their travels. I know you'll want to be there, and Frank asked for you to come too. The captain okayed both which is highly unusual. He wants this case solved. The Dawsons are a prominent family, and there is pressure coming down on him from the top."

"I guess you can't escape workplace politics anywhere." Peyton shrugged her shoulders.

"Of course, it helped that Frank comes with some solid endorsements from cases in Palm Springs, Montana, and several other cities and organizations. The list of officials who recommend him is impressive. So is his dog's ratio of convictions. I admit I'm looking forward to seeing him in action." Jaxon leaned back in his chair and took a sip of his coffee.

"Jessie has talked a lot about Radar's ability. It should be fascinating to watch." Peyton's phone rang. "This is Jeremy—you should listen in." Jaxon nodded. "Hi, this is Peyton."

"Did your cousin tell you I would call?" Jeremy asked.

"Yes. Detective Kincaid is here, and he's going to listen in if that's okay with you." She signed the bill to her room.

"Perfect. I wanted to talk to both of you," Jeremy added. "Hey, Kincaid. How's it going?"

"No complaints." Jaxon stood beside her and motioned for her to precede him.

"Jeremy, keep talking. We're on our way to a more private place to talk." They walked to the empty conference room which the resort said Kincaid could use during their investigation. He unlocked the door.

"Let me know when you're ready." Jeremy told her.

"We're set, and I have you on speaker." Peyton took out a notebook and pen.

"I did a bit of research and followed the money trail. Your boy had some large sums of cash deposited into his accounts in the past several months. I followed the money, and it originated from a bank in the Caymans. I'm still trying to find out whose account he was being paid from. I can tell you the amount of money we're talking about means some high rollers are involved. Big money from private accounts in offshore banks aren't easy to track. But I will. You can count on it," Jeremy said.

"You sound sure of yourself." Jaxon's brows rose when he glanced a Peyton.

"I'm good at what I do. It may take me time, but I'll track down the owner of the account. I can pull some favors if I need to. You follow the evidence and so do I. Mine is done through my computer and some fancy maneuvering around firewalls and encryptions. Like you, I'll get my man, and you'll have a name. What you do with it is up to you."

"It sounds like you love your job." Jaxon smiled at the passion in Jeremy's voice.

"I do. Jessie and now Peyton make it a whole lot more exciting though. I never know where their cases will take me. I'm sure you're already finding that out. You're in for a hell of a ride." Jeremy laughed. "Seriously though, from the looks of it you're dealing with some dark money and something bigger than your single victim."

"I think you're right. The murder of the Dawson kid might have been a mistake. It alerted us to an operation that may have gone undetected." Jaxon clicked his pen on and off.

"How are you feeling about all this, Peyton?" Jeremy asked her.

"That's a loaded question. I'm handling it the best I can." She paused. "Let's see, I'm a tourist new to the area, and I'm embroiled in a murder case. I've seen ghosts for heaven's sake, and not just a few. I've been shot at twice and saw people injured with the bullets that were meant for me. I'm upright and not on a plane headed home. I guess you could say I'm managing." All the while she answered she tapped her pen against the notebook faster and faster until it flew out of her hand, hitting the wall across the room. Missing Jaxon's face by mere inches.

"Peyton is a bit rattled but is holding up quite well. She's helped move this case forward and I couldn't be prouder of her." He reached for her hand to still her fingers drumming on the table taking up where her pen had left off.

"I'll call you as soon as I have more information. Hang in there, Peyton. From the sounds of it, you're doing great considering your past few days. If Kincaid is proud of you that's a step up from a few days ago when he thought you were a kook." Jeremy chuckled.

"You're right. At least we can be in the same room for longer than five minutes without having a major fight." Peyton laughed when Jaxon picked up her pen and rolled his eyes at her.

"I can't wait to hear where the money is coming from. Thanks, Jeremy." Peyton ended the call.

A sweet tension filled the air between them. Peyton gazed at him. "Did you mean what you said?" she asked in a soft voice. "You're proud of me."

"Hell yes. I can't imagine what you're experiencing, but you've been strong and helpful. It's bound to get worse before it gets better. At least if we find Carlee's body, you'll have fulfilled your promise to her and you'll be free to go." He still hadn't moved his hand or let go of her fingers.

"I want to know what the Tombstone connection

is?" She tried to slip her hand away from his, but he held tight.

"I'm still thinking about it. We need to start at the beginning and go over all your visions to this point again." Jaxon took out a small recorder. "Is it okay if I record you?"

"Sure. I don't want to forget the details. I wrote them down each time. I take copious notes. I always have."

Flipping open her notebook she started with the day she saw E J's ghost and Carlee's spirit standing behind him. They went through each premonition looking for something that connected them.

Jaxon asked several questions as she talked. "I'm missing something simple." He raked his hand through his hair. He turned off the recorder. "What stands out to you?"

"Lots of money means some kind of smuggling or trafficking don't you think?" She frowned, concentrating on the few notes she had jotted down. "E J obviously was involved with some hardcore thugs, and he must have messed up somewhere. Carlee was in the wrong place at the wrong time. Her death was a warning shot to E J not to mess up again. Still I think beyond the guys who break the bones there are some wealthy shadow figures who are making lots of money and feel untouchable while hidden from view."

"I like how your mind works. All those manuscripts you've read may pay off."

"When I've read some stories, I've thought there's no way this could possibly happen in real life. Then comes a news article or broadcast to prove me wrong. Sometimes I've wondered if the author had literally seen it. You need to ask Matt sometime about the Harvest Club. From what Jessie told me, they had to think outside the box. We might have to do the same."

"My suggestion is to go over each of the premonitions like a new manuscript. Try to anticipate where the story is taking you, and I'll work through them logically. Together we might find a path forward." He stood. "I need to get back to the station, but I'll be back to take you to dinner."

"I'll give it my best shot." She gathered her items from the table and followed him out of the room, shutting off the light. She turned to walk back to her room.

She had no idea how it happened or when, but Jaxon Kincaid had become almost tolerable. Okay if she were honest, she liked him. In another time and place she might even find him interesting and like to know more about him. She might even describe him as handsome to her friend. Thinking of Destiny reminded Peyton that she needed to call her and see how her mom was doing.

Chapter 22

Before she could make the call, her phone rang. "Hello," she answered quickly hoping it was her friend.

"Where are you now?" Jaxon asked.

"I'm almost to my room. Why?"

"I stopped at the concierge's desk on the way out. Yesterday before I left, I gave the manager strict instructions to make sure no one gave out information of your daily plans or whereabouts. Today he told me a man was asking one of his employees a lot of questions about you which he refused to answer. The troubling thing he told me is the guy showed him a badge. Smartly the employee explained that without a warrant your information was private and would remain that way until he saw one."

"That's good," Peyton said.

"On one level yes. But it also supports the idea of a leak in our department and someone stalking you. You need to be doubly careful, Peyton. Pay attention to your surroundings and the people you see. It's a man you need to be watching for. Someone who is trying hard not to be seen. You should be okay inside, but don't walk alone on the premises. Especially the parking lot after dark. I'll meet you in the lobby at six." Jaxon paused and then added, "This is important—your life could be in jeopardy."

"I'll be careful. Believe me, I know how to watch

those around me. Starting now this is no longer a vacation." She opened the door to her suite and walked in.

"Call me if you see anyone. If you can get a picture, take one and send it to me. I might be able to identify who we're dealing with and stop him before he does something."

"I will. I have another call coming in. I'll see you at six." Peyton ended the call. "Hey, Destiny, you're just the person I wanted to talk to."

"You promised to tell me what's going on. Now start talking." Peyton did.

Peyton found herself suspicious of every man who was in her line of vision. It was the one that she couldn't see that she should probably be worried most about. She found a shady spot by the pool where she spent the afternoon engrossed in her book. She had purchased it when she was in Tombstone on its history. There was a clue to be found somewhere in its pages, and she read as a person on a mission. Ah, the reward. She read over the few sentences several times. Maybe this was the connection she had been looking for. She read about the many sightings of lingering spirits walking the pathways in Tombstone. At its heyday Tombstone was one of the most dangerous places in the US. Gunslingers and lawbreakers kept sending each other and innocent bystanders to early graves. After reading about all the innocent lives lost in fires and several ghosts sightings at the Bird Cage Theater, Peyton began to put together clues in her mind. Was any of this real or was it wishful thinking on her part? Jaxon might find it amusing, but she was sure she was on to something. Many people who had died unexpectedly and violently were among the spirits that were regularly sighted according to local legends. It was as she had thought.

****

Jaxon found himself watching the men around the station. He knew a lot of them personally. He couldn't believe any of them were anything but decent, hardworking officers. He spent time talking it over with the captain.

Stolberg suggested that he should look through personnel files at candidates who might have been in line for a promotion that didn't come through. That would justify the theory of him being a target and Peyton too because of her connection to him. "Remember, Kincaid, no one really knows what is going on in another person's life. It could be anyone. The fact the man is showing his badge to get information makes me want to get him even more."

"I hear you," Jaxon said.

"My theory is someone is angry you got the promotion that he felt belonged to him. Can you think of anyone who has treated you differently since you started leading the homicide unit?" Stolberg asked.

"Not off the top of my head." Jaxon leaned forward in the chair.

"He may be quiet but seething inside. It might not take much to make him blow if he hasn't already."

"You're right. He might be the shooter in Tombstone. If that's the case, he will feel the noose tightening about him. We could have a desperate man on our hands," Jaxon said.

"Yes, and he'll have to act fast. The next few days will be crucial." The captain scowled. "I hope you can find a clue in those files. Time is a big factor now."

"I do too." Jaxon stood to leave. "Mr. Wagner and his dog will be here tomorrow, and we'll start the track the next morning at six a.m. When that gets out, I'm sure it'll be only a matter of time until our suspect comes unglued. I would like to stop him before it happens."

"Do your best." He leaned forward in his chair. "I plan to be on site for part of the track. I want to see how the dog works. We might need to use them more in the future."

"Chief Parker believes firmly in the ability of this one." He leaned his shoulder against the wall as they continued to talk.

"I know. I've talked to Parker a few times. You look surprised. I needed confirmation that I wasn't losing my mind letting you follow the strange, twisting story you've told me. I have a lot of respect for you, Kincaid, but my job is on the line. I'm not about to give my approval without checking out every source I can," Stolberg told him.

"I respect that, sir." Jaxon smiled. The captain did the same.

"You're a good man, Kincaid. Get out there and stop this guy. Both of our jobs might depend on it."

"I'll do my best, sir." Jaxon turned to leave.

"You may need do better than that," the captain muttered. "If it takes a ghost to solve their own murder, I'll not stand in their way. Not that I believe in ghosts, but at this point I'm up for any help wherever it comes from."

He left the captain's office wondering about the strange conversation he just had. Treading into unchartered water made him unsure what steps to take next. He went down to Human Resources with Stolberg's order for the personnel files from the last couple of years. Thankfully there were less than fifty. Manageable unless he had to add another couple of years' worth of files because he couldn't find what he was looking for.

Peyton's part in the case could be wrapping up soon, but he wanted her to stay. She should see it through to the end and maybe longer if he asked her. The truth was he hated to see her leave. Strange that after fighting with her, now he couldn't imagine her not being around. Placing the files on his desk, he grabbed the first one in the stack and began to read. Nothing to see there. Besides personally knowing the officer, the man had a stellar record in the community and was active in the Cops and Kids program. This guy was a gem.

After reading several files, he locked them in his drawer. More than ready to call it a day, he headed for the exit. He had enough time to change his clothes and make it to the resort in time to pick up Peyton.

Chapter 23

Peyton waved at Jaxon when he walked into the lobby. She met him halfway. "Did you have a good day?"

"Not bad." He smiled at her. "What did you do all afternoon?"

"I found a shady spot and hung out by the pool. I did a bit of reading about Tombstone and came up with some interesting theories that I want to run by you later." She showed him the book that had held her interest most of the afternoon.

He placed his hand on the small of her back and maneuvered her toward the door. The lobby was busy with guests checking in. "Sounds like you had a relaxing day." He held the car door open for her. "Did you remember to keep your eyes open?"

"Yes. As a matter of fact, I began to suspect everyone I saw. I didn't like the feeling. I didn't sense anyone around me that shouldn't be. I'll have to go with that for now." She slipped into the passenger seat, and he closed the car door once she was settled.

"I spent most of my day going through personnel files. Nothing stood out to me, but I still have several more to read." He turned the key, and the engine hummed to life. "Captain Stolberg is planning to join us on the track with Radar. I thought we should take Frank out to dinner tomorrow. He wanted to meet you." He pulled out into traffic, quickly changing lanes.

"I would like to meet him too." Peyton glanced out the window and watched as another amazing Phoenix sunset streaked vivid color across the sky.

"I am meeting with Carlee's family early tomorrow to get a personal item that we can use for Radar to get her scent. I admit I'm looking forward to watching Frank's dog at work. He comes highly recommended by several agencies." He stopped at the red light.

"I hope we can bring Carlee home to her family, then I'll be free to go home too." For some odd reason, once the words were spoken the thought depressed her. She wanted to leave for home but at the same time she wanted to remain. Of course, she could read how the case ended in the news, but it wouldn't be the same as being a part of it. Her thinking wasn't practical and made absolutely no sense after her constant struggle with Jaxon. Still in her heart of hearts she wanted to be around when the suspect was captured.

"I was hoping I could convince you to stay and see this case through to the end if we can bring it to a close quickly." His deep voice cut through her rambling thoughts.

"Why?" she asked, glancing at him.

"You're the one who discovered Carlee's connection to E J." He put on the turn signal. "Besides we haven't figured out Tombstone or the shooter's place in all of this yet." He glanced at her. "You're free to go, but I hope you'll consider staying and consulting with me on this case." He pulled into a parking space at the restaurant.

"I'll think about it." She smiled at him. Had he read her thoughts? He gave her a good reason to stay.

They walked into the restaurant.

The rest of the evening was a blur to her. Stunned that Jaxon had asked her to stay longer to consult with him on the case remained in the forefront of her thoughts. She wanted to shout yes right away, but she needed to be sure her decision was the right one.

Later, still mulling over the idea, she climbed into bed and shut off the light. The danger to her personally and those around her was real. Shot at twice, she needed to consider the fact that her luck might eventually run out. Not a nice thought to fall asleep to. But it had to factor into any decision she made. "Carlee, what should I do?" she whispered into the empty room. After tossing and turning for another hour she decided to shelf the idea for now, at least until after the track. Still, her mind traipsed from one random thought to another.

Would Radar find Carlee's body? In her heart, Peyton knew the answer. There wasn't a doubt in her mind that they would find the girl somewhere in the Superstitions. But even if they brought her home tomorrow, the questions would persist. Like why Carlee had shown up in her vision of Tombstone. What was her connection to the town? There were too many moving parts that didn't seem to fit together, and she wanted to connect them. She should stay to help. Plumping the pillow behind her head, she rolled onto her side. She would leave. She turned over on her back. It was settled in her mind, but then he asked her to stay.

Detective Kincaid seemed to be more charming as the days went by. A small part of her desired to stay and get to know him better. The other side told her to run—she would only get hurt. Happy endings weren't real, at least not for her. But she wanted to keep the dream of one intact. Life would seem awful without the possibility that true love existed. She hadn't found it yet, but maybe this was her time for happiness. She would stay or maybe…not.

****

Jaxon didn't know what to think. Peyton said she would consider his proposal to stay. He wasn't convinced that she would. They had come a long way in their working relationship and yet he felt like he was skating on thin ice every time he was with her. He would take whatever time given him, and hopefully their tenuous friendship would survive the case.

Peyton had been animated when she talked to him about what she read in the book. The ghost sightings in Tombstone were described in detail and managed to bring her some comfort that others saw spirits too. A lot of the sightings seemed tied to people who had suffered sudden and violent deaths or murders that were still unsolved. She had read to him a few stories from the book. He had to admit the author had made some interesting points.

Somehow E J and Carlee were connected to Tombstone like the others. How, was the question yet to be answered. He loved this about any case. Watching and waiting as the evidence answered the questions of why and how. When it came to ghosts—that was another story altogether—and the reason he hoped she would stay. If he were honest with himself, maybe he had a few other reasons too.

****

With the bagged teddy bear on the backseat, Jaxon merged onto the highway heading to the airport to meet

Frank. Mrs. Blair told him the bear was her daughter's most cherished possession. Carlee had slept with it every night since she was a little girl.

Frank had requested two dog crates to transport Radar and Kilo in while on the road. Jaxon was driving one of the station's SUVs so he could put the dogs' pens in the back. At passenger pick-up, he jumped out to help Frank with his suitcase and opened the back for the dogs.

"Nice to meet you, Mr. Wagner. I'm Detective Kincaid." He shook hands with Frank. "We appreciate you coming all this way to help."

"It's my pleasure." Frank patted the open door and helped Radar as he jumped up. Then he helped Kilo. He secured the doors once the dogs were in the crates. He gave them treats. "There you go, big fellas."

"He's a fine-looking bloodhound. A bit larger than I've ever seen before."

"Yep, he's a large-sized bloodhound. He knows his job and often surprises me. We make a good team, and most days when he's on a track there's no stopping him. Like humans, though, dogs can have bad days." Frank turned to look at Radar in the back.

"What's the other breed?" Jaxon asked.

"A Belgian Malinois. He's one tough dog," Frank told him. "I use him for finding drugs. I felt I needed to bring him. I don't know why."

"I guess we'll know soon enough." Jaxon drove out of the airport onto the highway. "How will Radar work in the heat?"

"If we start early enough in the morning, he should be okay. He worked Palm Springs, but it wasn't as hot as it is here today. Were you able to find a room that takes dogs?"

"I did. I'll take you there after we go by the station. I want you to meet Captain Stolberg."

"I look forward to meeting him. Will I get a chance to meet Peyton?" Frank asked.

"Yes, at dinner tonight," Jaxon told him.

"Perfect. I'm fond of her cousin Jessie. I've watched her struggle with her abilities. She's gone from overwhelmed to one strong woman. How's Peyton handling it all?"

"I think she's coming to grips with it. Like I am." Jaxon glanced at him.

"You've kind of answered my next question. Matt Parker was perplexed by Jessie for a while and often still is. He accepts it on some level but doesn't get it on another." Frank grinned. "It's been fun to watch him learn to deal with it."

"I'd say that describes me. She's been accurate. I accept it, but I don't pretend to understand how." Jaxon pulled into the station and parked. After Radar and Kilo were out of the crates and on their leashes, they went into the station to meet Captain Stolberg.

Radar took all the attention in stride. Mostly he lay at Frank's feet sleeping. Kilo, on the other hand, was attentive and alert, never taking his eyes off the others in the room. Jaxon tried to visualize the relaxed dog on a track and couldn't. He'd have to wait until tomorrow to see how it would really go down.

****

What was Kincaid up to now? He watched the three men in Stolberg's office. Edging toward the open door, he hoped to hear what they were saying. Suddenly, a ferocious looking dog jumped up, bared his teeth, and growled at him. All eyes in the room were on him. "Sorry, sir, I didn't mean to disturb the dog. I need to get my equipment, and I'll be on my way."

"Kincaid, shut the door," the captain told him.

He stared at the closed door, relieved. Dogs could spell trouble, especially that one. He shivered thinking about that bad boy sinking his teeth into his flesh. Were they here to search for the shooter at Tombstone or something else? Damn, he wished he could be a fly on the wall, but he didn't want to get near that dog. Pulling his cap down over his head, he went to the officer's lunchroom. He could fade into the background. Maybe he would hear something of value.

Chapter 24

Peyton understood why Jessie loved Frank. His calming demeanor at dinner the night before made her feel instantly okay with what was happening to her. He told her that bringing the family closure was why he did the job. He had seen some bad things in the years he had been doing tracks, but when a person was found or a case solved, it made it all worthwhile. Radar had helped to bring closure to lots of families over the years. He had some interesting stories to tell. Captain Stolberg pumped him with questions most of the evening and then turned them on her. She believed she held her own. He was an intimidating man, but he didn't scare her.

Jaxon would pick her up soon. Five came early but they wanted to start at six before it got too hot. She slathered on sunscreen. Putting on her hat, she grabbed her sunglasses and left the room. She wanted a coffee and bagel for the road. Rushing toward the coffeeshop she almost ran into a man who suddenly stepped in front of her.

"Where are you off to in such a hurry, little lady?" The man's booming voice startled her.

"Excuse me." She tried to move around him. He was a large man and on the tall side.

He stopped her by moving into her path and blocking her retreat. "Don't be rude. I asked you a question."

"I'm sorry. I don't know you, do I?" She frowned at him. "I don't need to tell you my plans. I'm in a hurry, and I didn't mean to run into you, but you stepped in front of me." She stepped around him and hurried off before he could try and stop her again. That was a weird encounter. Something about the man seemed vaguely familiar. Shaking off the odd sensation, she hurried to the coffeeshop for her to-go order. She added cream to her coffee and went into the lobby to wait for Jaxon to arrive.

She walked out to the car the minute he stepped out of it. "Good morning. You're right on time as usual." She slid into the backseat when he held the door open. "Hi, Frank. I hope you slept well."

"I did, thanks. You sound chipper this morning," Frank said. "I want some of what you're drinking." He smiled at her.

"I have high hopes of bringing Carlee Blair home to her family today. As hard as it would be to know she is dead, I think it would be better than always wondering where she is." Turning around in the seat she saw Radar in the crate. "You must be the famous Radar that my cousin is always talking about." The dog lifted his head when she said his name and laid it back down. "He's a handsome fella, Frank. Truly a sharp looking dog."

"I think he is. Radar is my best bud. Aren't you, fella?" Radar popped up, responding to Frank's voice.

"I see you already got coffee. Do you mind if we stop?" Jaxon asked.

"Not at all. I figured you would get it before you came. I went ahead and ordered mine. I should have asked if you wanted me to order you some too." Peyton latched her seat belt.

Jaxon drove to the nearest coffeeshop and pulled into the drive through. Giving the girl their order, he pulled up to the next window to pay. He handed Frank a coffee and a bagel. "That was fast. We beat the morning rush." He pulled into an open space to add cream to his coffee.

"Five is early, but Radar is ready to work in the morning. Since we have no idea how long the track might take or how many miles, it's best to start him early. The sun should be up soon. Hopefully the temps won't rise as fast."

"I heard on the news this morning the temperature should be cooler today. But I've still come prepared with lots of sunscreen and a hat in case they're wrong." Peyton ate a bite of her bagel, feeling almost too excited to eat. Carlee knew they were coming.

"I may borrow some of that sunscreen. I never remember to bring my tube, and I don't particularly want to get a sunburn." Frank took a sip of his coffee. "Ah, I needed this."

Jaxon checked his side mirrors as he pulled onto the nearly empty street. "Let's go find the Blair girl."

"Sounds good to me," Frank said.

The sun began its ascent in the morning sky as they pulled into the parking area of the trailhead. The one Carlee had shown her. Several of Kincaid's team were there, along with Captain Stolberg. The area was closed off to tourists during the track. The team gathered in a circle around Jaxon as he gave them instructions for how the morning would proceed.

Peyton walked away from the group. Studying the

rugged landscape in front of her, she tried to imagine Carlee walking down the path on her way to meet E J, carefree and happy. Carlee had no idea she was walking to her death. The sadness of the thought made tears form in Peyton's eyes. Unsuspecting, she had walked on. This trail now held the secrets of the last moments of her life. An eerie silence pervaded the area. Only an occasional bird could be heard through the abnormal stillness. It was as if nature muted itself in anticipation of what would happen next.

The abrupt chill took Peyton by surprise. She rubbed her arms, wrapping them tightly around her middle. It lifted, only to be followed by another cool rush of air swirling around her, dancing up and down her spine in a quick staccato fashion. Holding her breath, she saw the ghostly form flittering on the path, beckoning for her to follow. She took a few steps down the path and stopped. "Lead the way, Carlee. These people are here to find you and take you home. They will do all they can to find your killer." She paused, seeing the sadness on Carlee's face. "I'll try to stay until they do." Relief and disbelief filled Peyton as she uttered the words aloud. She couldn't stay away from work much longer, but she would remain as long as she could. With that decision made, she was ready to get started.

****

"Ms. Reynolds, are you ready?" Jaxon called out to her. He could tell something was happening with her.

"I'll be right there." She wiped the tears from her eyes and walked over to the group.

"Frank, you lead the way. We'll take our cue from you. We're here to aid and protect you and your dog."

He handed Frank the bag with the scent item.

Frank put Radar on his line. He placed the scent item in front of the dog's nose and then the vial with the decomp in it, explaining the dog would know the person was dead that he tracked. "Find the girl, fella, let's bring her home." Radar's head went up, searching for an indication in the air, and then his nose went down toward the ground. His ears moved back and forth, pulling the scent toward his nose. He began to scurry down the path, pulling hard on the line, tugging Frank along behind him.

Peyton and Jaxon started out beside Frank. "I have a question." She glanced at Frank.

"Ask away." He tried to slow Radar down.

"Do you think it's possible for a dog to perceive a spirit?" she asked.

"If there is one around, he could sense them," Frank answered as the dog led him down the trail. "Dogs are more sensitive than humans, and people can sometimes see ghosts. Look at you and your cousin."

"I think you'll understand when I tell you our ghost is leading the way." Peyton walked fast to keep up.

"Then we'll have a successful track." Radar tugged and Frank struggled to hold him back.

"I'm counting on it." She slowed her pace and let Frank give the dog his lead.

"I bet he's sore at the end of track," Stolberg mentioned to them.

"Frank told us last night bloodhounds are tenacious when they work. I'm beginning to believe it. I can see why he said it's hard to get them to stop once they begin a track. As hard as they work, I can see why they can become depressed if they don't find what they're searching for." Jaxon took a short video of Frank and Radar at work for his own record.

"If he finds the girl, would he be able to track the killer from the girl's remains?" the captain asked. "I didn't hear his answer last night. That's when I got the phone call."

"From what Frank said, Radar has worked some cold cases that have led to several arrests."

"Damn, I find this fascinating. What about you, Kincaid?" Stolberg wiped the sweat from his forehead and adjusted his cap.

"I do. If we find the girl in the next few days, I will be persuaded to use dogs more often. Carlee is an important link to find E J's killer. They could be one and the same." Jaxon wanted to find out what Peyton had seen earlier. He watched her talking to Frank.

As soon as the captain turned to talk to Amos, Jaxon picked up his pace and caught up to them. "I know you saw something. You want to talk about it?" he asked her.

"Carlee is leading us now. I saw her earlier. Frank seems to think Radar could sense her. I find that interesting." She paused, pulling her hair into a ponytail to get it off her neck. "Don't you?"

"Interesting might not be the word I would use to describe it. Have you thought more about what I asked you yesterday?" He watched a small lizard scamper across the path in front of them and onto the rocks.

"Yes. I'll tell you soon what I've decided to do."

"Fair enough."

"I remember seeing this place." Peyton pointed at the unusual rock formations.

"What do you mean?" Jaxon glanced at the area

that she indicated.

"In the vision I had. I remember seeing Carlee and E J sitting here when the men ambushed them." Her mouth dropped open. "Wow, I can't believe the whole thing was real."

"What?" Jaxon asked. "Are you sure?" She nodded.

"Radar seems to be following the path the men did when they abducted Carlee." She raced to keep up with Frank.

"I think he's on to something," Frank called out to them.

Radar went off the beaten path, winding through the cactus and low-lying brush. Scurrying over rocks and down a small hill along a gulley created from the water rushing down the mountain through parched ground. The dog had a single purpose, and they scrambled to stay close but ended up falling behind. Anticipating the unknown.

Chapter 25

Peyton heard Radar's bay before she saw where he had indicated. When she caught up with them, there was no doubt in her mind the dog had found Carlee's resting place. She had seen it. "She's down in this old mine shaft." She patted Radar's head.

"He's indicating as if she's in there." Frank pointed to the area when Stolberg arrived.

"What luck. No one would've ever thought to look for her there. I'm stunned." Jaxon shook his head.

"Who knows if it's your victim, but something dead is down there." Frank stroked his dog. "Good work, fella." He gave him a treat.

"Still it's something to watch him process all the odors in the air and zero in on one that he's picked up. We'll know soon enough if it's our missing girl. If it is, it will make it even more amazing. If not, someone else will have a loved one return home. I'd say that's a good day, wouldn't you?" Stolberg looked around at the faces of the team.

Frank nodded at him. "Yes, sir, I would." Frank sat down on the rock and watched Jaxon and his team. Radar lay down at his feet.

"Let's get to work, people. Finding the possible site is one thing, but extracting the body will take careful, precise work," Jaxon told his team as they unloaded the gear they had been carrying in backpacks.

"First we need to examine the site. Check the area near the opening to the shaft. It's been a few months, but you never know what you might find." He walked over to Frank. "How sure are you about this site?"

"All I can tell you is the dog has signaled this is the place. If he's on track, then she's here or something else dead is."

"I'm sure she is." Peyton rubbed on more sunscreen. The sun was higher in the sky and getting hot even with the slightly cooler temps. In the direct sunlight it still felt blistering on her skin.

"I guess we're about to find out how accurate this whole thing is. I hope you're prepared for the answer," Jaxon said as he leaned close to her.

"I am. I could ask the same of you. You're about to have to deal with your skepticism. Of course, if I were in your shoes, I would probably feel the same way you do." Peyton walked away from him and went to sit next to Frank.

Using a small fiber optic camera on the end of a cable, Amos lowered it down the shaft. "Kincaid, there's a body down here," he called out.

Jaxon went to look. "You're right." The image told the story. Only forensics could determine if it was Carlee, but he was beginning to believe that Peyton was right. It looked like he would be eating crow again. He'd been doing that a lot lately. Maybe he needed to surrender while he still had a bit of pride left. He walked over to where Frank sat next to Peyton.

"Frank, your dog did an amazing job." He bent down to pat the dog's head. "Someone is down there, and my guess is that it's probably our victim." Jaxon sat on the rock beside Peyton.

"Some days he impresses even me, and I work with him all the time. Today he might have had a bit of supernatural help." Frank winked at Peyton. "Hey, we'll take any help we can get."

"I hear you." She leaned toward him and spoke quietly. "Who knows better where they are than the victim themselves?"

"True." He smiled at her. "You're a lot like Jessie. To think there are two of you makes me happy."

"I'll take that as a compliment. My cousin is all right in my book." Peyton smiled back at Frank.

"In mine too." He removed his hat to wipe the sweat forming on his forehead. "I think I should borrow that sunscreen now. The sun is hotter than blazes and I'll be as red as a lobster soon if I don't." He reached for the tube she had in her hand. After he put the cream on his face and arms, he put his hat back on.

"How long will you be here?" She glanced at Jaxon.

"Most of the day. Captain Stolberg is going to leave in a few minutes, and I think you two should go back with him. There is nothing you can do here besides roast in the heat."

"Sounds good to me." Peyton stood, brushing the dust off her jeans.

"I'm with you." Radar jumped up when Frank did.

"Frank, we'd like you to try another track after we recover the body. I'll talk to you later about it."

"Sounds good."

"Peyton, as soon as our victim is ID'd, I'll let you know."

"You'll affirm what I already know." She smiled at him.

****

Talk about dumb luck. All of them had been so sure the cops would never find the body, yet here they were. The others needed to know. Not something he was looking forward to telling them. The body would soon be examined, and their own identities could be revealed. Only a matter of time. Not one of them had been careful. But they were counting on the summer heat and time to destroy their prints and alter any DNA that might have been left all over the kid. It had been a joke to them at the time. The guys would be mad as hell. He would be too if he had any feelings left, but he was dead to those ever since that night.

How could he forget what they did to her? The man shuddered at the thought. That poor kid didn't have a clue what she walked into that day. Such a pretty little thing, not much older than his own daughter. He stifled the groan he felt deep inside. The sight had come back to haunt his thoughts more times than he wanted to count. It was too damned late for him to have a conscience now. He followed them at a distance careful not to be seen or heard.

He watched them walk back to where they had left the cars. Killing the girl was probably one of the dumber things he had participated in. What a waste. At the end, Dawson ended up dead anyway. Shooting up Tombstone wouldn't gain him any favors. He was garbage, and they knew how dispose of trash.

He should've known Kincaid would be the one. If he had figured out this much, the rest wasn't far behind. Nothing seemed to be working right. When things went bad, they went there fast. Fated to face the one man who could probably take him out, his gut gave him a reality check. He'd played the game and lost, and there wouldn't be many more chances. He had used up plenty in the last few stupid choices he made. Dead either way, he might as well go out in a big way.

Chapter 26

Peyton listened to Stolberg and Frank talk in the front seat. She was almost hypnotized by the sound of their voices and the passing scenery out the side window until her mind finally drifted off in its own direction. Radar had been amazing to watch this morning. Whether or not he had unseen help didn't matter—the dog found Carlee's resting place. Fascinated to be an observer in such a unique experience, she still felt the awe of Radar's success. She had never imagined how accurate a dog's sense of smell was compared to humans. This would go down as one of the more memorable events in her life.

She wondered how long Jaxon's team would be at the site. Getting Carlee's body out of the mine shaft could prove to be noteworthy. From her reading, many of those abandoned shafts were dangerous. Of course, the experts would know how to go about extricating the corpse. One part of her had wanted to stay and participate in every part of Carlee's recovery. But her emotions were raw, and she wasn't sure she wanted to be there when the body was recovered. It made it more real somehow. Someone had murdered the beautiful girl, and she had seen it in her mind. The coroner wouldn't tell her anything she didn't already know. It was Carlee Blair that had been found today, and what the girl had suffered was beyond words. She could only hope that those responsible would pay a price for their crime.

Add to her emotions was the feeling she had all morning that they were being watched. It seemed highly improbable with Radar in the area. He would have barked if he sensed danger. Wouldn't he? The man who stood in her way this morning probably shaded her feelings, making her uneasy. All of this was so new to her and hard to separate facts from her own emotions. She wasn't bold, only uncomfortable, naïve, and a bit scared.

Where did she go from here? She had no idea how this worked. Carlee died because of something Dawson was involved in. How did Tombstone fit into it, if at all? Right now, she only saw fragments and nothing that tied it all together. She sent off a quick text to her cousin.

—*Call me later. I need to talk to you. Hopefully, you can make sense of all of this.*—

A quick reply of "okay" gave her peace. Back and forth she worked through the visions and dreams she had that involved Carlee, hopeful something would jump at her. It would be nice if Dawson could help too. She hadn't seen him since that first day at the murder site. Why? She had no idea.

"You're quiet back there. Is everything okay?" Frank turned to look at her.

His voice startled her. "I'm good, just thinking." She gave him a tentative smile.

"A murder case like this must be a bit overwhelming for you," Stolberg said.

"You could say that. I've read about murders, but I can't say I've ever seen one."

"What do you do for a living?" Stolberg asked, changing the subject.

"I'm an editor at a publishing house. I've read manuscripts about murder, but it didn't prepare me for the real thing." She paused. "I wonder what kind of person could murder and dump a body so unceremoniously without regard for the victim or their family."

"A question we often ask ourselves at any murder scene. I've learned over time there are some bad people in this world. A lot of good ones too," he added. "You hope you never meet the bad ones or be by one in the wrong place at the wrong time." Stolberg changed lanes.

"I'm not sure you'll ever get a good enough answer to make sense of it. There will always be a question unanswered." Frank frowned. "Sometimes the best we can do is bring the victims home to their families and get the ones who did it off the streets."

"Amen to that." Stolberg put on his turn signal and drove into the resort parking lot. "And we're going to solve this case." He pulled up near the entrance. "Jaxon talked to me about you, young lady. I want to thank you for all your help and for putting us in touch with Frank. Radar did a fine job. We are one step closer to finding the killer, and that's a good thing." He got out so he could open the back door for her.

"See you later." She patted Frank's shoulder. "It was awesome watching your dog at work."

"Have a relaxing afternoon and try to put this out of your mind. Kincaid will let you know when there is a positive ID." Stolberg stood beside the open door.

"Thank you." She stepped out of the car. "Get

some rest, Frank. I'm sure you could use it after the morning you've had."

"I plan on it." He waved at her before the captain closed the door.

She made it to her room before the full force of the morning hit her. Thankfully, no one knew about her display of emotion, except an empty room and Carlee, who observed her unseen.

****

For the first time at a crime scene he had thought about the possibility of the person's spirit observing what they were doing. Call him fanciful but there were times throughout the day where he felt they were being watched. Their experience at Tombstone left him feeling on edge. He walked over to a rock to sit as the coroner bent over the body and did his part to get the corpse ready to transport.

"I'd say from the condition of the body we're looking at time of death at a couple of months or more. Underground is cooler, and with any luck some of the evidence should still be intact. Where she landed was almost the perfect depth. A few more feet either way and the temps start to rise, and evidence is lost to the elements or heat. I'll know more after the autopsy. I can tell you right now the victim is a young female, probably in her late teens." Max zipped the body bag. "It's always a damned shame to see a young one like this. I'll let you know when I have an identity and results."

"Thanks. You know the protocol. We're looking for anything that can point us in the direction of a suspect."

"I'll do it by the book," Max told him. "How did

you ever find her?"

"We got a tip she was in this area."

"We're talking about a large area. You've got me scratching my head on this one." Max wiped the sweat off his brows, catching it before it could drip in his eyes.

"We had a bloodhound doing the tracking," Jaxon told him.

"Now that had to be fascinating to watch." Max sat on the rock beside Jaxon.

"It was. This skeptic is a firm believer now. He took an impossible, overwhelming task and made it seem easy." Jaxon handed Max a bottle of water. "Thanks again. Get out of this heat."

"You do the same." Max took a swig of the water and stood to leave. The coroner's crew carried out the body.

After the team packed up their equipment, Jaxon's crew got ready to walk back to the cars. "Amos, thanks for thinking of the camera." Jaxon walked up behind him and rapped him on the shoulder.

"When you said we might need to check some abandoned mines, I knew the camera would come in handy. I'm glad the captain requested the money for them in the budget last year. They're awesome for seeing into tight places."

"Money well spent by the department." Jaxon grabbed a couple of the bags to carry.

"I've been on various investigations over the past several years, and it doesn't get any easier than this one was. I really hate when it's a kid though." Amos carried the bagged evidence that had been gathered. "Are you riding back with me?"

"Yes, the captain left in the car I was driving. He took Ms. Reynolds and Frank back to their hotels." Jaxon was glad to see the parking area in the distance. He had enough heat for the day. After another ten minutes on the trail they made the last climb up to the cars.

"We had a successful day." Amos opened the trunk of the car, where they deposited the gear they were carrying. "There's no way we would have found that body without the help of that dog. Even with a tip, the area is vast, and it could have taken days—if ever."

"He made short work of it. All we had to do was follow him." Jaxon tossed his files on the front seat.

"I won't forget watching that bloodhound at work. He was awesome." Amos closed the trunk when the last bag was put in.

"I hear you." Jaxon latched his seat belt. "Radar made it a lot easier on us."

"If you don't mind me asking, who is Peyton and where did you meet her?" Amos started the car. "She seems like a nice girl."

Jaxon smiled, thinking about all the fights they had. "She is staying at the resort and tried to do CPR on E J when the staff pulled him from the pool. I met her when I interviewed the witnesses."

"Wow, that must have been hard on her. Wasn't E J shot in the head? Most women I know would be falling apart, not trying revive a dead man."

"I doubt that. Women are stronger than you think." Jaxon looked at the text messages on his phone. "She's only here for a short time on vacation and will be going home before long." Jaxon took another drink from his bottle of water.

"Too bad she's leaving soon." Amos glanced at him.

"Why is that?"

"You two looked perfect together, and I thought I detected a bit of chemistry. Besides being easy on the eyes, you seemed almost relaxed with her." Amos grinned. "Just a casual observation as a friend."

"Actually, we've been at odds from the beginning. I'll admit I find her fascinating. Who wouldn't?" Jaxon turned the air vent in his direction. "Man, the AC feels good."

"I saw several of the team noticing her, if you know what I mean," Amos goaded him

"Knock it off. We're friends and nothing more." Jaxon amazed himself for keeping a straight face as he told the lie. A real whopper. His feelings were already involved, but she didn't feel the same about him.

"Other than Dawson, how does she fit into this case? Why was she here today?" Amos asked.

"She's the one that connected the Blair girl to E J. She found her in a missing person's file on the internet. She was doing a bit of sleuthing on her own. I'm glad she did. It was a shortcut for us." Jaxon decided he could tell Amos the whole story. He explained all the ways Peyton had helped already.

"Okay, that's another wow. I wasn't expecting to hear she saw their spirits. You said her cousin has the same ability, too?"

"Yeah. Although this is the first time for Peyton. I've talked to Chief Parker in Blue Cove several times. What the girls have seems to be genuine. Parker is engaged to her cousin now. He was skeptical in the beginning too."

"How did you react when she told you?"

"How do you think I did?" Jaxon asked.

"Knowing you, I'd say you weren't nice about it." Amos chuckled.

"You've got that right. I was suspicious. I went as far as to call her a kook." He heard Amos laugh. "I'm not proud of it, but in my defense, I had never heard anything like it before."

"I don't get it. But we did find the girl." Amos turned onto the highway back to the city. "It explains a few things to me." Amos glanced at him.

"Like?" Jaxon asked.

"Like why Brice Delaney died with an absolute look of terror on his face. He must have had a part in our victim's death, and he saw her out there. Maybe there is justice after all." Amos shook his head. "How does Frank fit in?"

"Frank is friends with her cousin. He brought his dog here as a favor to her."

"I for one am glad he did." Amos glanced at him. "If I were you, I'd try to make myself charming and snatch that girl up. She's an asset."

Chapter 27

Peyton answered her ringing phone. "Hey cousin, you wanted me to call," Jessie said.

"I sure did." Peyton told her about the morning and finding Carlee's body. "Now I'm trying to figure out how all of these separate, evolving pieces fit together."

"It will come together soon enough. A clearer picture will form with time and evidence. You'll get some of it, and the detective will too. You can't do it alone. If you're there, you need to be a part of his team. Believe me—I found out the hard way, guys can be territorial when it comes to their job. Work with him and let him think he's the one in control. More peaceful that way."

"Did you work peacefully with Matt?" Her voice sounded skeptical even to herself.

"Of course not." Jessie laughed. "I kept telling the poor man that I was going to be involved whether he liked it or not. It's the feminist in me. What can I say? I'm only letting you in on the secret it took me a long time to learn. I fought the man every step of the way. Don't repeat my mistakes."

"I wish you were here. I have lots of questions. I have no idea what I should be doing. Besides you're fun and make me laugh. I could use that right now." Now she sounded pathetic.

"Start by working with the detective." Jessie

paused. "Peyton, I never told you, but my home life wasn't a piece of cake either. My dad was not easy to live with. Those brothers are more alike than you know. I didn't go through what you did, but Dad was stifling to me and my mom. The Reynolds men have bigger than life personalities. I'm convinced he is the reason I fought so hard for women's rights. I can't abide a man telling me what to do. You can imagine how that sits with Matt."

"From what I can tell, Matt loves everything about you, even the crazy parts." Peyton had seen the way he looked at Jessie.

"He sure does, and I'm better because of it. How about you, cousin? Is love in your future?" Jessie asked.

"I don't know. I find it hard to trust men. I think I'm ruined for relationships."

"No, you're not. You're afraid, and I get it. But the right guy makes the risk worthwhile. Whatever you do, don't fall for your detective. I want you back here where I can keep my eye on you as you fall in love. I want our kids to grow up together."

"Don't worry. I'm coming home soon. I've talked to my boss and offered him a proposal, and he's considering it now. Who knows? Maybe I'll live in Blue Cove. At least I'll be there until the end of next month for Katie's wedding."

"You mean the biggest event ever according to Katie. Believe me, all of us will be happy when the wedding is a happy memory. Katie isn't exactly a bridezilla, but she keeps all of us helping and hopping. I'm not kidding." Jessie laughed. "My friend is high maintenance but also the funniest person I know. Her wedding will be an absolute blast."

"Tell her I'll be there." Peyton closed her eyes, trying to picture Katie telling people what to do.

"I will. Oh, before I forget, Reba said she would call you tomorrow, and I will too. Love you, Cous. Katie's calling. She'll keep calling me until I answer." Jessie ended the call.

****

Jaxon answered his phone. "Kincaid, this is Jeremy."

"Hi, Jeremy. What's up?"

"I called Peyton, and she told me I should call you. I found something that might be of interest to your case." Jeremy went into detail about what he had found. "Do you know the company or who owns it?" Jeremy asked.

"I wonder if it is a real company." Jaxon wrote the name on an envelope sitting on the table. "It doesn't sound right to me, but what do I know?"

"I'm going to work at getting around the firewall on the company's website. I think you may be dealing with white-collar crime. They're trafficking in something illegal, but I'm not sure what yet. I will try to track down the real name, but we're talking about millions of dollars changing hands and shifting from one account to another. I have a feeling when you unravel this there will be lots of people involved." Jeremy paused. "You need to watch your back. If these guys think you're on to them, they'll come gunning for you. Peyton too, if she's near you."

"I hear you. Thanks, Jeremy. I appreciate all your help. I'll do my best to keep Peyton safe."

"If she's like her cousin she'll keep you busy. Those Reynolds girls are passionate about their commitments. Peyton is only starting out, but believe me, after talking to her she's in this all the way. If I know her, she's online checking out everything I've told her. Take care, Jaxon. I'll call you as soon as I know more." Jeremy hung up.

He needed to talk with her. Staying away from her wasn't working. He called her number. "Peyton, would you like to have a cup of coffee with me?"

"Isn't it a little late for coffee?" she asked.

"Not for me. You can have whatever you want. I need to talk with you. I want your perspective on a few things. My talk with Jeremy got my juices flowing, and I want to run my thoughts by someone."

"And you want to talk to me?" He could hear the question in her voice.

"As strange as this might sound to you, yes. You're the one who orchestrated this today. It's your friends that are involved, and I think it's important that we talk." He waited for her response, which seemed to be taking forever.

"Of course, we can talk. When?" she asked.

"I'm outside waiting. I drove here on the hopes that you would be open to coming with me."

"I'll be out in ten minutes." She ended the call.

That went better than he had expected. Things were getting better between them, or at least he told himself they were. He scrambled, searching for the questions to ask her. Although he did want to talk to her, he needed to know she was okay. His talk with Jeremy reminded him how serious this case was. Jeremy's findings had taken it up to a whole new level. Tomorrow he would inform the captain.

****

Peyton raced to get dressed. In for the night, she hadn't planned on going out. Grabbing her floral sundress out of the closet, she slipped it over her head. Why would he want to talk to her? It pleased her but at the same time it worried her. She had already told him everything she knew. Jeremy said he would call Jaxon earlier with the information he had found. She ran the brush through her hair, applied lip gloss, and slipped her feet into her sandals. Reaching for her purse, she shoved her phone in as she opened the door and left the room.

Glancing at her reflection in one of the windows, she could only hope she looked put together. Ten minutes wasn't a lot of time to dress, but she hated to make him wait too long. What man calls at almost ten in the evening and asks you out for coffee? Unless of course he has bad news to tell you. He couldn't. No one she knew would know to call him. Except for Matt or Jessie. "Stop it!" she admonished herself. "You're getting worked up over nothing. You have no idea what the man wants to talk to you about. Maybe he wants to be with you." She laughed at the notion. Yell at her would be closer to the truth.

She saw him before he saw her. Standing near the entrance, and even from here she could see the grim, tired expression on his face. *Be nice to him, Peyton. You'll know soon enough why he wanted to meet with you right now.*

"Good evening, Detective Kincaid. It's a bit late to be asking a girl out." She smiled when he turned toward her.

"I realized that while I was standing here. I thought of calling you back, but you had already said yes. Ten minutes, exactly." He looked at his watch. "You made it on time."

"I'm nothing if not punctual. I didn't give you any guarantee on how I would look though."

He gave her the once over, the approval written in his eyes. "I'd say better than perfect for ten minutes' notice." They walked out to the car side by side. He reached around her to open the car door.

As soon as they were on the road, Peyton asked him why he had called. "I did wonder what was so important that it couldn't wait until morning to talk to me about."

"You want the truth?" he asked.

"Yes." She turned to look at him.

"Jeremy gave me some disturbing information. I realized this case is much bigger than E J and the Blair girl. He told me I needed to watch over you. You could be in danger by virtue of being tied to me. I had to make sure you were okay even though it's late."

"And are you satisfied that I'm fine?" She touched her skin. "I'm all in one piece."

"I can see that." He smiled at her. "You look better than fine. But I still wanted to talk to you, which is my second reason for asking you out."

"I can live with that. What do you talk about?" she asked.

"How are you after the track this morning?"

"If you must know, I spent some time crying and more time talking to my cousin. I didn't realize how hard I would take it." Peyton glanced at him.

"I think you handled it well, all things considering. It's not easy dealing with murder. You've had some unusual experiences since arriving in town."

"True. Speaking of those experiences, have you heard any more about how Barbara Newsome is doing?"

"I'll check first thing in the morning. You can go visit her if you want to."

"Yes, please. I can always go during the day. I doubt I'll be busy the next few days."

"Which reminds me—have you made your decision about staying?" He turned on his signal and drove into the parking lot of the restaurant.

"I have. When I saw Carlee's spirit, I promised her I would be here until we found her killer. But that's conditional on it happening reasonably soon because my leave of absence is almost up."

"I'm happy to hear it." He reached for her hand when she got out of the car, and he didn't let go.

She didn't push him away. After what they had shared today, it seemed right for some reason.

Chapter 28

Peyton had a restless night. Her dreams were filled with frightful images of Carlee, E J, and others. Ghostly faces, haunted eyes, and anguished moans swirled around her. Some of what she saw made little sense to her but stayed clearly with her after she had awakened tangled in her sheets in a puddle of sweat. She reached for her notebook and pen, writing down the details she could vividly remember. Jaxon needed to hear about what she had seen. If the details were correct, it did involve someone at the station.

Reba confirmed it later in the morning when she called. Peyton recalled her ominous words. "Peyton, every time I think about you, I'm troubled. And for the detective too." There was a long pause on the phone. She heard Reba exhale a big breath. "Someone has revenge in their hearts. It started as a simple case of envy, but it's way past that now. Your lives are on a collision course. And I'm afraid there will be injuries. Be careful, sweet girl. Make sure you do what that officer tells you. Don't fight him. Now's not the time to be stubborn. He will be the one who saves you from death."

If that was meant to inspire confidence, Reba's words had the opposite effect. Peyton shuddered as she recalled them. Getting on the next plane home sounded perfect to her, but she refused to let fear rule her. But neither was she brave enough to leave her room for the day either.

She ordered room service and spent a good portion of the day reading or rehashing the words Reba had told her. Jessie called to make sure she was okay. Sadie called too. It seemed everyone knew what Reba had said and were worried about her. The one person she wanted to hear from hadn't called yet.

****

Jaxon spent most of the morning in Captain Stolberg's office going over everything Jeremy had told him. They also talked about the positive ID of Carlee Blair and their concern about a leak. "It appears this case is bigger than we anticipated, and the leak may be tied into it."

"How is your search going? Have you turned up anything yet?" Stolberg frowned, resting his chin on his hand.

Jaxon shook his head. "No. Is it possible it's someone who used to work here and quit?" Jaxon asked. "I've looked over the files and nothing stands out to me."

"That might be an angle to consider. Check out those files too." Stolberg leaned back in his chair. "What do you think we're looking at?"

"A company operating illegally and moving money around, trying to cover their actions. It could be a number of illegal activities. I should know more soon." He explained a few more ideas Jeremy had run by him.

"I'm concerned about the size of this one. Do we need to call in more help?" the captain asked.

"If it's what Jeremy thinks it is, the FBI will be involved whether we want them to be or not. This is a federal crime. Truthfully, we might need them. I should have a list of names to give you before long. At the very least, it might help us understand why they got rid of E J. The company he worked for didn't want the attention. The way he was throwing money around, someone would have noticed eventually and traced it back to them. The one big mistake they made as far as I see it was murdering the Blair girl and then E J. Otherwise, they might still be flying under the radar."

"And we would have never known any of it without Ms. Reynolds. We owe her a debt of gratitude."

"As unconventional as it is, we would never have gotten this far this fast without her help." Jaxon stood. "With your permission, I'm going to check on people who left the job recently who might still have attachments to someone here."

"Sounds good. Let me know what time the reservations are for. Taking them out for a fine meal is the least we can do for all their hard work. Besides, I want my wife to meet Frank and Peyton. Then she can put faces with names as I talk to her." He smiled. "She loves to know details, and I'm no good at describing people's appearances."

"Something we both have in common. My mom and sister can go on and on about the details of my sister's wedding, and I have no idea what they're talking about. They want those same details when they ask me questions. It'll never happen." Stolberg chuckled as Jaxon turned to leave.

Amos knocked on the captain's door. "Hey, Kincaid, Jordon down in tech has some evidence he said you need to see pronto." He motioned to Stolberg. "Good day, sir."

"I'll check it out and let you know what's up," Jaxon told Stolberg as he left his office.

Jaxon couldn't believe what he was looking at. The next hour was spent poring over the information on E J's computer. Once he was sure, Jaxon called the captain down to have a look. Jordon explained what the numbers they were looking at meant. Stolberg made an instant decision to call the FBI.

Later Jaxon made another trek to HR with a stack of files. He returned with several new ones. He spent his afternoon poring over them and only stopped to watch the custodian, Edwards, mopping the lunchroom. Amos described him as an odd sort of guy who kept to himself and didn't interact much with others. Cleaning up after the guys wasn't an easy job. Edwards' medium built was like half the men on the force. He had worked here for several months, and Jaxon knew almost nothing about him. Why was that?

He needed to get to know the guy. How would he describe Edwards? Nondescript. Nothing stood out about him except for the red ball cap that he always wore. He had never seen the man without it. The cap was his signature. He seemed to blend into his surroundings quite easily. Jaxon had a perfect view from his small office cubicle across the hall to where the man worked. There was something almost mesmerizing about his movements. He had some great moves. With earbuds in his ears, Edwards worked to some tune and the mop moved in rhythm with it.

If he didn't stop wasting time, he would be working on these all night at home. Still, he watched. The thought hit him. Maybe they weren't looking for a bad cop but rather someone working in the station. A plant. Jaxon knew all the guys around him, and they were solid. He didn't know all the new staff. The desk clerk at the resort said a big man showed him a badge, but they were easy enough to get hold of. He needed to explore the new direction that his mind was taking him. It was a possibility to consider.

Reservations were for six-thirty, and the captain, Frank, and Peyton were notified. He looked forward to a night out without thinking about the case. If it was possible. He smiled.

Last night, Peyton had captivated him, which wasn't hard for her to do. He wanted to see more of her. After they had been seated in the coffee shop, he watched as a young teen with Down's Syndrome, like his new niece, came over and sat beside her in the booth.

"I like your hair." The girl ran her hand over Peyton's hair.

Peyton didn't flinch. She let the girl touch the long waves, talking to her as the girl continued to stroke her hair.

"What's your name?" Peyton asked her.

"Blanche," the girl answered.

"That's a lovely name. My name is Peyton." He watched, fascinated, as the two of them talked like they had known each other for years. They talked about so many subjects Jaxon lost count. Blanche suddenly stood and slapped two one-dollar bills on the table. "This is on me," she said proudly with a smile and walked away.

Peyton had grown on him since they had quit arguing. After seeing her interaction with the girl, her estimation only grew in his eyes. There wasn't a doubt

199

in his mind, she should work with special needs kids. She'd be great. He knew his family would love her when he took her home. And he would. He was determined.

Chapter 29

Peyton had brought a special dress in case of a formal occasion. She got dressed with care. As Sadie always told her, "you only get once to make a good first impression." Not that she wanted to impress anyone, but it was always in a girl's best interest to feel confident and look great. She glanced at her image in the mirror as she passed. The blue-green color of the dress was perfect with the jade earrings Grams had given her.

Only Madison and Jessie knew about her desire to teach. She hadn't shared that with anyone else until Jaxon. Did the man put truth serum in her drink to make her talk? All she had to do was get near him and she was ready to spill all. She could only imagine how a criminal would be intimidated by him.

Peyton still needed to tell him about her conversation with Reba and about her dream. Hopefully there would be time tonight. Reba's words still shook her to the core, and so did the awful premonition she had when she heard them. She wouldn't tell him about the weird vision, or he would send her home.

****

Jaxon had studied Peyton most of the night. Something was up. Her demeanor seemed off. She looked stunning, but he could tell she was troubled about something. There wasn't time to question her until later in the evening as the group began to go their separate ways. As soon as he dropped Frank off, he asked her what he had wanted to all night. "Hey, what's going on? You seem preoccupied tonight. I hope it wasn't the company."

"It's not you. I didn't sleep well last night." She turned to look out the passenger window.

"Why?" he asked.

"I had bad dreams most of the night."

"Would you care to elaborate?" He drove through the traffic and stopped at a light.

"I wrote the images down so I wouldn't forget. There's a lot to this, and it might take a while to explain it to you. I think you need to know. I'm not sure how to tell you though." Her voice softened. "To tell you the truth I'm spooked, and nothing much scares me anymore."

"Now you've got my interest. We'll talk this through. Let me get out of traffic. I'm taking you to my place. It's quiet, and we can talk there. I promise to behave."

"Okay." Her voice was barely audible.

He parked his car in the small garage, and they went into his condo. "Make yourself comfortable." He motioned her into the living room. "Would you like something to drink?"

"Water would be nice." She sat in one of the leather chairs. "You have a nice space. It's neater than I thought it would be, which may be a stereotype. I thought most guys weren't that neat. At least, most of the married friends I have always tell me how messy their husbands are."

"Thanks, I think. I can't say I never make my share

of messes. Especially when I was growing up. It was a constant point of contention between my mother and us boys. I think around high school I figured out that I felt better when my space was tidy. My mind likes things organized. It's a better environment for me to work in." He chuckled. "My mom might be shocked at that confession. I hope I can count on you to keep my secret." He placed her glass of water on the glass-topped table beside her. "I still like her to wait on me when I go home."

"Thank you." She reached for the glass, taking a sip of water.

"Before you start, can I tell you something?" he asked.

"Of course." She smiled.

"The longer I know you the more impressed I am by your character. When I saw how you treated Blanche last night in the coffeeshop, you won my admiration. I don't think I told you my brother's new baby has Down's Syndrome. She has already stolen all our hearts. Your kindness with Blanche encouraged me. I was worried my niece would have it rough as she grows up. People aren't always kind."

"No, they're not. The thing about these kids is that they are the angels among us that are here teaching us how to be better people. Their impact is far reaching, more than we often understand. What is your niece's name?" Peyton reached for the photo he showed her.

"Emma. We all call her Emmie. Her smile lights up the room."

"She's adorable." She handed the picture back to him.

"Anyways, it gave me hope. I wanted you to

know." He sipped his water. "You can start when you're ready."

For the next few hours, they went over every detail she could think of. Her nightmares, Reba's words, the man who had gotten in her way at the resort. They talked about Jeremy's call and how the case had expanded in a new direction.

"I wasn't going to tell you, but I feel I should. While Reba was talking to me, I had an odd premonition." She rubbed her arms as goosebumps trailed down her back and across her shoulders.

"Odd in what way?" He waited patiently for her to reply. He could sense the hesitation and fear around her.

"I saw myself lying on a stretcher with people working frantically around me. Flashing lights, sirens, and the sense of urgency scared me. Am I going to die?" she asked in a hushed tone, her voice trembling.

"Not if I have any say in the matter." He tried to reassure her, but he had to admit her fear was contagious. She had been accurate in the past. Was she seeing something as a warning or was it about to happen to her? "There is something you need to know."

"You sound serious." She sat forward in the chair.

"The tech department found some files on E J's computer. He has two sets of records—one he kept for anyone to see and another hidden one. I swear he might have been trying to do the right thing. We should know what it all means soon, but this case got a lot bigger and I can't imagine what we will find and who's involved. I'm not free to talk about it. I'll tell you when I can."

"Sounds like Jeremy was right. We need to watch our backs."

"Would you like to have protection? You've helped us, so we can certainly cover you," he asked, fighting the panic rising in him. It was too big with too many possibilities to consider—it would take all-hands-on-deck with this one.

"No, I think I'm safe at the resort. I don't know where the scene took place only that I saw it." She stood and started to pace. "It's late, and I'm tired. I would like to go back if that's okay."

"Sorry, I lost track of the time." They exited the condo and he walked her out to the car. "Promise me if you become concerned at all for your safety you'll call. We'll get someone there right away."

"I will." She leaned her head back against the headrest and closed her eyes for a moment. "I'm not sleeping." She smiled. "I'm simply resting my mind."

He handed her a piece of paper. "Barbara, the lady you assisted in Tombstone, is ready for visitors, and her husband said you are the first person she asked about when she woke up."

"That makes my day, or should I say night." Peyton lifted her head. "She's going to be okay. I want to go visit her."

"I'll take you tomorrow."

"You don't need to. You're busy," she added. "Besides, I have a car."

"I would rather drive you until I have time to assess what you told me tonight, if that's okay with you."

"That's a reasonable request." She turned to glance at him. "I can be rational. Especially after what I told you. I don't, however, expect you to babysit me or watch me twenty-four seven. You have a murder to solve, and I don't want to get in the way of your investigation. I'll play it safe and stay near the hotel until I feel it's time for me to leave. Hopefully, that will be soon, and our lives will return to normal." She unlatched her seatbelt when the car came to a stop. "Thanks for the dinner and a nice evening."

"Wait a minute. I'm walking you to your room. I don't want you to have to put up with another out-of-control hotel guest."

After walking her to her room without incident, Jaxon sat outside in his car for a while. What she had told him disturbed him more than he let on. Her fear was palpable. Rattled by what she had seen, how could he possibly reassure her it would all be okay. Not after what he saw in those computer files. He'd never been in a situation like this before. He warned himself not to get involved with her, but that hadn't stopped him. Now the thought of losing her or not seeing her again was more than he wanted to deal with. He would see to her protection and not tell her.

Chapter 30

Jaxon spent the morning in meetings. The minute he walked into the station Amos told him he was wanted in the captain's office.

Jaxon knocked on the closed door, opened it slightly, and stuck his head in. "Amos said you wanted me."

"Come in, Kincaid, and close the door. You need to meet these folks. You'll be working with them as our representative until this case is closed." Stolberg introduced the two agents in the room. Agent Miller's tall frame pushed away from the wall to shake Jaxon's hand. O'Donnell, the shorter of the two men, pumped his hand with enthusiasm.

Jaxon instantly liked both men. "Nice to meet you." They continued with small talk until they were joined by Jordon from tech.

They spent the next few hours going through the files that E J had encrypted on his computer. Jordon and Agent Miller pointed out certain highlighted entries and explained what they meant. The facts didn't look any better in the daylight. The men analyzed the impact of the crime both in the US and several other countries that would also be affected. No one in the room doubted for a minute when the news came out that lives would be altered as result of this company's actions. How many may have already died?

"Damn, why would someone do this?" Jordon shook his head.

"Money, greed, you name it. To me these guys are scum in suits." Miller pointed to the picture of the board members and the CEO. "We're going to nail them and close their operation down. We are preparing the info for a search warrant now."

"What time frame are we looking at for searching the premise?" Jaxon asked.

"The operation is scheduled for first thing tomorrow morning." Agent O'Donnell crossed his arms over his chest. "We don't want to give them another day to peddle this junk."

"Could this be the reason they killed Dawson?" Miller pointed at the computer files.

"It's possible someone found out. I'm more prone to believe that Dawson was drawing too much attention by spending lots of money. All I know is that his murder and that of his girlfriend have alerted us to this bigger problem." Jaxon leaned his hip against the desk. "They were under the radar until we found E J's body."

"This kid did a thorough job of documenting the company's actions. He knew his way around the computer. He made it easy for us to unlock his files." Jordon scrolled to the next page.

"When this is over, maybe it will be a consolation for his parents. In the meantime, some civic minded folks in our community will be going to jail. The backlash is liable to be substantial." Jaxon drummed his fingers on the desktop. "Where do we go next?"

"To the bank," Agent Miller said. "Dawson's safety deposit box has a flash drive stored there, according to this notation. I'm curious to see what he left us on it."

Jordon printed the text of a note Dawson had written. "He explains some of it here."

"I know they're getting wise to me. They thought killing Carlee would stop me. It almost did. You have to believe me I never thought they would hurt her. But there are too many lives at stake to stop now. I hope this can right some of the wrongs I've done and make my dad proud. I've saved all these files and more from the company's computer, including offshore bank account numbers, to a USB flash drive locked in my safety deposit box. My dad has a key and can take you there."

"Kincaid, you're friends with his father. Call him," Stolberg told him.

"Yes, sir." Jaxon left the office to make the call.

"I'd like to go with you." Agent O'Donnell stood in front of Jaxon's desk.

"Let's go." Jaxon motioned to O'Donnell. "E J's dad will meet us there in fifteen minutes." Jaxon told the captain the plan, and the two men left the station together. On the way to the bank, he told the agent about how Radar found Carlee's body.

"Hell, that sounds like a story my friend Tom Maxwell told me. He's an agent back east. What's the dog's name?"

"Radar, and his handler is Frank Wagner." Jaxon turned into the bank parking lot.

"I'll be damned, it's the same dog. Don't tell me that Jessie Reynolds is working the case with you."

"You've heard of her?" Jaxon couldn't hide his surprise.

"Hell, yes. Tom swears by her. Is she here? I want

to meet the woman." O'Donnell took off his seatbelt.

"No, but her cousin Peyton Reynolds is, and she seems to have Jessie's ability to see things. She's quite remarkable." Jaxon told O'Donnell about her premonitions and their accuracy. "The only one we haven't figured out yet is the Tombstone connection."

"I'm sure you'll know soon enough." He slapped his leg. "Damn, I can't believe there's another one. How is it you detectives get to work with them, and the FBI has yet to snag one?"

"We're lucky, I guess. She came here on vacation." Jaxon opened the car door when he saw Elliot Dawson pull into the parking lot.

"You sure as hell are." Agent O'Donnell followed Jaxon and Dawson into the bank.

****

Peyton received a text from Jaxon telling her he would be tied up most of the day. He would pick her up to take her to see Barbara after work. It seemed like the perfect time to do a bit of online searching with help from her new friend Jeremy. The Tombstone vision fit into this strange scenario some way, but at this point she still had no clue how. There had to be a simple connection even if it had nothing to do with the town now.

She sent off an email to Jeremy and got to work. Had E J and Carlee gone to the tourist town together? That was an angle to investigate, or maybe something from the past would answer the question. Bank records were Jeremy's expertise not hers. All she knew was that the visions she had were somehow connected to something going on now. She devoured everything she could find on Tombstone at its heyday.

Later in the day, Peyton founded a shady spot to relax after taking a dip in the pool. She dropped her head back on the chaise lounge, closing her eyes and smiling at the sounds of children playing in the shallow end of the pool. It was hot but tolerable in the shade. She imagined how wonderful the warmth would be when everyone else was freezing in the snow. Still, it wasn't enough to tempt her to move here. She took a sip of her iced tea after squeezing lemon into it. Give her four seasons any day, at least at this point in her life. She liked it that way. Her lips puckered—the lemon tasted bitter. Relaxing, the heat made her feel drowsy.

The sound of heavy breathing caught her attention. She struggled to sit upright, but nothing would move. Her vision blurred. She couldn't focus. Dang, what was happening to her. The bitterness—a drug in her drink sent panic racing through her mind.

"If I were you, young lady, I'd be moving along if you know what's good for you." A strange face appeared blurrily in front of her. His breathing heavy and his breath strong, he moved closer until his face almost touched hers. "You wouldn't want to be hit by a stray bullet meant for someone else. It happens all the time."

"Who are you?" Her slurred words struggled out her mouth. It all sounded wrong as the humming in her head grew louder.

"I'm warning you to leave while you can still walk." His head bobbed back and forth.

She struggled. "Stop moving," she told him, slapping her hand over her mouth. "I think I'm going to be sick."

He moved his face back from hers. "Just do what I tell you."

"What did you do to me?" Panicked, she struggled to move away from him.

"Don't worry—you'll be fine after you sleep it off. Go home while you can and stay out of things that don't concern you. I'm the nice one. Tell Kincaid we're coming for him." He squeezed her arm.

She struggled and slapped at the stranger. "Who are you?" He didn't answer, or if he did, she didn't hear it.

Chapter 31

Jaxon called Peyton several times and got no answer. He found her at the pool area. "Peyton, wake up." He shook her gently. She seemed slow to respond. "Are you okay? I called several times, but you didn't answer."

Still groggy, she struggled to sit up. She shook her head. "I remember drinking my tea thinking it tasted funny. I thought something was wrong with the lemon. It's all a bit muddled after that." She explained what she had seen through her mental haze. "He told me to go home. It was a threat, and he said he was coming after you." She frowned in concentration. "I wish I could tell you how he looked. He was a blurry blob with bad breath, and I had a distorted brain. I tried to fight him, but I felt like I couldn't move."

"Let's get you up and moving." He helped her up, reaching for the glass of tea. "I need to have this tested. It sounds to me like GHB, also known as the date rape drug. It acts as a depressant on your central nervous system. GHB causes drowsiness, acting like a sedative in your body. Believe me we've seen this used too often." He held onto her. "How are you?" He walked her back to her room. "I think you should wait until tomorrow to go see Barbara."

"You're probably right."

"Are you sure you're okay?" They stood outside

her room. He opened the door when she slid the keycard in. He gave her a gentle nudge through the doorway.

She whirled around to face him. "No, I'm not okay. I'm mad. I want to know how he slipped that into my tea. The glass was beside me the entire time. Did one of the wait staff slip it in or did he when they weren't watching?" Her hands on her hips and with an indignant look on her face she looked him in the eyes. "I want answers."

"Yes, ma'am." He saluted her. "That's what we detectives do. We detect." He grinned. "Why don't we order room service when I get back, and we'll talk some more. You're still a bit loopy, and I want to talk to folks before they change shifts." He pointed to the glass of tea he carried in his hand. "I'm going to run this by a friend to have it checked, just to make sure."

"You can have it." She waved her hand. "Good riddance."

"I want to question the staff to see if anyone saw anything. I'll be back in a few. Don't open the door to anybody but me. I don't care if they show you a badge. Hear me?"

"Sounds good. I know I have something important I wanted to talk to you about, but right now I can't think of what it is." She plopped down in the chair. "I don't know if you noticed I'm not my usual self." She giggled.

"I've noticed. You think about what you want to tell me, and I'll go do my job. I want to get this guy before he hurts you." He started toward the door.

She jumped up, tripping over her feet. He turned in time to catch her before she hit the ground. "I'm not steady yet, am I?"

"Hardly." He smiled at the goofy look on her face, messy hair sticking out in a strange fashion, and her sunglasses angled precariously on her head, but she was still a knockout. He was hopeless. He needed to get out of there before he kissed her.

"I don't understand why I don't seem to be working right." She started to close the door.

"It will get better soon." He ruffled her hair, brushing it away from her mouth. "Be sure you lock this after me. I'll call you when I get back." The door closed and he waited until he heard the deadbolt slide into place.

Damn. They must be getting close. Whoever the man stalking her was, he wasn't afraid to show his face in public and seemed to be getting more aggressive. He had drugged her in daylight with people all around the vicinity. Jaxon questioned the staff who worked the pool area. A couple of young men remember the man as tall and big. Not heavy but muscular with brown hair. One thought it strange the woman never left the pool area all day. Twice he had checked on her. He said she was breathing and seemed to be sleeping peacefully. One of the rules all the staff knew was that they were to see to the guests' wants and needs but not to disturb them. Most of their guests vacationed there to relax and bothering them was at the top of the not-to-do list. Jaxon couldn't fault them for not waking her. He clenched his fist. He called his friend, who came to get the tea. He had a drug spiking test kit. He would know soon if it was GHB.

****

After she changed her clothes, Peyton sat to wait

for him to get back. The fog slowly lifted, but her anger seemed to intensify. Ready to go to battle, she wanted to yell at someone. Anyone. She took a deep breath as she tried to calm herself. Anger never worked out well for her. How did Jessie put up with this? She was over it already and she had only just begun.

Reaching for her phone, she called her grandmother. "Hi, it's me." Peyton held back a sob.

"Is everything okay, dear?"

"That's a loaded question. Are you busy?" Peyton asked.

"I'm helping Jessie close up the store. I did one of the children's story hours today. I had such a fun time with all the kids. Those little ones can keep you hopping. It's good for me. We aren't too busy to talk to you though. The store is closed. I'm putting you on speaker so Jessie and Reba can hear too. Is that okay?"

Peyton had no idea if anything she said made sense. The minute she knew someone was listening she cried, she yelled, and then she cried some more. "Which brings you up to date on what's happening in my life. My tea is being tested for GHB now."

"Goodness, dear. No wonder you sound upset," Sadie said.

"What is troubling you the most, Peyton?" Reba asked. "You're afraid of something."

She told them about the premonition she had about herself. "I don't know what to think. I admit it spooked me, and today didn't help. I still have no idea who the man is. He didn't hurt me—there were too many people around, but if he had tried, there was nothing I could do to defend myself."

"I know the feeling." Jessie told her about the time

she was drugged and thrown in the trunk of a car. "I was scared and alert to what was happening, but my body wasn't working. I'm sorry, cousin. I know how hard it has to be when you're out there alone."

"We'll put our heads together and come up with a plan. You shouldn't be there by yourself. It's too much for anyone." Sadie took a deep breath. "Jessie knows all about plans, don't you, dear?"

"I can't work without one," Jessie said.

"I'm sure I'll be okay, but I needed to tell someone. It's been building up inside me for several days now." Peyton wiped the tears running down her cheeks and reached for another tissue for her nose.

"I can imagine. We'll do our best to think about it. One of us will be coming to be with you until you feel free to come home. All we need to do is figure out who," Sadie told her. "I'll probably be the one coming, dear."

"Grams, I don't want to put you in danger. I'm sorry I fell apart on you. Please don't worry. My emotions got the best of me is all. Detective Kincaid should be back soon and hopefully he'll have some answers for me."

"I'll wait for you to call me then I'll make my travel plans. I'm not sure how much help I'll be, but you won't have to be alone. I think that's important."

"Barbara, the lady I told you about who was shot, is doing better. I'm going to see her tomorrow." Peyton changed the subject. Sadie sounded worried.

"I'm happy to hear that," Jessie said.

"Peyton, this is Reba. I've been listening in, dear. You'll go through a dark time, but you will see the light again. It will all end well. Many people have suffered, and many have even died because of these people. It may take years for all the truth to be fully realized. You are the reason their crimes have come into the spotlight."

"Thank you, Reba. I'll try to remember that it will turn out okay. Boy, am I glad I called you guys. I needed to hear your voices. Detective Kincaid will be happy too. I would be yelling at him if I hadn't talked to you."

"We'll wait to hear from you," Sadie told her again.

"Goodbye, love you all." Peyton disconnected the call.

Chapter 32

Finally, Jaxon called to say he was on his way to the room. Her stomach grumbled, reminding her she hadn't eaten for a while. Food sounded good, and she felt happy he was on his way, a good sign. Purely for the investigation, of course. She smiled as she ran the brush through her hair. She wasn't fooling anybody, much less herself. Peyton found Jaxon unnerving—he seemed able to look right through her. At the same time, his sense of humor and good looks drew him to her. What could she say? Her dad had ruined her for a serious relationship with any man, and this might be as close as she ever got. Unless, of course, all the therapy she was going through worked. Lots of things had already changed.

—*You can open the door*— his text said. It was followed by a knock which sent her to check out the peephole.

"Peyton, I know you're looking at me. Open the door." He grinned at her. "Please."

"Nice to see you too, Detective Kincaid." She motioned him in. "I'm starving," she said, her hands planted on her hips with her foot tapping the ground.

"I could use some food too. Let's order and then we'll talk. At least you seem more coherent now. I might be able to take you out without people thinking you've had too much to drink."

"Not nice, Kincaid." She tossed the room service menu at him. "Make your choice. I've already made mine."

"Jaxon," he reminded her.

She flashed him a smile. "Whatever." She gestured with her hand.

With their dinner choices decided and ordered, they sat in the comfortable chairs provided in the room to talk and wait. "What did you find out?" she asked.

"Your tea had GHB in it," he told her bluntly. "There doesn't seem to be a nice way to tell you."

"I'd rather have the truth out in the open. My cousin likes to know the facts because she wants to plan. Me, on the other hand, I want details. I need to know what I'm dealing with. I feel more in control and less afraid. When I heard my parents yelling but I couldn't see what was happening—it was scary. I would sneak out of the room to watch them. I would grab anything I could find to use as a weapon that I thought would make me safe. It made me feel stronger and more in control that way. Of course, my dad could have snapped it in two if he had ever caught me. Today, the drug was one of those scary out of control moments for me." She pursed her lips and sat forward in the chair. "With his face in front of me, his distorted voice, I was in the closet all over again."

"I'm sorry this happened. I should have had protection for you." He raked his hand through his hair. "You shouldn't have to deal with this."

"I won't be taken by surprise again. Twice is two times too many. I'm angry, I have a weapon of my own, and I'm not afraid to use it."

"What kind of weapon are we talking about?"

"I'm a master in self-defense. I've spent years perfecting the techniques. I teach advanced classes for New York PD and at the community center near where I live. I'm sure I could stop my father or any other man if I needed to now. That's why I'm bothered I let this guy intimidate me twice. Next time I see him, he'll rue the day if he approaches me for any reason."

"That's not what I expected you to say." Jaxon went to answer the door. He let the man bring the cart in with their dinner on it. "Let's eat. This steak is calling my name." He settled himself back in his chair, cut off a piece, and began to eat.

Peyton lifted her glass, hesitating before she drank. "How do I know if this drink made it here without someone tampering with it?"

"Do you want me to test it? My friend gave me some test strips. I figured you might want to have them for assurance. I know your experience was a scary one."

She handed him the glass. He followed the instructions his friend had given him. "You're good to drink it." He explained how the strip would look like if it had tested positive. "For now, you might want to buy everything bottled and get your coffee at a coffeeshop away from here. Although, I don't believe any of the staff here are involved. I talked to two who remember seeing the man around the counter. He told the waiter he'd deliver it but was told it was against resort policy."

"Were they able to describe him?" she asked as she tentatively sipped the tea. No unusual taste made her feel a bit better.

"They described him as a tall, big man with dark hair. Not heavy, but muscular."

"Yes, that's right. He reminded me of a body builder. His arms and chest seemed to be muscle and not fat. I'm not sure if he's the same man that blocked my way in the hall. He seemed familiar to me when he placed his face inches from mine. Blurry, but I kind of recognized him. His voice too."

"I won't be able to take you to see Barbara until later tomorrow. I'm working with the FBI searching a company's property tomorrow." Jaxon explained what else the techs had found on E J's computer. "This is big. And it will take some time to understand the full magnitude of the crimes committed by this company. It's safe to say this is one of the reasons why E J was murdered. Something he did or said didn't set well with the organization."

"Wow, he walked into a mess, didn't he?" Peyton straightened the napkin on her lap.

"The short answer is yes. I'm not telling you all the facts or what was in those files. It's hush-hush for now, and it's better you don't know. They've murdered two people that we know of, and they will add to that number if they think we are getting close."

"I'd rather not know. I don't need any more trouble." She ate a bite of her salad. "What's next?"

"Tomorrow should be a surprise." He stroked his chin. "With the arrests of several prominent citizens there's liable to be a few shock waves felt. The FBI had been watching this company already after a whistleblower complaint. And E J gave us the ammunition we need to take them down. I don't want you to go anywhere tomorrow. It would be great if you remained in your room until I pick you up. I have no idea how this will go."

"I'll stay here. You've given me a lot to think about. I'm working on a theory about this case and how it's connected to the vision in Tombstone. I've been doing some research. I'll talk to you about it when I see you tomorrow. Thank you for spending time with me. I admit today shook me a bit."

"More than being shot at?" Jaxon asked.

"In some ways, yes. To see someone who could possibly hurt you but have no ability to move or do anything was terrifying. I don't ever want to feel anything like that again."

He stood, his fist clenched at his side. "I need to be going."

"Okay." She followed him to the door.

He paused before he opened the door. "You and I have some unfinished business. We are in the middle of a case right now. That won't be forever." He traced her cheek with his finger. "The thing is, Peyton, I didn't want to get involved with anyone when I first met you." He placed his finger over her lips when she started to speak. "All that has changed. I've made a few decisions that involve you. You're on my radar now, and I find I like having you there. I'm going to spend whatever time we have left together to convince you that I'm a man you can trust." He opened the door and closed it behind him.

She turned the deadbolt. Peyton had no idea what she would do about Jaxon. He interested her, but no way would she live in Arizona. It was too far away from Madi. If she got out of the state alive, she would be grateful.

Chapter 33

The early morning raids took place simultaneously at WorldStar Drug's headquarters and several homes across the city. The element of surprise aided the operation. Obviously, the informant at the station hadn't gotten wind of the operation and no suspects were tipped off. They were all on their way to jail, phoning their fancy lawyers as the search was going on at their company.

Jaxon liked working with the agents. The search warrant was presented at the front desk reception area, and the agents began to seize records, computers, and any evidence they could find. Jaxon and Agent Miller questioned employees. They took down their personal information as they tried to ferret out how much they knew about the company's practices. Most of the lower-level employees had no idea anything was going on and were taken by surprise. They were let go and told appointments would be scheduled for each of them to appear for an interview. Several people in senior management knew more about the operations. They were under investigation, along with the owners and CEO of the company. They would face the allegations and lawsuits that would be made against the company. Figuring out who was complicit would be crucial. The number would rise as the extent of the criminal activity unfolded. Prison time appeared to be in many of their futures, including several researchers who worked in the lab. What a sad waste. Who would do what WorldStar Drug Corporation had done to people at a vulnerable time in life? The press was already lining up to take pictures.

"These guys make me sick. Wearing their high-priced suits and Italian leather shoes, they systematically executed people. Others did the dirty work while they sat in their fancy offices and played God." Miller frowned at one of the men being led out of the office in handcuffs. "The decisions they made lined their pockets while sending others to their death. Guilty of murder not up close and personal, but they murdered people nonetheless. How many died because of the decisions made here we may never know." Agent Miller leaned his hip against the desk where one of their tech people was packing up a computer. Another cleaned out the folders from the filing cabinet, boxing them up as she did.

"I imagine the lawsuits this company will face will be massive when news of this gets out." Jaxon placed several files in the box with others.

"All the company's accounts have been seized, as well as any connecting property in a few other states. Eventually, the lawsuits and courts will determine how much money will go to the victims and their families. Let's put it this way—these folks won't be spending one more nickel on their lavish lifestyle," Miller stated.

"To that I say, amen. Putting them out of business sounds like a gift to the world. The problem is a lot of people will be hard pressed to trust anyone with their health again. It's a damn mess." Jaxon leaned against the wall and folded his arms across his chest. "You wonder if at any time they felt guilty about what they were doing."

"If they did, it didn't last long. I wonder what their defense will be. Hopefully one of them will sing and turn on the others." Agent Miller walked over to where the tech was working. "Take everything from this area. When they make bail—and they will—there'll be nothing here to destroy or change."

"What are the odds of putting the top guys away?" Jaxon asked. "It seems to me the legal system differentiates between white-collar criminals and the rest of society. I want these guys to get time."

"Let's just say they'll try to blame it on someone in the lab and walk after a few years. If I have a say in it, I want an ironclad case that will put them behind bars for years to come," O'Donnell said as he grabbed an empty box and filled it with more files.

Jaxon couldn't believe the evidence they carted out of the offices and labs. At the end of the day, the building was padlocked and would remain that way for a while. He had always trusted the doctors and the pharmaceutical companies. The government agencies and the laws that ruled the industry had never given him any cause for concern. Like anything, people could find a way around the law to the detriment of others. What other areas should he be concerned about? Criminals had infiltrated every area, it seemed. He had liked working with the agents. He was happy now that one of the applications he had sent out involved a position at the FBI near home. He thought he might like the change of pace.

Jaxon called to let Peyton know he would pick her up at six. The clock assured him there was enough time run by his place, change, and get to the resort. The drive home in rush hour traffic gave him time to think. As of today, the case had taken on national implications. Bigger than either one of them could've imagined the day Dawson's body was lifted out of the pool. Peyton steered him toward the size and scope with her premonitions, which were instrumental in getting them to this point. Their accuracy troubled him, especially after the incident yesterday and the foreboding she felt about her own life. He couldn't take her intuition lightly. She hadn't been wrong, up to this point, and her fear concerned him. Hearing her voice earlier calmed the tension that had been building all day.

****

Peyton spent the day in her room reading. Being idle wasn't easy for her. Activity made up a big part of her routine. Thankfully, she found an exercise channel and did a workout to break up the monotony of the day. She wondered what Jaxon found out in the raid. She listened to the news throughout the day. Riveted to the TV when the news broke, she saw the agents carrying out boxes of evidence. Hoping for a glance of Jaxon at work, she kept the news channel on most of the day. Finally, her patience paid off. She caught a fleeting glimpse of him standing near a desk by the agent that was speaking to a member of the press. Kincaid took her breath away. With that said, she still wasn't going to do anything about it. Maybe if it were another time or place, it would be different.

Somehow the story unfolding on the quick news flashes was linked in a strange way to all the ghosts she had seen. Heaven only knew how, but hopefully soon she would too. With each piece of the story that emerged, she found herself wondering what was happening to the world. Was it always like this, and she had never noticed it before? Most people were kind and cared about others, or was that part of an illusion too? When did being kind go out of style? Or had it ever been in? No, she still believed most people were decent. Every day good people lined up to save lives and give because they cared. She needed to remember that no matter what.

Changing her clothes into something more appropriate to wear to the hospital took her mind in a safer direction. Yoga pants were out—she threw them across the bed. She reached for the hanger with her white slacks and teal blouse on it. Boredom had made her too philosophical for her own good today. She didn't want Kincaid to have to worry about her.

One thing growing up with abusive parents taught her was that she didn't want to treat anyone else the way she had been treated. People could change, and she had great hope her parents would because they were getting help. She wanted to love them and see them again. Did that mean she could also learn to trust people again? Her therapist said she could. "Enough with the thinking. Go read your book, young lady."

Picking up her book, she began to read where she had left off. Hopefully Jaxon would be here soon, or she would leave this room.

****

Glued to the TV all day, he watched and listened until he felt physically ill. He knew this day would come. His time was running out. Forgotten were his plans to take his wife and kids and leave quietly before it all hit the fan. Damn, his family would be devastated.

Seeing the shock written on the faces of his friends and watching them be hauled off to jail in handcuffs made his decision easy. No way would he be taken alive. He couldn't be on that side of the law—he'd rather die first. He pulled out the dreaded note to his wife and family, reading it over several times. It didn't sound any better than when he had first written it. What a mess. With the letter folded, he placed the paper in a stamped and addressed envelope and stuck it in the mailbox. With that task finished, he made plans for how he would exit on his terms.

Chapter 34

Jaxon knocked on the door to her room and she greeted him with a smile. "Not a moment too soon. I was considering climbing the wall. I'm not used to being idle all day. You can only read and watch so much TV."

"You didn't leave the room I take it." He closed the door behind her, checking the lock. "Thanks."

"I stayed in like you asked me to. It might have been a different story if you had told me to stay inside and not go out."

"You would have left. Is that what you're telling me?" He chuckled.

"I probably would have found a way to show my rebellious side. I learned fast when I was young that I could make my stand in secret. I didn't have to bend from being who I am. My dad would yell at me to sit down and stop my wiggling. I did, but I was standing in my heart. Now, I'm free to go ahead and stand no matter who tells me to sit. However, when the word please is used, I'll take the request under advisement. As my Grams used to tell us, please is the magic word that makes many things possible."

"I'll make a note of that. No orders without the word please." He grinned.

"Smart of you." She fluttered her lashes at him. "You'd be surprised how far a simple please goes to win me over."

"Duly noted. Seems reasonable enough even for me."

They walked into the hospital side by side after they arrived. He carried his laptop in one hand while his other brushed hers as they walked. "Mrs. Newsome is on the fourth floor in room 412. I'm going to stay here in the lobby and catch up on reports. That way you'll be able to have a private chat with her. She's been asking to see you, her husband said." He squeezed her hand. "You don't need to hurry. Enjoy your visit."

"I will." Peyton walked to the elevator and turned to smile at him. She made a detour to the gift shop for flowers and a card.

****

Peyton rode the elevator up to fourth floor. The door to Barbara's room stood open. She paused before entering. Barbara looked good considering what she had been through. The smile that lit up Barbara's face when she saw Peyton made her brush aside the moisture building in her eyes.

"Come in, please come in. I was hoping you would come tonight. I want my husband to meet you. He stepped out of the room to get some coffee."

Peyton sat in the chair beside the bed. "You look good, Barbara." She patted the woman's hand.

"I'm getting stronger every day." She stared out the window, a faraway look in her eyes. Rubbing her arms, she shuddered. "Better than that day. Ugh." She sighed. "I was afraid I was going to die. But you stayed by my side, and I'll never forget it. I'm in your debt. Holding that shirt against my wound, applying constant pressure. You didn't think about your own safety. The doctor told me your quick actions helped to save my life. You kept me focused and hopeful that I would survive. My husband told me it was touch and go for a couple of days. But thankfully, I'm here."

"I wish I could have done more." Jessie patted her hand.

Barbara's eyes teared up. "I got great news from my daughter yesterday. I'm going to be a grandmother. I'm grateful to be alive. I can hardly wait to see my new grandbaby." Barbara reached for a tissue. "Sorry. I'm so emotional. I cry at everything."

"I'm sure it's normal after a traumatic experience." Peyton moved the box of tissues closer to her.

"It could have ended differently." The tears ran down her cheeks. "I thought for sure I was a goner but owe a lot of thanks to all those who saved my life. They're my new heroes."

"I can see why. And a grandbaby is wonderful news. Congratulations to all of you, Barbara." Peyton stood when Glenn Newsome walked in the room.

"Glenn," his wife called to him. "This is Peyton Reynolds, the woman who helped me."

"Ahh, I finally meet the red-haired angel who helped my wife." He smiled at her and extended his hand. "Your hair isn't as red as she said, but we'll let that be our secret."

"It looks redder in the sunlight, and it was quite sunny that day," she whispered to him.

"Barbara has talked non-stop about your kindness. I want to thank you for caring. Not many people would have with bullets flying around." He gave her hand a gentle squeeze.

"I'm glad I could do something. Truthfully, I was

scared. But I know a few basic life saving techniques and wanted to help. She looks much better than that day." Peyton glanced at Barbara who was struggling to stay awake.

"My wife's prognosis is good. She is making steady progress, and the doctors expect her to make a full recovery. The surgeon told her today she would be able to go home in a couple days as long as there was no sign of infection," Glen told her. "The bullet was designed to break on impact, the more pieces the greater the damage inside her. They had to repair quite a bit. It's amazing what they can do."

"It sure is." Peyton stood beside Barbara's bed. "I'm going to let you get some rest. I'm happy you'll be around to see your first grandchild and many more birthdays. Please let me know when you get home. My number is on the card." She pointed to the card next to the flowers on the cart next to the bed. "I want a picture of you with your first grandbaby."

Peyton left when the nurse came in to check her vitals. It was the perfect time to leave. Barbara needed to rest.

When the elevator doors opened, she found Jaxon where she had left him. Engrossed in something on his computer, he wasn't aware she was there. "Hi, you." She touched his shoulder.

"Sorry, I didn't see you. I lost track of time." He closed his laptop, putting it back in the case. "How was your visit?"

"Perfect." She smiled a knowing smile.

"Would you care to enumerate for me?" Jaxon remained sitting.

"First of all, her prognosis is good, and she may get

to go home soon. Next, she is grateful to be alive and be able to see her first grandchild. I can concur with her that's a wonderful thing. I got to meet her husband and they both thanked me several times. My only regret is that she had to suffer any of this to begin with. If I hadn't been in Tombstone, the shooter wouldn't have been there either. Still the visit was awesome, and I left a drowsy Barbara, who should be sleeping as we speak." She sat in the chair beside him. "I'm glad she will be around for many more special events."

"I've been thinking about Tombstone and its connection to this case. Do you remember what you were telling me about your visions of the area?"

"You mean about all the people who were killed unjustly? Or about the ghosts who haunted the town?"

He shook his head. "The part about seeing Carlee Blair at the sign pointing to the Mexican border."

"I remember. Why?" she asked, leaning closer to him.

"Each picture you have seen and told me about is a part of a puzzle that is only beginning to come together. I hope to give you a total picture of how it all connects soon." He stood and reached for her hand. Gently he pulled her to her feet. "We should go."

"I would love to see how it all connects," she told him the minute he got in the car and closed the door. "I understand why I saw Carlee. Her family will be able to say their goodbyes. For many of the ghosts walking around Tombstone that wasn't true. They were simply forgotten in time." She latched her seat belt. "How many people has that been true for? One dictator kills millions, he dies, to be followed by another in a different place and time. It could be depressing if you let it." She frowned. "Now you can understand why I'm an activist where I can be. You have to try to do good when you can."

"I agree. Take it one day at time—that's the best we can do. Embrace the great moments when you get them. Pay it forward whenever you can." He started the car. "I'd love for you to meet my family. You'd fit right in. All of my siblings are passionate about something."

"What are you passionate about, Kincaid?" She smiled at his frown.

"Jaxon." He exhaled. "Me, I'm passionate about the law and putting those who hurt others behind bars for a long time."

"I'm glad you are. Carlee's and E J's families will have closure because of it." She turned her head and glanced out the window.

Peyton did a great deal of laughing over the next several minutes when Jaxon changed the subject to his siblings and their antics growing up. She told him about some of Destiny's and her escapades as well. His family sounded wonderful, making her sigh quietly within. It left a strange feeling of emptiness inside her long after he had walked her to her room and left. Family was something she longed for. She wanted to belong to a real family, to care and have someone care for her. Was it a pipe dream or could she find it for herself?

Getting into bed, she stacked the pillows behind her back. Tired, but wide awake with a mind that refused to shut down, she sorted through the events of the past twelve hours. Peyton recalled Jaxon's parting remarks after he walked her to the room. With a serious warning to keep her eyes open, he reminded her that their shooter had probably heard the news along with everyone else. It was only a matter of time before the police tracked him down. Feeling trapped would make him more unpredictable and dangerous. Jaxon wanted her to be aware of those around her. She didn't have to stay in her room, but she couldn't let down her guard either.

She smiled into the dark room. The biggest surprise of the night was that in a quick one-eighty he changed the subject and asked her on a date. Talk about being taken off guard! She muttered a quick yes and went in the room, closing the door in his face. She didn't know what she was more afraid of—the unknown assailant or a man she was coming to care for. Both had the power to hurt her, and she had promised herself never to let another man have power over her. It would be a long night of recriminations. She palmed her forehead. What possessed her to say yes?

Chapter 35

Peyton awakened early and left the resort. Checking her review mirror several times to make sure no one followed her, she relaxed when the traffic around her seemed normal. After a workout at the local rec center, she went to a coffeeshop and then on to a boutique. Shopping for a new dress would take her mind off the situation she found herself in. The concierge told her about a small store that was among their guests' favorite places to shop. Hers as well. Peyton loved the look and the style of the place the minute she walked in the door. The prices weren't bad, but she was used to New York. Almost anything was cheaper than shopping in Manhattan. After trying on several outfits that the sales associate helped her put together, she settled on the one which gave her the wow factor.

"Impeccable," the young woman told her when she walked out of the dressing room. "It suits you perfectly."

"I like it." Peyton turned to see a sideview in front of the mirror. "The color is fantastic with my complexion. I'll take this one with the accessories and shoes you suggested. You really have an eye for what looks good together."

"I love fashion. You could say this is my dream job. I'm taking a fashion design class in college." She held a necklace against the dress. "This looks great against the color of the dress, don't you think?"

Peyton nodded. "You're so good. You may as well add the necklace to my ticket too. It's nice to love what you do." She handed her credit card to the woman. After paying, she took the bag and walked out of the store. She was excited—the dress really did look great on her. The blast of hot air hit her, taking her breath for a moment. "Whew, it's going to be another hot one." She put on her sunglasses as the bright sun was blinding.

She might be nervous about going on a date with Jaxon, but she planned on looking her best. On the top of her to-do list was enjoying every minute of their time together. She had earned it and probably wouldn't see him again once she left town. No one else would ever need to know. Except for Jessie, of course—she always seemed to know everything.

She made it in the car and was turning on the AC when her phone rang. "Hey, cousin, I was just thinking about you. What's up?"

"I wanted to make sure you're okay. Reba has been calling me every few hours to check on you. I finally told her I would call. We heard about the FBI raid on the news. There's another branch of the company outside of Boston too. Matt is trying to get the skinny on it because they aren't saying much on TV. Reba is sure it's somehow connected to the case you're involved with. Is it?" Jessie asked.

"Yes, to both of your questions. I'm fine, and they're related, but I'm not sure how yet." Peyton studied the person in the car that pulled in beside her. Thankfully it was an older woman. "Detective Kincaid promised to tell me more as soon as he can. The investigation is ongoing."

"How is the good detective anyway?" Jessie laughed.

"He's fine and at least we can talk now without arguing, which is progress." Peyton smiled when she said it.

"I'm sorry to say we are more alike than we let on. We are lucky if we can even look at a man without turning around and running. Ask Matt—he'll tell you. He turned on the charm and I started running as fast as I could. Oh, I was interested all right, but I didn't want another man to have any say over my life. I've made him promise some strange things." Jessie chuckled. "He's been amazing, waiting for me to come to terms with him in my life."

"I hear you. I've spent years running. I'm not sure I would even know how to stop."

"Matt is wonderful, but sometimes his need to protect me is so great he can't help himself. That's when I remind him, not too gently I might add, that I don't need him to tell me what to do. I've been taking care of myself for a while without his help. Of course, he also tells me when it comes to a case the niceties don't apply. It's a game we play all the time." Jessie gave a dramatic sigh. "I let him think he is winning, but I always get the last word."

Peyton laughed. "I'll remember that in the future. Sounds like good advice to me."

"Before we hang up, I need to tell you from Reba to be careful. She's worried about the premonition you had. If it is still with you, listen to what you're sensing."

"I am, and I will. But will it do me any good? I mean if it's true, will the premonition happen no matter what I do?" Peyton mused.

"Reba said that it will most likely happen as you sense it, but in the end you'll be okay. She wants you to remember those words above everything else. I'm the bearer of mixed news I'm afraid."

"I'll try. This supernatural junk is new to me. I'm stumbling along as I go." Peyton took a quick look around the parking lot.

"I still do. We'll muddle our way through it together. Stay in touch, cousin."

"I will." Peyton disconnected the call. Unsettled, she started the car and drove back to the resort, making a stop at a deli to buy a salad along the way.

****

Jaxon spent the morning poring over personnel files and searching the internet. He found what he was looking for. Shocked by what he discovered regarding a veteran cop no longer with the department, his next stop was Captain Stolberg's office. "Sir, do you have a minute?"

"Kincaid, you're just the man I was looking for. What's up?"

"I need your opinion about what I found." Jaxon showed him the file and what he had found on the suspect's media sites.

"You need to bring him in for questioning. Take a team and pick him up. If he's not already in hiding after yesterday."

"My sentiment exactly. At the very least, it will alert his wife that something is up if she doesn't already know." Jaxon pulled a team together and left for the suspect's last known address.

Jaxon wasn't surprised when his wife told him her husband was out of town for the week.

"Is there a problem, officer?" she asked.

"We think he has knowledge of a company we're investigating and wanted to question him is all." Jaxon handed her his card. "Please see that he gets this when he comes home and have him contact us."

"I will." She closed the door.

The scenario didn't sit well with Jaxon. His gut told him the man was in town hiding and that he wouldn't go down without a fight. His back was against the wall. From the description of the man who accosted Peyton, this was the same guy. Which meant he had been hanging out at the resort and observing her. Why? Unless he was there when she tried to save E J. Somehow, the suspect had connected Peyton to him. It was starting to make sense.

Peyton wouldn't appreciate Jaxon acting like her protector, but he had to come up with a good idea of how to do so without her knowing it. At least tonight, she'd be with him and half the police department at Dan's engagement party.

When he asked her out, her response still made him smile. If he had a fragile ego, he would have given up. She muttered a scarcely audible yes and promptly slammed the door in his face. At least she didn't say no. It was a start. Given time, he could bring her around.

Chapter 36

Peyton glanced in the mirror. Jaxon would be there in a few minutes. For the first time in a long time she liked what she saw. Perfect. She smiled. It had to be the dress. She ran her hands over the soft material that followed the curves of her body. Sadie used to tell her when you least expect it everything comes together just right. Your hair does what it's supposed to, the dress you put on suits you perfectly, and lo and behold your skin glows with your happiness—it makes for magic. Maybe it was her time to live in her own fairytale instead of reading about others'.

For one awful moment a sense of foreboding tried to crowd its way into her mind, but she shook it off. *Not tonight. This is my time and I'm going to live in this moment.* The knock at the door rescued her from any more bad thoughts. The expression on Jaxon's face sealed the deal.

"Hey, Kincaid. How was your day?" She smiled at him coyly.

"Jaxon," he said, grinning at her. "No complaints about the day." He reached around her to close the door. "Are you ready, or do you need anything else?"

"I'm ready." She clutched her purse in her hand.

He pulled the door shut, lacing his fingers through hers. "I hope you like dancing."

"Why is that?" she asked.

"Because once the guys get a load of you in that dress, there'll be no rest for you."

"I like to dance, and I don't want to sit at a party for heaven's sake. It's all good." She squeezed his hand.

"Who are you and what have you done with Peyton Reynolds?" He glanced at her.

"Let's just say she's gone for the evening, and I'm taking her place for a few hours. She'll be back tomorrow. But tonight, I plan on having a blast. There will never be another evening quite like this one." The minute the words came out of her mouth the dark cloud forced its way to the surface of her mind. She shook her head, refusing to allow it, but Peyton knew it was only a matter of time before she would face the great unknown threat.

****

Jaxon watched her go from animated to staid in a matter of moments. "Are you okay?" he asked before he started the car.

"Yes. I was thinking is all." She fastened the seat belt. Her hands fiddled with the purse on her lap.

"About what?" He glanced at her, placing his hand on hers.

"A conversation I had with my cousin earlier. It's not important." She quickly changed the subject. "Where are we going?"

She wasn't being truthful with him. He let her have her way for now. "We're headed to a local club. My friend is celebrating his engagement party and has the place for the night. It should be a great time. Like I said, the guys won't be able to leave you alone. Promise me you'll save a couple of dances for the man who brought you." He saw her smile, and the dimples that attracted him to her the moment he first saw her tugged once again at his heart Yep, he was in big trouble. She wouldn't be easy to forget.

"I've been thinking about what we talked about last night. Do you think the border crossing might play into this somehow? The first time the word cowboy was used in Tombstone was not in a nice way. They were stealing cattle and bringing them across the border to unload. For considerable profit, of course."

"The answer to your questions is a resounding yes. The border crossing has something to do with this case. We'll see over the next few days how it plays out. What your premonitions have done is point us in the right direction. And remind us that men have always been greedy." He checked his rearview mirror. He wanted to make sure they weren't being followed.

"True. It seems every crime, unless it's a crime of passion, involves money and greed. Throw in power and you have a trifecta. I'm frustrated that I haven't been able to put all the pieces together to get a clearer picture. Having never done this before, I'm not sure how to go about it." She glanced at him.

"And I've never worked with anyone with your ability before. I would say we've muddled through all right so far. The next couple of days should be quite interesting. You should be on your way home before too long. Did you ever hear from your friend?"

"Yes, she won't be coming before I leave. At least her mom is improving, which is good news." Peyton reached into her purse and pulled out her lip gloss. She applied it to her lips. "Grams doesn't want me here alone, and she is making arrangements to come. I don't want her to. It would be too stressful for her. I told her I would let her know if I needed her." Peyton paused. "I figure if I wait long enough she won't need to come. I don't want to put her in jeopardy."

"I'm glad your friend's mom is better. When it comes to Sadie though, you can tell her not to come. But I doubt it'll keep her from coming if she thinks she should be here." He pulled into the club parking lot. "She's got a mind of her own."

"True. She's a bit feisty."

"Not unlike someone else I know." Grinning at her, he unlatched his seat belt. "Remember you owe me a couple of dances. I'll cut in if I have to." He got out and went around to open her door.

"You sure know how to flatter a girl." She smiled at him.

He could see how the night would play out the minute he walked in the door with her by his side. Amos strutted over and asked her to dance before she could even place her purse on the table where their name cards were. Damn, he wanted to tell him to get lost, but he had no claim on her. Knowing Amos, he was doing it on purpose to get a rise out him. "Remember what I told you." He watched the gentle sway of her hips as she moved away. It seemed he would be seeing the same sight several times before the night was over.

****

Peyton enjoyed all the attention. She couldn't remember ever feeling like this before. For years, the only words she remembered were the condemning words that she wouldn't amount to anything. Spoken by both parents repeatedly until she believed them and set about to prove them wrong. To hear someone tell her she was attractive and mean it felt heady. Refreshing. She would face reality tomorrow. Today she would drink it in and pretend it was all real.

Jaxon, true to his word, had cut in twice already. This time she decided to ask him. He was standing with a group of the young officers when she touched his shoulder. She leaned close and said, "I believe this dance is yours."

"I believe you're right." He turned, taking her hand, and he led her onto the dance floor. The music began to play a slow song perfect for the couple who had requested it. Peyton smiled as he took her in his arms and said, "Someone up there must think I've been a good boy. I was hoping for a slow one."

"Oh yeah, why is that?" She glanced up at his face.

"What healthy American male doesn't want to hold a beautiful woman in his arms for an entire song without getting himself in trouble?" He gave her a lopsided grin. "Here you are in my arms, and you haven't hit me yet."

"The song is not over. There's still time." Peyton laughed. "I do know how to behave in public though."

"Good to know. With that in mind, I'm free to tell you that you're the most beautiful woman in the room, and I'm glad you're with me." He pulled her tighter.

"I'm glad I am too." Peyton had no idea what song was playing, but for the first time in a long time she didn't care about the details. She simply enjoyed the moment.

When the song finished playing, he held onto her hand. Weaving through the crowd he led her to the buffet table. "Let's get something to eat. They can't take you away from me if we are eating."

"Sounds good," she whispered.

In some ways, the night passed by too quickly for her. She savored every dance, all the compliments, and the atmosphere. She would describe the night as life changing for her. Which made no sense whatsoever. It wasn't that big a deal, but at this moment it was everything. Sadness filled her when the evening started to wind down. For some strange reason her emotions were on the edge and her senses were heightened. Amos brought her back to Jaxon for the last dance. The dance was magical. Okay, maybe she inflated it a bit in her thinking, but it felt more than all right to her.

When they left the club, they stood out front with several of Jaxon's friends and their dates. She moved away for a moment and that was all it took. She heard a strange popping sound like a firework. She glanced skyward but winced when something hit her leg. When she reached down to swat what she thought was a bug, her hand came up sticky and red with blood. The popping sound came again. "Kincaid, help," she moaned when an awful sting tore through her side, sending her crashing to the ground. Jaxon sounded garbled and the noise around her deafening. The pain took her breath away.

"Hold on, sweetheart." Jaxon's face seemed to be floating.

"Hold on to what?" Her voice sounded strange to her.

The whir of sirens, people yelling back and forth, more popping sounds filled her head until it all went silent.

Chapter 37

He refused to let go of her hand. In his mind, letting go might mean she would be lost to him forever. Powerful emotions shook him. He didn't have time to analyze them or the moisture filling his eyes. He swiped at the tears streaming down his cheeks. He never cried. But kneeling by her prone figure all his feelings rose through his body and spilled out his eyes. He gulped for air and was grateful for the strong hands of his friend that squeezed his shoulders to steady him.

"Let them do their work, Kincaid, you'll need to move." Captain Stolberg's words penetrated his thoughts.

Jaxon let go of her, placing her hand softly to the ground before he stood. "I should have known. How could I have missed the possibility he'd show up here?" Jaxon watched the paramedic insert a drip line. He turned his head and grimaced.

"None of us saw this coming. No recriminations— we have work to do. You can follow the ambulance when it leaves. You'll have people to contact." Stolberg patted him on the back. "The guys went after the shooter. I've heard more gunfire."

"Were there other any other injuries?" Jaxon sensed his training beginning to take over.

"A couple of minor ones, and I'm waiting on the status update about our suspect. Amos called in a 10-

33, and backup is standing by."

"Our suspect is down. A 10-52 is requested." A voice called over the radio. "Another one is running. I repeat one down, but we had two, and he's on the run."

Another ambulance came into the parking lot. Directions were given to where the suspect was on the ground. Jaxon made his way to the area where a group of his team stood. "Will he make it?"

"He's in a bad way? He refused to throw down his weapon but continued to fire on us. I think he had a death wish. It looked like a suicide by cop." They talked among themselves and agreed.

"Damn, this is a mess. I can't believe he came after her. What did she do to him? He didn't even know her." Officer Dunnigan shrugged his shoulders.

"Not a damn thing." Jaxon's fist clenched at his side. He called Frank to have him come by the site. Explaining what happened to Peyton, he wanted to see if they could track on the other shooter's fresh scent.

"Is she going to be okay?" one of the officers who had danced with Peyton asked.

"I hope she will be. I can't believe I didn't consider this scenario," he muttered. "Although I think she might have." Jaxon started to walk away. "Thanks, guys. You know what needs to be done. I'm headed to the hospital as soon as the ambulance leaves. I'll call in her status once I know it."

That is what she wasn't telling him tonight. He should have questioned her more thoroughly. She had seemed happy, and he hadn't wanted to spoil the mood. Hell, it was spoiled now. He would have to call her family. The worst part of his job.

With the stretcher loaded in the back, the

ambulance pulled out of the parking lot. "She's stable enough to transport. Call me when you know her condition," Stolberg told Jaxon. "I'll be at the hospital as soon as things are under control here. Harris is following the suspect's ambulance and will update us on his condition."

"Frank is bringing Radar to see if he can track the second shooter. I can stay if you want. Peyton saw three or possibly four men attack Carlee. Maybe he's one of them."

"Get out of here—we'll take care of this end." Stolberg pointed at Amos. "You drive. Kincaid, do your job."

Jaxon handed Amos the keys. "I will." Amos followed the route the ambulance had taken a few minutes earlier.

They walked in the hospital through the emergency entrance. The attendant at the desk told them she was on her way to the second floor and headed into surgery. The man called ahead to let the nurse's station on the second floor know that the detectives were on their way up and would need any updates on the patient's progress when they became available.

Taking the elevator, they made their way to the second-floor Surgical Ward. After checking at the nurse's station, Jaxon headed to the waiting area.

"The nurse told me she would bring us updates when they were available, but that she would probably be in surgery for a while. You want a cup of coffee? I could use one." Amos paced in the hall. "Hospitals make me uneasy."

"Yeah, it might be a long night." Jaxon leaned against the door frame.

"You want cream or sugar?" Amos asked.

"Cream. I'm going to make calls to her family." He started by calling Chief Parker.

"The hour your calling tells me something is up. Is Peyton okay?" Matt asked.

"No, she's been shot." Jaxon couldn't think of an easier way to tell him.

"Damn. What happened?" Matt asked.

Jaxon told him the events of the night. "She's in surgery now and they've promised to update us. The nurse said it might be a while."

"Where'd the bullet hit her?"

"I'm not sure. It appeared to be her side. She got hit and she went down fast."

"Did you get the shooter?" Matt swore under his breath.

"One of them. He's in surgery too. My guys think it was a suicide by cop. He seemed to have a death wish. He's involved in a big case that is only beginning to unfold. The shootout gave the second guy time to get away."

"Damn. I'll call Jessie and her grandmother. They'll want to come. I'll make the arrangements. Call with any updates as soon as you get them. What is your gut telling you?"

"I don't know. It looked bad, but until I hear from the doctor, I don't want to speculate. She had a premonition of something happening to her. She told me Reba said she'd make it, and I guess I'm holding on to that."

"Okay, well that's about all any of us can do right now." Matt paused. "The minute you hear call us."

"I will." Jaxon disconnected the call.

In the waiting room Jaxon flipped mindlessly through several magazines, glanced at the clock on a regular basis, and checked in at the nurse's station to see if there was any news.

At two thirty a.m., the nurse came out. "The patient is stable, and the doctor estimates it will be at least another hour before she is in recovery. He will be out to talk with you as soon as he's done." She started to leave and then turned back to them. "She's holding up well. Try not to worry."

Easier said than done. Jaxon jumped up and started to pace. He went into the hall to call Matt Parker with the update.

"At least that's somewhat positive. I'll wait to hear more as soon as you have news. Sadie and Jessie will be there tomorrow, and Madison is flying in also."

"Jaxon, the nurse's station called." Amos tapped him on the shoulder. "They're closing up now and she'll be in recovery soon."

"Matt, I'll get back to you. We should know more soon."

At four a.m., the surgeon came out to talk to them. Jaxon knew because he had been watching the clock for the past fifteen minutes. The doctor held up an X-ray and pointed to the place of two bullet wounds. "One bullet grazed her upper thigh. You can see it right here." He showed him. "I had to do a few stitches, but the wound did minimal damage to the muscle and tissue. This, on the other hand, was a bit more complex. The rib cage took the brunt of the bullet's force slowing it down a bit, but I had to repair damage to surrounding areas. As you know, detective, a bullet doesn't always take a nice, neat path. She did well through the surgery and her vitals are stable. Barring any complications or infections, she should make a full recovery. She'll be monitored in ICU tonight."

"I want to be with her until her family gets here tomorrow."

"That's fine." The doctor left and the nurse said she'd let them know when she was in ICU.

Jaxon called Matt with the final update for the night and promised to let him know if there were any changes. Stolberg stopped by and got the news before heading home. Amos left soon afterward, and Jaxon finally was alone with his thoughts.

He was in love with Peyton. The vision of her lying on the payment with her blood pooling around her was still fresh in his mind, forcing him to face facts. While she recovered, she would have to come to grips with the idea that he loved her. He couldn't think of the possibility she wouldn't make it. He wouldn't tell her tomorrow or even for a while how he felt. It would send her running but he was determined.

The nurse took him to the unit's ICU. "Don't let the monitors and tubes scare you. She's stable and doing fine at the moment."

He nodded. She had been so vibrant and full of life tonight. Glancing at her motionless, pale form, his emotions got the best of him. His chest tightened, making it hard to breathe. Moisture filled his eyes, and for the second time tonight he fought back tears.

Chapter 38

Her eyes fluttered, but they would barely open. A blurry face came and went in front of her. Where was she? Somebody kept poking her and talking gibberish. A searing pain hit her every time someone touched her. Why wouldn't they leave her alone? Water. Please. No one heard her cry. Nothing came out when she tried to talk. Her legs wouldn't move, and her arms were too heavy to lift. She must be dying, but she didn't want to. Seeing Carlee watching her surrounded by a beautiful light didn't help. Both Carlee and the angel behind her watched her intently. But she didn't want to go. Why couldn't anyone else see them? A heavy weight pressed down on her. Had they come to get her? Bizarre images swirled around her. Eerie-looking faces, needles, and drug vials danced in front of her while strange, disjointed images dashed through her mind. Darkness mixed with bright lights floated in and out, getting dimmer until only peace remained.

****

Jaxon slept off and on through the next few hours. Awakened each time a nurse came into check on her, she hadn't stirred the entire night except for a few groans when they checked her. The shift was changing, and he stood when a nurse came in to check her vitals. He walked out in the hall but could hear the nurse talking.

"Good morning, Ms. Reynolds. It's nice to see those pretty eyes of yours." Jaxon heard her go about her routine, then the nurse finally called out to him. "You're free to come back in. Our patient is awake. She can't have any water yet, but you can use the oral sponge to moisten her lips." She handed it to him once he reentered the room.

The nurse patted her hand. "You just push this button if the pain gets to be too much."

Peyton stared at him. "Why am I here?" Her voice was hoarse and hardly audible.

"Don't you remember?" He dipped the sponge in water and let her suck on it for a moment. Her blank look told him she didn't.

"You were shot." Jaxon touched her arm, being careful not to hit the IV in her hand. "Are you in pain?" *Of course, she is.* What a stupid question on his part. He didn't dare roll his eyes—she wouldn't understand.

"Right now, I don't feel anything. I'm sure it'll change at some point. From what I've been told, it's painful. Why can't I remember what happened?" Her brows furrowed.

"I'm sure it will come back to you. You went through major surgery and you're still a bit groggy."

"But I remember you, and we were together, weren't we?" She studied his face. "I can remember bits and pieces. I know I saw Carlee standing over there. A light was all around her. I thought they had come for me."

"You're not going anywhere." She opened her eyes wide at the vehemence of his answer. "We were at party last night, and we had a great time. After the party ended, we went outside to talk to a few people. There was a popping sound." He saw the light come on as her memory came back.

"Like fireworks. I remember." She sighed with relief. "I looked up to see them, but it went blank after that. Please tell me what happened. I need to know." She clutched his hand and begged him. "How bad is it?"

"The doctor should be in soon, and he'll be able to give you more details. I can tell you what I remember him saying. You were shot twice—once in the side and the other grazed your upper leg. Your ribs took some of the impact of the bullet but not all. You were in surgery for several hours. The doctor said you held up well." He squeezed her hand in his. "I'm sorry that this happened. I should have known he would show up."

"I had an odd feeling something would happen. I think that's why I worked hard at enjoying every minute last night. Does my family know?" As she spoke, he reached for the tear spilling from her eye and rolling down her cheek.

"Yes. Jessie and your grandmother will be arriving soon. Your sister will be here later." He wiped her cheek with a tissue and moistened her lips again.

"I should've told you what I was sensing, and I'm sorry I didn't. Still, I think it was bound to happen." She rubbed her tongue over her lips.

"I held on to Reba's words to you that you would be all right." He let go of her hand to pull the chair closer to the bed.

"Please don't go. I don't want to be alone." She reached for him.

"I'm not going anywhere until your family gets here." He sat beside her, holding her hand until she fell asleep. He dozed from time to time but knew the minute her family had arrived. He could hear Sadie at the nurse's station asking for Peyton's room. He slipped her hand from his and stood.

"You must be Detective Kincaid," Sadie said as she walked in the room followed by Peyton's cousin, Jessie. He would have known Jessie in a minute from Peyton's description of her curly-haired cousin. Sadie had beautiful granddaughters, and that was a fact.

"I am. I'm sorry to meet you under these circumstances." The tears shone in both of their eyes.

"If I would have thought this could happen to her, there's no way I would have let her come out here. Poor, dear girl. She's been through too much." Sadie sniffed and reached for a tissue.

"You couldn't have stopped her. Peyton has a mind of her own. Something we both get from you," Jessie said and hugged Sadie. "She'll be okay. She has to be."

"Has she been awake yet?" Sadie glanced at Jaxon.

"Yes. She was a bit groggy and struggled to remember what happened but eventually she did." He explained to them what had happened the night before.

When the doctor came in, Jaxon chose that time to leave. The family needed to ask questions, and he didn't want to be in the way. He got an update on her condition from the nurse and walked out of the hospital feeling a bit better than when he arrived the night before. Sadie had made him promise to come back later. As if she could keep him away. Even if it meant getting drilled, he wanted to be near Peyton.

The first thing he did when he left the hospital was make a call to find out the status of the case. Stolberg told him Radar was going to do another track today.

They would wait for him to arrive. He rushed to the address after grabbing a quick shower and change of clothes.

As soon as Jaxon arrived at the scene, Amos met him at the car and brought him up to speed. "Radar tracked to this house last night, but we didn't find anyone. Today we're armed with a search warrant, and the team is already in the process of searching the house and bagging up evidence. Frank seems to think his dog can track from here. We all wanted to wait until you got here to begin. Stolberg thought you'd want to be a part of it."

"Thanks, man." Jaxon leaned his against his car.

"How's Peyton?" Frank approached them with Radar on his leash.

"She's in pain, but I know she's relieved her family has arrived. Sadie and Jessie made me promise to bring you by the hospital after she's out of the ICU."

"I'd like that." Radar plopped down at Frank's feet.

"Seeing you would be good for Peyton too. The doctor said barring any unforeseen complications she should recover nicely."

"That's a relief." Frank smiled.

"Do you think your dog can track our suspect from here?" Jaxon asked Frank.

"We know the guy came to this house at some point after the shooting. Radar tracked him the ten miles from the club to here. I think he can give us an indication which way he went. Even if he drove from this site, the dog can scent a direction," Frank replied.

"We have reason to believe this suspect is injured and will need medical help or be found dead," Amos added.

"Why do you think that?" Jaxon pushed away from the car.

"There were two different blood types found at the crime scene last night. We found a few spots of blood along the trail that the dog tracked, and some in the house this morning, along with some bloody clothes."

"What do you know about either suspect?" Stolberg asked when he walked over to them.

"I did a bit of research on the name I had from the file," Jaxon said. "He worked as a security guard for the corporation under investigation, WorldStar Drug. He came over to work at the station as an officer. I have a feeling about the other suspect. I'll know soon whether my theory is correct. I didn't think before—and I still don't—that any of our hard-working officers are dirty. I believe that will bear out soon." Jaxon folded his arms against his chest.

"Who did the leaking then?" Stolberg frowned. "I want to nail him."

"Someone working at the station, but not one of our officers." Jaxon took out the small notebook from his pocket and looked at the notes he had scribbled during the night.

Agent Miller and O'Donnell walked up to them. "We're here to help. This case is moving fast and one of your suspects has ties to the other case."

"We appreciate any help you can give us," Stolberg told the agents.

"How's the victim this morning?" Miller asked.

"Her vitals are improving, and her family is with her." Jaxon pulled out his phone and read a text. "The hospital said our suspect can be questioned now that he's awake."

"Send Amos and Dunnigan to question him. Let's get this track underway." Stolberg walked away. "We want this guy in custody before the day is done."

****

Peyton tried hard not to complain. Pain, though somewhat manageable with meds, kept her sleeping when she didn't want to be. When she wasn't in dreamland, her emotions teetered somewhere between ecstatic to be alive and feeling sorry for herself. Sometimes within seconds of each other. One thing for sure—she wasn't fun to be around, but she didn't think anyone knew it but her. She talked little but teared up lots, especially every time the nurse would say something sweet to her right after she had a terrible thought about doing the woman bodily harm for poking at her. Yes, she knew the nurse was only trying to do her job, but dang, it hurt. And when the woman told her with sunshine in her voice, "We will try to get you up soon and moving," Peyton wanted to smack her. Was she nuts? Better yet, what kind of person was she? Moving wasn't something she intended to do for a long time.

Chapter 39

Jaxon would run by the hospital at night after working all day. The routine became a familiar one—as soon as he arrived Sadie, Madison, and Jessie would go down to dinner while he stayed with Peyton. No longer in ICU, Peyton walked the halls twice a day with nurses or family members, according to Sadie's updates. Her grandmother also told him the doctor said Peyton would be able to travel home in a few days if she kept progressing.

He had a few things he wanted to say to her without her family present. Tonight was the night if she was alert. Most of the evenings while he sat by her side, she slept. The walks tired her out. Rest was what she needed to heal Sadie told him repeatedly. He thought maybe she was concerned Peyton was sleeping too much. It had only been a few days since Peyton had been shot and had her lengthy surgery. Her body had been through a lot as had her emotions. He wondered if a victim's advocate had talked to her yet. It was something he needed to check with the nurse about before he left for the night. If not, he would request one visit her.

He heard the laughter when got off the elevator. Peyton begged her cousin not to make her laugh anymore—it hurt. He paused outside the door to enjoy their happy chatter.

"Are you ladies about ready for dinner?" Jaxon walked into the hospital room.

"Right on time. My stomach has been talking to me." Sadie smiled at him. "Doesn't our girl look better today?"

"Yes, she does. And if the laughter I heard when I got off the elevator is any indication, you're all happy to see the improvement."

"You can only imagine how thankful this old lady is." Sadie stood. "Sit." She pointed to the chair. "We'll leave you to chat. Peyton, don't forget to tell him what you told me earlier."

"Okay, Grams." She leaned her head back against the pillow and closed her eyes.

"Are you tired? You can tell me later if you want." Jaxon sat in the chair next to the bed.

"I'm a bit tired. Mostly, I need a moment of quiet. Those three can talk me under the table, especially when they're worried. And boy, can they hover. I can't reach for a glass of water without one of them anticipating it before I move my hand. Some things I need to do for myself." She paused to take a breath and glanced at him. "Before you think I'm ungrateful, I love every minute of it, but it can be a tad exhausting trying to keep up with all their conversations going on at once. And darn, it hurts to laugh. Sometimes I give up and feign sleep." She smiled. "Don't judge me—I'm not used to being idle."

"No judgment here." He grinned. "What did Sadie want you to tell me?" he asked.

"The first couple of nights I saw lots of puzzling images. I don't know if it was the effects of the drugs or more of my strange visions. I'm trying to remember them. I don't know the enormity of the case you're involved in or why someone targeted me, but I do know lots of people have been hurt and more are dead than you know about. The connection that links it to Tombstone and many other places is the power and greed. Power tells them they have a right to do what they've done, and greed keeps them wanting more. They never have enough. It's the same old story: the strong oppressing the weak, the greedy taking from those that don't have much. I've seen their faces, and I know their pain."

"You're right. I promise as soon as I can tell you everything I will. Whether you are here or back at home, you will hear it all from me face to face. You are the reason this case is on its way to being solved."

"Thank you. I know as soon as I can travel, they're going to take me home. I hate not being here to see this through to the end. I believe I'm beginning to see the reason I've seen what I have."

It was now or never. "Peyton, you and I have a lot of unfinished business and there's no way I'm ready to let you go. When I saw you lying on the ground, it hit me you could die, and I never told you how I felt about you."

"How do you feel?" She reached for his hand.

"I want to get to know you more." He stroked her hand as he held it. "The sparkle in your eyes intrigues me. Every time you smile, your dimples make me want to be the one that makes you smile for the rest of your life. You're unlike any woman I've ever met, and truthfully you fascinate me. I'm not good with words like you, but I want to find out more about you. I want to see where this goes. I don't want to push you. I'm simply telling you that you haven't seen the last of me. Not by a long shot."

"I'm glad." She sighed.

He watched her eyes slowly drift shut, and her breathing became soft and even. "Enjoy the quiet and sleep, sweetheart. It's bound to be noisy soon." He leaned close and kissed her cheek.

Jaxon heard their happy chatter when the elevator opened. "Sadie, I have an idea," he said when they walked in the room. "Why don't you ladies go to your hotel and I'll stay here tonight? She's out of the woods now. You could use a good night's sleep. I'll call you if something comes up."

"That sounds like a good idea, young man. We could use the rest and a nice hot shower. We'll be back tomorrow, but if you need to leave before we get here, I think she'll be just fine."

"I couldn't agree more." Jaxon stood.

Sadie took his hand. "I hope you'll come to Blue Cove to see her young man," she said softly so only he could hear.

"I plan on it. I promised her that she'd hear about the case from me, which means I'll be in Blue Cove at some point to fill her in on what happens."

"Good. I like you, and I'm never wrong about these things. You came into her life at the right moment."

"Vice versa." He smiled as the ladies left. Sadie must have been something when she was young. He got a kick out of her. There was nothing subtle about her. A truly remarkable lady, and Peyton, Jessie, and Madison were cut out of the same cloth. The desire to get to know this woman beside him was stronger than ever.

He pulled out his computer and began to work on

the report. The track a few days ago had been successful. He needed to write how it went down while it was fresh in his mind.

****

She could fake sleep when she needed to. Her body was tired, but her mind didn't want to submit. Trust didn't come easily for her, but oh how she wanted to believe this man was for real. It would be great to have someone take care of her. A luxury she had always dreamed of and never thought possible.

His kindness extended to her family too. Peyton could see how tired Sadie looked. The past several days had worried her. And then he offered to stay here tonight so they could go back to the hotel and rest. She didn't need them to stay anymore, but Sadie wouldn't hear of it. He somehow understood that. The rotating shift nurses and doctors making their rounds would keep him from sleeping much. *Is he real*? Possibly. No way would she jump into a relationship. She could wait and see how he fared under fire.

Yet she wanted to believe. She sighed inwardly. For now, she would believe. The last nurse had put something in her IV and she drifted slowly to sleep. Her body relaxed, her mind silenced, and once again she found herself in the company of strange ghostly visions floating through her dreams. Spirits danced through the corridors of her mind. When one would fade from sight, another one would take its place.

Chapter 40

Jessie walked into the room arm in arm with Sadie. Peyton still slept soundly. Jaxon said his goodbyes and headed home before he needed to get to the station.

Today Frank and Kilo were going to run a track through the lab and warehouse. The agents wanted to see if there were any illegal drugs mixed among the others. Something Peyton had said to him about her strange dreams the first night made him think they would probably find more than they had bargained for. The FBI had spent the past few days boxing records, and today they wanted to catalog and check inventory. Their labs would test several of the meds randomly. Miller had agreed with him that it would be confirmation and probably nothing new.

Radar had been amazing to watch tracking from the house to their suspect. They needed more dogs to work with law enforcement. Without Radar's help they probably wouldn't have found Carlee's body. But now they would be able to bury her and have closure. Max, the coroner, had released the body to her parents a couple of days ago. His report wouldn't bring them any comfort. No one should go through what that daughter had.

Jaxon walked into the station. "Hey, Amos, how's it going?" He saw Agent Miller sitting in the captain's office.

"Not bad. How's Peyton?" Amos followed him to his cubicle. He nodded toward the captain's office. "They're waiting for you"

"I figured." He placed his files on his desk. "She's improving every day. We'll talk later." Jaxon paused before he moved on. "You've done a great job on this case. Everyone has. I appreciate it, man." Jaxon smiled.

"Thanks. We held it together, considering." Amos smiled back and pointed to the office. "You'd better get in there." It was Jaxon's turn to nod.

"Good morning, sir," Jaxon said as he walked in the office. "Hello, Miller." He acknowledged the agent. "How's it going, O'Donnell? Amos said you wanted to see me, Captain."

"Yes, Miller told me your plans for today. I'm ready to see what the dog finds. I know these guys are dirty. The question is, how dirty are they?" Stolberg sat on the corner of his desk.

"We'll leave as soon as Frank arrives. He's on his way. We've been in touch this morning. I'm glad you let him use one of the cars. It's given him more freedom with his dogs."

"What are you searching for?" Miller asked.

"Peyton told me about seeing bottles with names. I wrote down what she told me. Believe it or not, they were all real names for meds. She said they had killed people already. She also said it was almost like they were putting poison in their veins. It makes sense. If they've been tampering with the meds or diluting them, the impact could be far-reaching." Jaxon opened his laptop and showed the names he had researched.

"Wow. You want to bet that we'll find these in their laboratory and warehouse? When our labs test the drugs, they'll probably find major issues with them," O'Donnell said.

"Does this make you as angry as it does me? I guess I'll be able to tell Elliot Dawson his son became a hero in his death. It might give him a measure of peace. E J did all the hard work of documenting what these crooks were doing. We should have enough evidence to put them all away for a long time."

"Hell yes, I'm angry. We still have to find all the victims that have been devastated by this." Miller's hand fisted at his side.

"The best part of having this record from Dawson is that we will find some of the victims or their families. Think about all the folks who have been murdered and treated unjustly that no one even knows about," Stolberg said as he nodded. "This should help Elliot. You'll have to tell him soon."

"We got lucky with this one. Too many victims have no witnesses to see what they've suffered. At least this time there will be a payday for these criminals and their greed," Miller said and stood as Frank walked into the room.

"No luck about it. Thanks to Peyton, E J, and Radar we have evidence." Jaxon clapped O'Donnell on the back. "Let's gather some more and put them behind bars."

They walked with Frank out to the cars. Jaxon said, "You have your other dog today, I see. Where's Radar?"

"Radar is in his crate back in the room where it's cool. I brought Kilo along this morning. Remember when I first got here, I told you I had no idea why I brought him along? Now I get it. I don't usually bring two dogs when I fly. They're a lot to handle. This is one time I'm glad that I did. If there are drugs to be found, this is the dog you want on the job. He's the best."

"We'll be there in a few. It's a big warehouse, and if your dog finds what I think he will, it'll go a long way to putting some bad people in jail." Jaxon pulled into the parking lot and helped Frank get Kilo out of the crate. They walked into the lab area and the track began where the agents were at work cataloging lot numbers on the bottles ready for shipment. Thankfully they weren't going anywhere.

Frank bent down next to Kilo. "Find the drug, boy." He let the dog smell the heroin in the bag. Kilo went through the warehouse and hit on several spots. The agents took samples to test from several lot numbers of bottled drugs.

Kilo worked through the morning. Several items were on their way to the FBI lab. "Your dog did a fantastic job," Miller said, standing next to Frank.

"What are you looking for, exactly? I imagine some of these drug derivatives are used legally," Frank said, addressing Agent Miller and Jaxon.

"We're looking to see if they were used in the amounts legal for medical consumption. If any were sent in the pure form. If they've added more to make them addictive or not enough to help. This company has been using unsafe and unfair practices. One of the employees left a road map for us before he was murdered by their hired thugs," Agent Miller said.

"Not exactly a poster child for the pharmaceutical companies." Frank shook his head. "It's a sad day when the people you trust to help you are harming you. I'll be interested to hear how this one turns out."

"Peyton will know, and you will too. I'll make sure of it. You both were a great help in this case." Jaxon looked at a text on his phone. "Speaking of Peyton, Sadie said the doctor told them she'll be discharged tomorrow and free to travel with a few restrictions. I wonder how Sadie managed to talk the doctors into it. It will be rough for her to travel for a while yet."

"I'm happy to hear it. Sadie can be very persuasive." Frank paused and studied Jaxon's face. "Look, I've been through the whole romance thing with Matt and Jessie. I can tell that you're interested in Peyton." Frank slapped Jaxon on the back. His eyes crinkled at the corners and his lips curved into a smile. "What are you going to do about it?"

"I'm going to take it slow. She's been through a lot and doesn't exactly trust men. I get it. I've told her what I plan to do. It may take a while, but I think she might be worth the wait." Jaxon's smile acknowledged his feelings were positive ones. "I'm hoping to secure a job back near my hometown. No matter what, though, I'll be going to Blue Cove when this case is wrapped up. She'll have to come back here for the trial of her shooter. We are bound to meet a few times and I'm a patient man." Jaxon leaned his hip against the door frame. "An extremely patient man when it's something I want."

"You won't be disappointed—she's a keeper," Frank said.

"Couldn't agree more."

"I'll be happy to vouch for you with the FBI, Jaxon. I'll write a report for your dogs too, Frank. You'll have to come back to testify in court, as well, Frank." Miller leaned his side against the wall.

"I know the routine. I'll be happy to do my part to put these guys behind bars." Frank shook the agent's hand. "If you guys are through with my services, I want to stop by the hospital to see Peyton. Oh yeah, Sadie hired a private air ambulance service. That's how she convinced the doctors."

Agent Miller whistled. "Wow, that's a major expense.

"Not any more costly than more days in the hospital and at the resort until she's up to traveling. The doctor is letting Peyton leave early because of the air ambulance service and their reputation. She'll be monitored, able to rest, and have the care she needs. It would be tough to fly on a commercial airline for a few more weeks. Sadie wants her granddaughter home where she can care for her. She'll go first to the hospital in Boston and in a few days be transferred to Blue Cove."

"Sounds like a good plan." Jaxon shook Frank's hand. "Tell them I'll be there to see them later. I want to say my goodbyes before they leave in the morning."

"I'll tell them." Frank's movement caused Kilo to stand up close to his side.

"Thanks for coming. I know this wasn't an easy trip. I think you've convinced Captain Stolberg a tracking dog needs to be available to the department."

"They can do a lot that we humans can't do." Frank grabbed Kilo's leash.

"Expect a check for your expenses and services. We all agreed it's worth every penny."

Jaxon walked down the hall with Frank. "When you book your flight, let me know. Someone will get you and your dogs to the airport."

****

Peyton had mixed emotions about leaving. Everything inside her seemed out of her control. She cried one minute and laughed the next. What was up with her? The victim's advocate told her it was normal to have a certain amount of anxiety after a stressful event. But for heaven's sake, to fall apart when Destiny called her? They both were crying before she hung up. Now, "guilty" described the thoughts rolling around in her brain. She was anything but normal. How long would she be like this? Hopefully this wasn't the new Peyton, or she'd have no friends left.

The tears started all over again when Jessie told her about flying home. "It's too expensive, and I don't want Grams to pay for it."

"Listen, Cous, Sadie wants to do this. She wants you taken care of by the best. It's her way of making up for all the years your dad wouldn't let her." Jessie handed Peyton a tissue. "If you keep crying, you'll have my reputation. Tears are my release, as you know. I've never known you to cry. Let Grams do it."

"Okay, but all these tears make me think I've caught more from you than only seeing ghosts." She dabbed at her eyes. Jessie's words had wrapped around her like a big loving hug, which had her crying again. More tears flowed when Frank stopped by and when Jessie left to walk him down to the lobby. All she needed now to completely lose it was for Jaxon to walk through the door.

Maybe if she could see him as the handsome cowboy of her dreams, she could hold it together. But one thought led to another and before she knew it, she remembered E J, Carlee, and all the nameless ghosts, and once again there were tears.

"Oh, sweet girl, what is the matter, honey?" The nurse who had walked in the room handed her the box of tissues.

"I can't seem to help myself. Everything seems to make me cry today." She sounded pitiful even to her ears.

"Let me talk to the doctor and I'll be right back. This sometimes happens after a trauma and during the recovery process." Nurse Sally walked out and came back a few minutes later with a shot. "This should take the edge off a little."

"Thank you. I don't want to worry everyone with all these tears. My cousin is the crier not me. My poor grandmother didn't want to leave me to go for dinner. She was worried."

"I'll talk to her for you," Sally said.

"Thank you. I'm feeling calmer already." She closed her eyes, sighed, and drifted off to sleep.

Chapter 41

Peyton had slept through his entire visit. Jaxon had wanted to talk over things with her. Instead, he talked to Sadie. She had been worried about Peyton's emotional state. The nurse and victim's advocate had reassured her it could happen after a traumatic event. He enjoyed Sadie, even though it wasn't the evening he had hoped for.

He put his shades on to see traffic through the glare of the bright morning sun. The clock on his dashboard reminded him that Peyton would be on her way to the plane. Nothing was settled between them. But Sadie had made him promise not to give up on her granddaughter. She told him she would call as soon as they arrived in Boston and Peyton was settled in the hospital for the night. The drive seemed longer today—it had to be the traffic.

Jaxon finally arrived at the station. With a cup of coffee in his hand, he headed to the interview room where Agent Miller and Amos were interviewing the president of WorldStar Drug Company. He stood on the other side of the glass to listen in with Stolberg.

"How's it going?" Jaxon asked the chief.

"About as expected. He's trying to throw the lab workers under the bus. You got here in time to hear them use the documentation against him. This ought to be interesting." Stolberg paused. "Can't wait to see how he jumps over this hurdle."

Agent Miller started giving him facts and reading through the recorded information E J had provided and that Jeremy had corroborated. The man's mouth dropped open. His high-priced lawyer kept telling him not to respond, but the guy couldn't help himself.

"Man, that's a beautiful sight." Stolberg crossed his arms across his chest. "I want you to go to see Elliot Dawson today. He needs to know what his son did. He'll have to keep it quiet for now, but it'll help him as he grieves."

Jaxon nodded. "Damn beautiful." The next few interviews were equal to if not better.

After a quick call to make sure Elliot was home, Jaxon found himself driving once again the familiar path to Dawson's home. He knocked on the door. "Elliot, your wife told me you were home. Do you have a minute to talk?" Jaxon asked when the elder Dawson opened the door.

He nodded and motioned him in. "I take it you have some news for me."

"I do. I think your wife should hear it too," Jaxon told him.

"I'll go get her. Make yourself comfortable."

As soon as they were seated, Jaxon began. "What I'm going to talk to you about you'll have to keep quiet for a while. The captain wanted you to know. It might help you get through this hard time." He explained all that Dawson's son had done and how it was helping to solve a major crime that impacted many lives. "E J left us a record of everything he saw. It has made our job easier and will probably in the long run save many lives. You can be proud of your son. In the end, he was a hero."

Elliot wiped at the tears in his eyes and handed a tissue to his wife, who sobbed openly. "Thank you. Our boy wasn't an angel by any means, but I couldn't believe he would do anything to hurt someone, either. This means everything to me."

Jaxon left a while later feeling like a weight had lifted off his chest. He sat in his car for a time, absorbing his visit with the Dawsons. That's when the call came from Sadie. He answered immediately. "How is she doing?"

"The move tuckered her out. She's already sleeping for the night," Sadie said. "You be sure to call her in the morning. She wanted to tell you goodbye before she left and was sorry she had slept through your visit. Be sure to look us up when you get back this way."

"You can count on it." Jaxon started the car.

"I know I shouldn't interfere, but my granddaughter lights up when you're around. And if I don't miss my guess, I think you like her too."

"When you're right you're right, Sadie." He grinned. "Don't worry. I'll find my way there. But it has to be our secret for now."

"I'm good at keeping secrets, especially if they have happy endings."

"Given time, I think this one will." Jaxon drummed the steering wheel with his hand. "I'll turn up and surprise her one day, hopefully in the near future."

"I'm glad. I look forward to seeing you soon. You know the perfect time might be an open house party given by Katie and Dylan a couple of weeks before their wedding. They've tagged it as a celebration with friends before the big day." Sadie told him all the details. "I hope you can make it. You have a few weeks to make arrangements."

"I'll give it my best shot. The investigation is moving quickly," Jaxon told her.

"What about the shooters? she asked.

"Bob Edwards, the one who shot Peyton, was found dead. He had been wounded when he fled. The next day Radar tracked him. He had succumbed to his injury. We are waiting on the cause of death. It could be complications from his wound and exposure, but other evidence points to a possible suicide. The second shooter is improving and being interviewed daily as he recovers."

"Such a tragic waste of life. All the people who fight every day to live and others who throw away their lives. I'm not sure I understand the logic of it, or maybe there is no rationale for it. Life simply overwhelms folks sometimes."

"I see it all the time." Jaxon cranked up the AC. "I'll let you know any plans I have if it works out. We'll talk soon." He disconnected the call and continued on to his office.

The next call after arriving back at the station made Jaxon's day. For weeks he had been waiting for this one. Now it appeared that all his plans were coming together. He couldn't wait to call his mom and tell her the good news. For now, it would have to wait. His job wasn't finished yet. He couldn't move on until it was.

Afternoon meetings gobbled up most of his time. Still, there was enough left over to work on the charges against two of the defendants in the case— impersonating an officer and falsifying job applications were minor compared to murder, rape, and attempted murder chargers. Assault with a deadly weapon, attempted murder of a police officer, and the list went on.

"How did Dawson handle the news about E J?" Stolberg asked when he stopped at his desk.

"It meant a lot to them," Jaxon answered. "His wife cried."

"I was sure it would be hard but welcomed. Elliot may have overindulged his son's bad behavior, but I know for a fact he loved his boy. They'll need all the help they can get as they go through the process of loss. No parent ever thinks their child will die before them. It's not supposed to work that way."

"I can't imagine. I know how much my brother loves his little girl. He'd do anything to protect her. Elliot is a decent man."

"I didn't know your brother has a little girl." Stolberg leaned his hip against the corner of Jaxon's desk.

"She's a great little girl. We all love her. Her smile is enough to make you happy." Jaxon smiled thinking of Emmie.

"My kids are grown, but my grandkids are the best. You think you can never love anyone more than your kids and then your grandkids come along and completely steal your heart. There's something pretty incredible about your children's kids."

"I hope to find that out one day." Jaxon stood.

"Keep working—you'll want to get this case behind you so you can move closer to your family. I know about the offer. I'm the one who told them they would be fools not to hire you, but damn I'm going to miss you around here. Congratulations!" Stolberg clapped Jaxon on the back. "You've done a damn fine job for this department."

"Thanks, sir. I've liked my years of working here. I admit, though, I'm looking forward to being closer to my family."

"And a certain young lady, if I don't miss my guess." The captain smiled.

"That too." Jaxon grinned.

"Good luck on both fronts. I'll leave you to your work." Stolberg walked on and stopped to talk with Amos.

The captain was a good man to work for. Jaxon had learned from one of the best. He would remember his days here in the Phoenix area with pleasure, although it was past time for him to put down roots.

****

Over the next couple of weeks, Jaxon checked all the boxes of things he needed to get done. Indictments were handed down and several more arrests made in the case against WorldStar Drug Corporation. The president and the top executives were held without bail because the state proved the case of flight risk against them.

He talked to Peyton several times. She seemed cordial but distant. He needed to get back there before she forgot him. Jessie had dropped the hint more than once that Matt's brother, Evan, was interested in Peyton, as well as Matt's best friend, Chad. Jaxon wasn't sure if she did that to warn him off or to get him moving. The only real encouragement he got was from Sadie and his mother, who had a way of dragging out information from him. Yep. He patted the airline ticket in his pocket. It was almost time for him to go east to the Bureau and fill out the paperwork on his new position with a side trip to Blue Cove.

Chapter 42

She had felt sorry for herself long enough. Looking out the window at the cove, she made an important decision. No more letting people wait on her and no more moping around. It was past time to get back into the game of life. Jaxon had called her almost every night, and she hadn't treated him well at all. Why he kept calling she had no idea. He said he wanted to talk over the case with her. She couldn't figure out why he wanted to talk to her at all.

The bullets hadn't killed her. She had another chance at life, and she didn't want to mess it up. She laced up her walking shoes. With a clean bill of health in her mind, she walked out the cottage door and headed down the path she saw her cousin jogging every day. The faster she walked the more alive she felt.

She hadn't been completely idle the last few weeks. She worked from home for the publishing company and sent out a few resumes. She had three telephone interviews and had a couple of face-to-face interviews set up for the next several weeks. Excitement pulsated through her as her feet pounded the dirt trail.

Life seemed strange at times. When she first got to the cove, she had thought it wasn't a place where she could ever live. The town was too small with no possibilities for a social life at all. But now, she could see herself living there easily. If everything worked out, it might be possible. Only time would tell. At first, she thought Evan Parker might be the guy for her, but there was no spark and he seemed more interested in some redhead who was too young for him. Men. "Don't go there, girl," she muttered. Chad was a handsome man, but he wasn't for her. Both were great guys. She kept her distance from them. What had she expected? She never gave them any encouragement.

"Good morning," she said as she walked by a strolling couple. Everything had changed for her since Phoenix.

Pulling her phone out of her pocket, she called her cousin. "How's business?"

"Listen." Jessie held out the phone so she could hear. "The mystery book club is meeting, and they are having a great time. Reba said she is stopping by later, and Molly has some great new treat for us to try. I'll bring you something home."

"You don't need to. I'm going to stop by later myself. I've made some decisions and it's time for me to get busy. I want to thank you for putting up with my moodiness, but I'm done letting people take care of me. It's time for me to take charge of my life again." Peyton picked up her speed, rushing to get back to the cottage.

"Good for you, cousin. I've been waiting for this day. I knew it was coming. I know you well enough to know you wouldn't let this get you down much longer. You have too many dreams to sit back and let life pass you by. Where are you going to start?"

"As soon as I get back from my walk and make myself look decent, I'll stop by the store and tell you all about my plans." Peyton waved at a runner that passed her.

"I'll be waiting. I can't wait to hear."

Later, Peyton walked into Idle Time Books and took a deep breath. She could see why Jessie loved this place. The atmosphere vibrated with energy. Reba, Molly, and Sadie sat at the big table in the center of the store, merrily chatting away. Grams looked lovely in her blue pantsuit. Always attractive and full of life, people would never guess her age. Reba, equally pretty, sat close to Sadie, and they were talking like two high school girls. The two of them together brought a smile to her face. Reba always seemed perfectly put together. Her words were an anchor through the worst storm of her life. Molly started telling a story and the ladies laughed right along with her. All her cousin's friends had opened their arms to her, and she wanted to thank them. There was no time like the present.

Sadie saw her first. "Oh, Peyton, I'm glad you decided to join us. Are you feeling well, dear? You look a bit flushed."

"I look alive, Grams. I've been out for a long walk and feel great." She stood behind her grandmother's chair and gently squeezed her shoulders.

"Hey, cousin. I told these ladies you were coming by and had some news to share. Don't disappoint them," Jessie said and pulled out one of the chairs for her to sit. "The stage is yours. Talk away, girl."

"I wanted to thank you all for your kindness toward me. You made some trying days quite tolerable for me. I haven't had many people whom I could lean on in my life, but you have changed that for me. I'm happy you are the first ones I will tell the changes I intend to make."

"I'm happy to have played a small part in this amazing journey in your life. Like with our dear Jessie, I don't believe it's over for you. You're only at the beginning." Reba reached for her hand.

Peyton shared with them her plan to work from home as an editor for her publishing company and to put her degree to work teaching special needs children. "I have a few interviews lined up over the next couple of weeks, including here. I never thought I could live in such a small town, but I love Blue Cove. The support each of you has shown me has been amazing, and I can't thank you enough."

"What will be your outlet for your new-found ability?" Reba asked her.

"I have no plan. Seeing ghosts might have been a one-time experience for me. Only time will tell. I guess I'll cross that bridge when I get to it." Peyton sat in the open chair beside her grandmother.

"You'll be crossing it soon, dear. It's not a one-and-done affair for you. Your ability, just like Jessie's, is necessary for the times we live in," Reba said and smiled at her. "It's only a matter of time and you'll be in the thick of it again."

"I agree with my friend." Sadie turned to look at her granddaughter. "You've seen what few have ever seen. You've been given a great opportunity to help others. You must consider an outlet for the gift. What say you, Jessie girl?"

"If it's true that she has a gift, then she won't have to see an outlet, rather it will seek her. I didn't go in search of anything except to help the person requesting it. It pushed me into Matt's path until we started working together. I figure she'll know what to do when it happens to her again. First thing, though, will be to stay out of the path of bullets." Jessie scrunched her face. "I'm serious."

"You've got that right." She glanced into the coffeeshop. "I want a coffee to go with one of Molly's treats. The coffee or tea is my treat to you all," Peyton told the ladies. "I'll let you surprise us with one of your specialties," she said to Molly.

Molly asked what they wanted and went to the shop to get their drinks and her new mint chocolate cupcakes. The small chocolate mint cupcake was presented in an edible chocolate wrapping with green mint frosting and was topped with a yummy chocolate mint.

"Molly, these are beautiful." Jessie took a bite. "Oh my gosh, they are heavenly. I've never tasted a cupcake this good before."

"I agree, dear. These are wonderful. I need to take six of them home. Lawrence needs to have a couple after dinner with his tea." Reba dabbed at her mouth.

"Peyton, should we make it unanimous that these are absolutely scrumptious?" Sadie asked.

"I'm in. I want six to take home tonight, too," Peyton said.

"How about three of these and three of my turtle delight cupcakes? It's another new menu item." Molly had brought one of them that she had cut into four pieces for each of them to taste.

"I'll do the three of each. I can't tell which one I like the best now. I'm happy with chocolate anything," Reba said as she took a sip of her tea. "Molly you do make amazing treats."

Peyton left the bookstore a while later with a box

of cupcakes in hand. Would she see any ghosts again or have another premonition? She had no idea, but she liked what Jessie said to her best. She didn't need to look for anything—they would find her if she was needed. Peyton could live with that.

She went back to the cottage and made dinner. It was past time for her to do her fair share of work to help her cousin out. She would stay here until she knew whether her job would be in Blue Cove or one of the surrounding towns. Then she would look for an apartment of her own. Katie had mentioned Liam and Connor were moving into a place down by Seaside Village and she could rent their place once she fumigated it. Katie wasn't joking. She had meant every word. She had said, "Liam is a slob, and he won't change till his wife makes him, if ever there's a woman stupid enough to marry him." Peyton liked Katie, and the apartment sounded perfect. Jessie's best friend was a hoot to hang out with.

Katie turned every small gathering into a party, and Peyton looked forward to what Katie called "a simple dinner with friends" at the end of this week. There was nothing simple about it if she knew Jessie's friend—unless a dance with several people coming, including several single guys, was a simple dinner. Peyton knew she would have at least one or two dances for the night. Right now, the walk today had pretty much done her in. After dinner, she would call it an early night.

Chapter 43

Jaxon boarded the plane with the consent of Captain Stolberg. After several grueling days of interviews, reports, and criminal arraignments at the courthouse, a scheduled job orientation seemed like a piece of cake. He still remembered how nervous he felt on his first job interview for the Phoenix PD. He got the job, but it had taken him across the country away from his family and friends. Looking back, he knew it was exactly what he had needed at the time. Separation from the familiar challenged him to grow up and make it on his own. His dad told him at the time, "Son, it'll make a man out of you."

After a slated meeting with the Human Resource Department and a few days at home, he would drive to Blue Cove. Only Sadie knew he was coming. The knot in his stomach every time he thought about seeing Peyton reminded him of how unsure his instincts were when it came to her. Would she be happy to see him or want him gone? He had no idea. Talking with her on the phone the past few weeks, he couldn't tell if she wanted to see him or had moved on. Damn, the uncertainty took him back to his awkward teens.

Sadie encouraged him make time to stop by Blue Cove. He would, but he wasn't confident Peyton wanted him there.

As soon as the plane pushed away from the gate,

Jaxon closed his eyes. He needed the down time and worrying about what might or might not happen wouldn't do him any good. Once the plane took off, he slept and didn't awaken until the captain told the crew to prepare the cabin for landing. Lifting his seat to the upright position, he was rested and ready to hit the ground running.

****

Peyton had three interviews over the next few days. Driving back to the cove from the last one, she had a positive vibe. The day school had made a favorable impression. Besides being brand new, the colors were vibrant and perfect for learning. The attitude of the staff seemed positive and caring. All in all, the place gave her a good feeling. Her phone rang while she drove.

"Hey, where are you?" Jessie's voice sounded through her headpiece.

"I'm in the town of Hanover." Peyton stopped at the stop sign.

"Oh, that's such a pretty town."

"It's gorgeous. I'm driving through the canopy of trees right now. I passed the ice cream parlor you told me about." Peyton gave her a description of her route as she drove.

"There's a great little boutique there. You should stop and buy a new dress for the party on Friday. Better yet, I know the perfect place for us to go when you get back. Stop at the store as soon as you get in town. I have someone you need to meet."

"Okay, I'll be there in a while." The lovely scenery had Peyton considering Hanover as a possible place to live. The only downside to it was no ocean view. She never thought she could be happy living anywhere but the city, but Blue Cove had changed her mind. She loved the city because she could fade into the background, but she didn't want to be invisible anymore.

She went first to the bookstore when she arrived back in Blue Cove. "Hi, ladies," Peyton said as she walked up to Reba and Jessie, who stood at the counter.

"Reba is going to watch the store until we get back. You're coming with me." Jessie took her across the street to First Community Church. Opening the front door to the church, she motioned for Peyton to walk in before her. "There is someone who wants to meet you. Follow me." They walked down the hall together to the office.

"Hey, Blondie, it's been a while since I've seen you around here." Melinda, the church custodian, glanced over the top of her glasses and acknowledged Jessie. Her ponytail balanced oddly at the side of her head.

"Hi, Red. This is my cousin, Peyton." Jessie stopped at Melinda's desk to talk. "Peyton, this is Melinda. She knows about me and all the strange things I've seen."

"Nice to meet you, Melinda."

"I would call you Red, but that's what they call me." She chuckled. "I'll think of a name. Give me time."

"She will too." Jessie smiled at her friend. "Melinda knows what's up."

"Is she another one?" Melinda's brows rose with the question.

"She is," Jessie told her.

"That's fine and dandy. Another one. That

probably means more ghosts will come to town. I think I'll call you Hazel 'cause green won't do. You've got pretty eyes."

"Thank you." Peyton smiled at her.

"Pastor John's going to get a kick out of there being two of you. I bet you're here to see him, aren't you? A regular ghost-seeing crime-fighting team. Are there any more of you?" She slapped her leg and laughed. "I'll be."

"Anything is possible. I'll talk to you later." Jessie moved toward the office door. "Hi, Audrey," she said to the office manager.

"Hey, Jessie. How can I help you?" she asked.

"We're here to see the pastors. This is my cousin, Peyton Reynolds."

"We met briefly a few times at the store. How are you, Peyton?" Audrey gave Peyton a hug.

"I'm good. Although I'm wondering why my cousin brought me to a church to meet the pastors. I hope she doesn't think I'm going bonkers too." Peyton made face at Jessie, closing her eyes and pursing her lips.

"You'll see." Jessie tugged on her hand to get her moving. She knocked on Pastor John's office door. The door opened, and the pastor looked out.

"Come in, Jessie. And this must be your cousin Peyton. Please, ladies, make yourself comfortable. Pastor Kevin will be right in." He motioned at the chairs in front of his desk.

Peyton leaned close to Jessie and whispered, "What are you doing? Trying to tag team me?"

"Hardly." Jessie smiled at her. "I'm trying to help you see yourself in a new light. These are the guys that helped me."

Introductions were made again once Pastor Kevin walked in the room. "I know you're wondering why I asked to meet you, Peyton. After Jessie explained to me all that you've been through in the past few weeks, we both wanted to meet another one of the amazing Reynolds girls."

His kind smile put Peyton instantly at ease. "I'm not sure what to say about the amazing part. Thank you, I think."

"Cous, I told him about your father, seeing the ghosts, and being shot. The combined stress of all of it made me worried for you."

"If I remember correctly, Jessie, you've had a few near misses too. Not to mention a stalker from your past who made life awful for you." Pastor John turned his attention on Peyton. "It all overwhelmed her until she saw the good she was doing for others. It made an activist out of her and turned crime in the area on its head. What I'm trying to say is that what you have is rare, but there is a reason for everything. You both get to see and describe what others have to go by faith to even glimpse."

"I never thought of it that way," Peyton said.

"I know. Me either. He has a way of making sense out of it all." Jessie smiled at Pastor John.

"Tell us your story, Peyton," Pastor John said.

It felt great to put into words all the emotions that had built up over time. Once the floodgate opened, all her feelings gushed out. Words tripped over one another to rush from her lips, freeing her from walls she had built around her heart. "I'm still trying to figure out why me?" She reached for the box of tissues he handed to her.

"It's simple, really. You were available and the path was meant to be healing for you too. Life isn't a book where you discover one truth for all time and that's all there is on a subject. Life is a journey to be taken one step at a time. I learn as much from you girls as I have from all the books I've read. Your experiences tend to blow my rational mind right out the window." John leaned back in his chair, clasping his hands lightly together in front of him.

"Sorry, sir," Peyton mumbled softly.

"No need to apologize, young lady. It's a good thing to be challenged from an unmovable position from time to time. I call it sacred cow tipping. A lot of good people have died trying to defend the indefensible. Your experiences also renew my faith."

They talked for a while longer. John and Kevin had her feeling good about her life when she walked out of the church. Pastor John commended her on the idea of working with special needs children. He also assured her to live her life and told her that her gift would make room for itself when needed.

The cousins waved at Audrey on their way out the door. "Can you see why I wanted you to meet them?" Jessie asked. "Pastor John called me a blooming miracle at a time when I needed to hear it most. I've had my doubts about all of this, Peyton, and I know you did and will again. You must have a way to release it all, and these men understand us."

"Thanks, Jessie. Talking about my childhood isn't easy for me. Although I know it's something I need to do in order to ever have a family of my own someday."

"All those disjointed puzzle pieces will start

coming together and you will understand why you saw Carlee, E J, and all the other faces along with them. I love you, cousin. You're a blooming miracle too."

"I sure hope so. What's next?'

"I have a new gal working at the store during the summer extended hours. I'm free for the evening. Matt is busy tonight. We are going shopping for a dress and out to dinner. I know just the place to end our girls' night out on a fun note."

Chapter 44

Jaxon had a few relaxing days. The job belonged to him if he wanted it. Boy did he. The papers were signed, but the starting date was left flexible until his case in Phoenix concluded. A lead FBI agent in a field office under Tom Maxwell sounded almost perfect. He would have to go through their training, but he welcomed it.

His family couldn't wait for him to move back. He knew the decision was right at this point in his life. Besides enjoying his mom's home cooking, he liked searching for condos and houses near where he would work. The place would be determined after his talk with Peyton. Right now, his plans included arriving early tomorrow to talk about the case with hopes of staying for the party on Friday. Plans could change, but he was hopeful. He grinned, leaning back against the pillows stacked behind his back. Tonight, when he talked to her, she seemed upbeat and animated, almost flirty. It gave him hope. He wanted to tell her he would be there, but Sadie had made him promise to surprise her.

****

Jaxon reached Blue Cove about eleven the next day. He called Sadie. "Hi, you told me to call when I got here."

"I'm glad you're here, Jaxon." She gave him directions to Jessie's cottage. "Jessie's at the store. It'll be a perfect time to talk with Peyton alone."

"How's she doing?" Jaxon asked.

"Better, I think. For a while, she seemed a bit depressed. Everyone told us it was a normal response to a stressful event, but her depression seemed extended. Even with all their reassurances, it didn't make seeing her that way any easier. A few days ago, she told us she was through letting us take care of her and that she had made some decisions. Frankly, I think it was a turning point for her. Peyton, unlike Jessie, who says exactly what she thinks about most everything, always seemed to enjoy being in the background. I never bought it for a minute, but she rarely departed from her controlled actions. Until the other day. I caught a glimpse of who Peyton really is." Sadie paused. "You've seen our real Peyton, haven't you?"

"Yes, ma'am. She's a strong, remarkable woman. I also believe that there's a witty, playful side to her that you'll be seeing more of if what you told me is true. And I have no reason to doubt you."

"You've told me what I've known all along. I could knock my son upside the head for what he did to his girls. I don't believe that we know the half of it yet. It may take years for it all to come out. But it will. In the meantime, our Peyton is on a brand-new journey. I'm excited for our dear girl. Go, Jaxon, and make your case. I'm rooting for you."

"Thank you, Sadie. I plan on giving it my best shot."

Jaxon followed Sadie's directions, which led him past the inn to parking behind. Following the path to the cottage, he paused to look at the beauty of the gardens. The fragrance of the blooming flowers was all around him, and beyond was a view of the cove. A beautiful spot to live. A small slice of paradise. Taking a deep breath, he knocked at the door and waited.

She was as beautiful as he remembered. It was his only coherent thought when she opened the door. "I thought I would surprise you." He grinned at her.

"You did." She held the door open and motioned him to come in.

"I told you we had unfinished business between us." He touched her cheek seductively as he walked past her. "Besides, I promised to bring you up-to-date on the case you helped us with."

"Is the case over then?" she asked, following him into the living room.

"Not quite but almost." He stood in front of the window, looking at the cove. "What a beautiful view from here. This place sits perfectly to take it in."

"It's a lovely spot." She stood behind him. "There's another cottage on the property with an equally beautiful view of the cove. Katie's brother and his friend live there now."

He sensed her nearness. "How are you?" He turned around. Face to face with her, he reached for her hand.

"I'm well. Feeling better and stronger every day." She tugged him toward the chairs. "Sit. Can I get you something to drink or eat?"

"I'd like to take you to lunch if you'll go with me." He gazed at her face, taking in the sparkle in her eyes and the flush on her cheeks.

"Why wouldn't I? I mean, you did come all this way. I'm hungry, and I'd rather not eat alone." She smiled, fluttering her lashes at him. "Let's talk for a few minutes, and then I'm going to take you to a place where Jessie took me. It's a blast from the past."

He reminded himself to breathe. "Sounds good. You have the floor." He sat in one of the floral chairs, enjoying the many expressions crossing her face as she considered what to say. Finally, he could tell she had made up her mind.

"I want to apologize for sleeping the last night when you came to visit me at the hospital. I had a lot I wanted to tell you. I didn't even get a chance to say goodbye." She stood and paced, stopping occasionally to look at him.

"You don't need to apologize." Why was she so nervous? What was going on in her mind? Patience. Give her time, he told himself. "I'm glad you let me in the hospital room after all you went through."

"Why wouldn't I? We did have a nice time at your friend's party." She smiled at him and quickly looked away. "What I want to know is…" She stopped in front of him. "Did you mean what you said to me that night at the hospital?" Her voice softened as she spoke.

"About wanting to get to know you?" he asked, and she nodded.

"That, and when you told me I hadn't seen the last of you. Can I count on you?" She sat across from him on the sofa. "I want to trust you," she whispered.

"I'm not going anywhere. I meant what I said. You fascinate me, Peyton. I would like to get to know you and find out where our friendship might take us. I'd like to believe it's far more than a friendship."

"Okay." She exhaled. "I can live with that. What's next? I mean, you live in Phoenix, and I have yet to determine where I will eventually live. I know it's time for me to leave the city. My last few weeks here have taught me one thing. I want to live among people who care."

"I'll be moving back to the area. I got hired as an FBI agent in one of their field offices. I will need to go through their training for a few weeks. The details haven't been finalized yet, but any of the locations Tom Maxwell talked to me about are not far from here and would be nice places to live. I've already taken time to look around." He sat forward in the chair with more hope than he had arrived with.

"Congrats! That's great news. It is what you wanted, right?" she asked.

"It is." He smiled.

"I've had a few interviews myself." Her fingers toyed with the fringe on the pillow beside her. "I loved the special needs day school in Hanover. It's a beautiful facility with a caring staff. I could commute easily from here. There is another one in Pinedale which is only a ten-minute drive from here. I can continue to work at the company I'm working for now. I will work from home in the afternoon and teach in the mornings at the school. I'm excited for the first time in a long time."

"I'm happy for you, sweetheart." The endearment slipped out naturally. He chose to let it hang in the air between them. "I say we have a celebratory lunch on tap. Later we can talk shop. A lot has happened in the case since you left. I'm sure you have some theories of your own to add after you've had all this time to think." He stood. "While you're at it, you can show me around town."

"My cousin took me to a fun place last night. If it's okay with you, I want to take you there." She tossed the pillow aside.

"I'm game." He reached for her hand, tugging her gently off the sofa. "Lead on."

"At some point, I would like to take you by Jessie's bookstore. It's a great place to hang out, and the coffeeshop right next door is equally wonderful."

He loved the way her eyes lit as her excitement grew. When they got to the door, he stopped her before she went out. "It seems I'm in need of a date for a party tomorrow night. I don't know that many people in the area and could use someone to show me the ropes." He waggled his eyebrows at her.

She laughed, her dimples coming out into full view. "Are you asking me?"

"More like I'm begging you, sweetheart." His body relaxed at the sound of her laughter.

"Since you put it that way, the answer is yes. I like the feeling of control that gives me. I don't remember anyone begging me for a date before." She did a quick curtsey. "Your wish is my command," she stated before she strutted out the door.

Chapter 45

She enjoyed the changing expressions on his face when Franny at the diner called him son. Each of Franny's flamboyant actions found him stifling outright laughter. Lunch had been fun. He asked her several times about any complications of her injuries. She had a few minor setbacks that required antibiotics, but her greatest struggle had been emotionally. He understood. How cool was that?

Later, she took him to the bookstore, where all the ladies fawned over him. His red face under all that gorgeous tanned skin made her laugh inside. Peyton couldn't wait to get him alone. She wanted to talk about the case. Since coming to terms with the new normal in her life and all the rapid changes, it was important for her to understand the why. She owed it to the two scars she carried on her body, as well as to all those who worried about her for the past several weeks.

There were more than a few times she thought this day might never come. Jaxon could be trusted—she would stake her life on it. The fact that he came in one attractive package made it all the better. He thought he had the upper hand, but she had a few surprises of her own for him. It was time to rescue him.

"Okay, ladies, you've taken up enough of Detective Kincaid's time." She leaned close to him and whispered, "Let's make our escape."

"It was a pleasure, ladies." He smiled at them. "I'm sure I'll see you again before I have to leave." He held the door open for her as they left the store. "Thank you." He opened the driver's side of the car for her. "Where to now?"

"One of my favorite spots." She drove to the parking area of the marina. "I sat here many times over the past few weeks. There's something about the ocean that seems to put things in perspective." She put the car in park and unlatched her seatbelt. "I want to know everything you can tell me." She turned to face him as she talked.

"Where do you want to start?" he asked.

"It's your case. You can tell me in the order you want. If I have questions, and I'm sure I will, I'll ask." She leaned her head against the window and waited for him to start.

"It's our case," he corrected her. "Since it started with Carlee and E J Dawson, we can begin there. Carlee, just as you said, was simply in the wrong place and with the wrong person. They had met online and were in the first stages of a crush."

"He liked her, no matter what his friends told you." She closed her eyes. "The first vision I had of them together I saw the way they looked at each other."

"I know he did. Her death broke his heart and deepened his resolve to take them down. Carlee didn't deserve what happened to her. Her parents were heartbroken but thankful to bring her home. They know you had some part in finding her, but with minimal details, of course. They were also grateful for Frank and Radar's part in finding her. Because of that vision and Frank's help, her family and friends were able to lay her to rest and begin the process of grieving. Hopefully, now they can begin to heal, but I doubt parents ever get over the loss of a child."

"Did her autopsy show how she died?" Peyton stretched out the leg that was falling asleep.

"Yes. If you want, you can read the coroner's report. Suffice it to say that it was sad and the details are not comforting. We know there were four different individuals involved because of the DNA found at the crime scene. Two of the suspects are dead, one is recovering, and we're tracking the fourth one. He was the man you must have seen in the shadows. I must admit I was surprised by the details surrounding one of the suspects. I'll tell you more about him later."

"All right, but don't forget. You've got my attention." She reached into her purse for her small notebook and scribbled down the reminder. "Who killed E J?"

"Brice Delaney or his brother, George, which takes the story back to the fourth man." Jaxon frowned. "Remember Brice blamed me for what happened to George?"

"I remember." She searched her mind for any details she could remember. "I admit I'm curious to know who the fourth man you're talking about is. I wasn't sure if he was even real." She shook her head. "So much has happened. It almost seems long ago and strange to me."

"I bet." He paused. "My testimony put George Delaney in prison. He nearly beat his ex-girlfriend to death. His rap sheet was long, including a convenience store robbery, assault with a deadly weapon, and pistol whipping a young store clerk. The teen suffered severe head trauma."

"He sounds like a real loser." She frowned. "I don't understand the rationale for hurting another person. Take the money and leave, for heaven's sake."

"I couldn't agree more. It does make you wonder about some folks." Jaxon's jaw clenched.

"Does his background give you any clues?" she asked.

"The brothers are something of a mystery and the investigation is ongoing." He leaned his head back against the seat. "They had some issues growing up. Broken family, abusive stepfather, in general not a good family life. George never finished high school, and both he and Brice were in and out of trouble over the years."

"Geez, you wonder why some folks even bother to have kids. I know this story all too well." She shook her head. "Sorry to interrupt. Please continue," she encouraged.

"A few weeks before E J's body was found, George escaped from detention. He was cleaning trash on the highway with other prisoners and managed to get away. It wasn't noticed until a bed check later in the evening."

"I don't understand. How is that even possible?" She folded her hands in her lap.

"One of the guards had been paid to turn the other way. Delaney's mom's house and Brice's apartment were under surveillance, but George never showed up there."

"Wasn't Brice the shooter at the Lost Dutchman Mine Museum? I think I remember you telling me he ended up dead there."

"He's the one." Jaxon raked his hand through his

hair and nodded. "He died of a cardiac arrest. Amos told me Brice had a look of terror on his face. I think he might have seen Carlee."

"I bet you're right. Seems like such a waste." She paused to flip through her notebook. "Why did they kill E J?" She glanced at the questions she had written down over the past few weeks. "I remember you said he left a record of some kind. I've also seen several of the reports on the news."

"E J turns out to be a bit of a hero in the story. He got a job at WorldStar Drug Company. After working there for a while, he noticed some unethical practices were going on. In his typical bad boy fashion, he tried to blackmail the president of the company. He was paid to keep his mouth shut. His lavish spending is what led to Carlee's death—it was a warning to him."

"That's so sad. Why is it they always kill the girl to get at the guy?" Her eyes grew misty.

"They did beat him that night, too," Jaxon reminded her.

"Yeah, but they murdered her. They shot at me to get at you, too."

"Point taken. Women have never had it easy. It's a wonder any of them would ever trust a man."

"I guess I should be glad they left him alive long enough to tell the story." She paused. "Sorry again. I'll try to let you finish, but I'm not making any promises I won't interrupt again."

"What the company didn't know was that he had created a digital record and locked a copy in a safety deposit box at the bank." Jaxon reached for her hand, lacing his fingers through hers. "One of the Delaneys killed him. Until we catch George and he talks, we'll never know which one for sure. So far, we haven't recovered the weapon that killed him."

"What did you find on his computer?" she asked. "If it's okay to tell me," she added.

"The company was diluting chemo drugs. People weren't getting the true dosages that were needed for their cancer treatments. With the details he documented, we were able to track to what states and countries the bottles were sent. Also, life-saving antibiotics had been altered. We're only beginning to see how many lives were impacted by the corrupt practices of this company. There were also illegal drugs found at the company's labs—it seems they were also dabbling in heroin, and several patients overdosed. Kilo, Frank's other dog, found evidence of opioids and cocaine, along with magic mushrooms and other hallucinogens. The list was numerous, as I'm sure you've read. E J also left proof of the thugs who worked for the company, along with the names of a few of the people who had been threatened or murdered. Each one had gone to the company's Human Resources with their concerns about the company's operation in some way. They were considered a liability. Several were paid off and let go. A few were threatened, and some simply disappeared."

"Whoa, I guess you have to be careful who you work for." She shook her head.

"All I can say is that this will impact a few of Phoenix's high society members when all the details come out. This part of the case is still under investigation, and charges will soon be filed."

"No wonder I saw all the ghosts of people who were murdered. Without Dawson's computer data, no one would've ever known. Any patient given one of the diluted drugs who died would have simply gone down as victims of their disease not of a corrupt, greedy company. Let alone the mixture of the illegal drugs that they were dealing. I was shocked when I read the list of drugs. I knew the street names from living in New York. We're talking about some dangerous drugs in MDMA, LSD, and the synthetic psychoactive drugs with their speed-like or psychedelic effect on the user."

"You're right. That's exactly what happened. Doctors we talked to that had used these meds said it answered questions for them. Patients who were progressing suddenly got worse and died. I'm sure stories will continue to come out and lawsuits will pile up." He squeezed her hand gently in his.

"How can they sleep at night?" she asked.

"Probably not well now." He changed the subject. "The shooter in Tombstone was ID'd from prints and evidence found on the rooftop." Jaxon glanced out the window at a person jogging by.

"Who was he?"

"A man named Harper. He worked at the station and quit not long after I was made lead detective. He was a plant. His records and schooling had been falsified. Harper wasn't a cop but one of WorldStar Drug's hired thugs. He came highly recommended by a friend of the police commissioner. Harper sent a letter to his wife and kids telling them how sorry he was for what he had done. He is still alive and will face life in prison. He planned to die in a shootout with the cops the night you were shot."

"You can't make this stuff up." If she didn't stop shaking her head, she'd look like a bobble head. "Did you ever find the leak in your department?"

"Yes," he said.

"Let me guess. It had to be someone who knew Harper and could pass along what he heard at the station. Right?"

"Yep. After Harper quit, the custodian, Edwards, another employee of the company, still worked there. He fed information out to the others. Edwards was also one of the shooters the night of the party. He was wounded but escaped. Radar tracked him and he was found dead. The autopsy found something strange though. The coroner is still trying to figure it out."

"What? Don't leave me hanging," she pleaded.

"According to the coroner, Edwards' DNA matches exactly another man's who died several months ago. He's running more tests. As of now, it's a mystery to him—another strange twist to this case. Edwards' signature red hat he always wore was gone. The bullet from Edwards' gun was the one that struck your leg."

"Wow, that's strange." Peyton paused. "Why me? I mean, how did I become a target?"

"Two reasons. You tried to save E J, and you had a connection to me. For that, I'm deeply sorry." He brought her hand to his lips and kissed it.

"Why? It's not your fault. Remember, Carlee is the one who ultimately brought me into the case." Her stomach fluttered. His action was gentle and reassuring.

"True." His thumb stroked the palm of her hand.

"At least it's almost over." She watched him shake his head no.

"Not quite, and I'm concerned. We lost track of George Delaney. He fled the Phoenix area, and there's a manhunt. We have no idea if or when he'll show up. If he ever does," Jaxon mused.

"I guess you'll cross that bridge when you come to it." She patted his hand. "I'm sure you'll get your man." She smiled reassuringly at him.

"My gut tells me that we will." Jaxon took a folded paper out of his wallet. "When I say we I mean you and me. Here's a picture of Delaney. If you see him around town, call Matt. This guy is not a nice person."

She glanced at the photo. "I will. Didn't you say you'll be working under Tom Maxwell?"

"I did. Why?" he asked.

"He's good friends with Matt and Jessie. I thought you should know. Tom has tried to recruit Jessie many times."

"Agent Miller told me that. Once Maxwell hears you're like her, he'll be trying to recruit you." He rubbed his forehead. "As it happens, news travels fast, and Tom is already working on me to recruit you. But I'm selfish. I want to keep you to myself." He held tightly to her hand. "I want you to know your insight and premonitions started and saved this case from becoming a cold case. Stolberg told me to tell you dinner is on him when you come back to testify at the trial."

"I'd like that. Your captain is a nice man. He brought me flowers when he came to visit me in the hospital. I liked his wife too."

Peyton took him around town, showing him all the places that were coming to mean a lot to her. She drove him to Hanover and showed him the school where she might be working. They then went to Pinedale, where she might also have found a job. All in all, it had been perfect. They arrived back at the cottage where they had started the day.

"I'll be here tomorrow at six-thirty for our date. Technically, this is a second date, but I'm calling it our first. A girl needs to be kissed on her first date and not shot." He kissed her cheek and walked out the door. "I'm staying at the inn. I'm not far if you need me."

Chapter 46

Jaxon whistled all the way back to the inn. He could see himself marrying this girl easily. The key would be to take it slow and easy and not to spook her. He smiled at his play on words. How could he spook a woman who saw ghosts? Taking a deep breath of the fresh air fragrant with blooming flowers, he understood why people wanted to live in a place like Blue Cove. Matt Parker had a pretty sweet setup here.

The sound of the surf hitting the shore made the Blue Iris Inn seem almost magical. On a night like tonight, it was hard to believe any of the stories he had heard earlier about the cases that had found their way to this small slice of heaven. They had solved some big ones.

Jessie's friend Katie seemed perfect for her job as the innkeeper. Her guests were treated well. More like pampered to be exact. Jessie had told him all he needed to know about staying there, and about her best friend, including that she was marrying Matt's friend Dylan. She repeated that several times. Jaxon smiled. A not too subtle reminder that her friend was off limits. She made him promise to make it to the inn in time for dinner and reassured him he would be glad that he did. Jessie was adamant that he be there on time.

Jaxon planned on a nice, quiet evening but as he knew all too well plans had a way of changing. After a quick shower and change of clothes, he made his way down the stairs to the dining room. The room was packed with familiar faces and several strangers.

"Everybody. this is Peyton's friend, Jaxon Kincaid," Katie announced. "Be sure to introduce yourself to him."

"Nice to meet you in person. Thanks for taking care of Jessie's cousin." Matt extended his hand.

"Matt Parker?" Jaxon shook his hand.

"That would be me. You already know Sadie and Reba." Matt pointed to where they were seated.

Jaxon acknowledged them with a nod of his head. "I met Reba earlier."

"This is Lawrence Thomas, Reba's husband," Matt said as he introduced them.

"Nice to meet you." Jaxon shook his hand as well.

"One thing you'll know soon enough—if you haven't figured it out already—is that Katie loves for people to have a good time, to eat well, and to get know each other. It's her way of welcoming people to town. The tall, blond guy in uniform standing next to her is her fiancé, Dylan. He's one of my top officers."

"Is this a party then? I thought the party was tomorrow night."

"Not the party. Only a pre-party of sorts." Matt chuckled. "Jessie and Peyton will be here in a few minutes to have dinner with us. The other thing you need to know is that Katie is notorious for matchmaking. She never lets up. I'm giving you fair warning. I can see her eyeing you now. Enjoy the evening, and welcome to town." Matt clapped him on the back. "If you think you're under pressure tonight, wait until tomorrow night. Here she comes. You're on her radar."

Matt wasn't kidding. Katie wasn't hiding her intentions. She never stopped hinting at him all evening. Peyton seemed flustered, which bothered him.

"I'm sorry for Katie pestering you." Peyton leaned toward him. "She can be a bit intense sometimes, but she has a great heart. She and Jessie have been friends forever," she told him.

"It's okay. I have siblings. I've been ribbed and done my share of teasing too. I'm fine. I can hold my own." By the end of the evening, he wasn't still sure he could. He had met his match. Katie was a master at the art of matchmaking.

"Walk with me." Peyton grabbed his hand and pulled him to her side. "I'm happy she did this get-together for you. It's her way of thanking you for taking care of me." She took a quick looked around the room. "They're all wonderful people, and you haven't met everyone yet. Tomorrow there will be even more. You'd better sleep well tonight." She winked at him.

"I will. Thanks for the warning." He liked this flirty version of her. He walked with her through the kitchen to the back door.

"I wanted to tell you all night how beautiful you look," he said.

"That's nice." She stopped at the door and turned to face him, wringing her hands as she stood there.

"Are you okay?" he asked, fascinated by the emotions playing across her face. He knew the moment her decision was made.

"Yes." She sighed, lifting her hands to frame each side of his face and gazing into his eyes. "Thank you."

"For what?" Her touch felt light as a feather but

like liquid heat on his skin.

She leaned closer until he could feel her breath near his mouth. "For restoring my faith in men." She didn't move.

He waited, fixated on her lips only inches from his. And then she kissed him. One long, deliberate, hot kiss. It left him breathing heavily. He couldn't imagine how he looked standing there with his mouth open. Shocked. Stunned perhaps. But before he could gather his senses enough to respond he watched her leave.

She simply squeezed his shoulder before she walked out the door with a coy smile on her face. "Sleep well." She sauntered out, closing the door quietly in his face.

Like that was going to happen. He had dreamed about this moment. Jaxon laughed to himself. And he had been worried about needing to go slow so as not to scare her. Still dumbfounded by his reaction or lack of it, he made his way to the stairs. "Sleep. I don't think so," he mumbled on his way to his room. It would be one long night, but damn, he was happy.

****

What had possessed her to be entirely too bold last night? She had surprised him. What must he think of her? He had given her a brotherly kiss earlier. She laughed. She hadn't meant for hers to be sisterly. Maybe she had gone a bit overboard, but it gave him something to think about. Hopefully, he thought about it all night. He had kissed her senseless once and left her standing alone. "*All is fair in love and war,*" *isn't that what they say*? At least he wouldn't forget her if that kiss had anything to say about it. Her stomach still fluttered when she thought about it.

She wasn't afraid of the new feelings rushing through her. She knew what she wanted and was given a second chance to go for it. She wouldn't let this moment pass her by without giving love her best shot.

She glanced at her new dress hanging on the closet door. The garment was soft as her hand glided over the beautiful material. She could imagine his face when he saw her in it. She wouldn't have long to wait. They say a man shows what he's feeling through his eyes. She planned to watch Jaxon's to see. Jessie had made her try on several outfits until they both knew this was the one. Turning to glance at the clock on her nightstand, she noted he would be there soon. And Jessie should be running through the door any minute.

Picking up the brush she ran it through the hair, pushing it behind her ear while she put on her makeup. Lip gloss with a touch of color on her cheeks, and a bit of mascara topped off by a squirt of perfume, and she was armed with the essentials to meet Jaxon Kincaid. The dress would be the last item in her arsenal. If the past few weeks taught her one lesson, it was you never know how much time you have, so live life. She planned on seizing the day and hoped Jaxon was ready. The kiss last night was round one. The dress and how she looked in it was round two.

Peyton heard the door open. "Is that you Jessie?"

"Yes," Jessie replied, her voice sounding strained.

Strange. Peyton never knew Jessie to be quiet. She always came through the door talking a mile a minute. She tied her robe tight and went to check. Her cousin stood inside the door with a man behind her holding a gun to her back. Peyton knew who he was, no introduction needed.

"Sit!" He pushed Jessie forward hard enough for her fall to the ground. "You're the one I'm looking for." He waved the gun in Peyton's face.

"You." He motioned at her. "Sit down and keep your mouth shut." He shut and locked the door, never taking his eyes off the girls. "Are you going somewhere?"

"I have a date coming in a few minutes."

"Let me guess. Kincaid. My night is complete. I can take you both out at the same time. Damn, this is my lucky night."

"Do you know this jerk?" Jessie asked.

"Shut up!" He pointed the gun at Jessie. "Don't say another word, or I'll shoot."

"George Delaney." Peyton frowned.

"You've heard of me." He puffed out his chest. "I'm famous."

"More like infamous," she hissed at him.

"Who is he, Peyton?" Jessie called out, drawing his attention.

"A wanted man and escapee from an Arizona prison. You know the type. A big tough guy that beats his girlfriend," Peyton answered back. She needed to keep him talking. The louder the better. Jaxon could be walking into a trap. "But not a smart one."

"Does he know my fiancé is a police chief and the place is literally crawling with cops?" Jessie followed Peyton's lead.

"Shut up! You, over there." He motioned at Jessie, shoving her in the back. "Don't open your mouth again," he yelled at Peyton.

****

Jaxon walked down the path from the inn to the

cottage. His hand was ready to knock at the door when he heard a man's voice yell. "I told you two to not to talk. You're driving me nuts." He heard a slap followed by a shriek.

He moved away from the door and moved to a window where he could see in the cottage. Jaxon saw George Delaney holding a gun, pacing in front of the two women. Peyton held her cheek where he had slapped her. His hand fisted. George had sealed his fate the minute he laid his hand on her. Taking his phone out of his pocket, he called Matt Parker.

"Where are you?" Jaxon asked.

"I'm pulling into the inn, why?" Matt asked.

Jaxon explained what was happening inside the cottage. "He has them at gunpoint and nothing to lose. I'm telling you up front. He hit Peyton, and I'm going to do something about it."

"You have to do it by the book. You know I'm right," Matt said.

"Right, but he hit her in the face. Tell me what you would do if it were Jessie?"

"I'd wait for him to resist in some way and then you can guess the rest. Don't do anything until I get there. I'm bringing a few reinforcements." Before he disconnected the call, Matt added, "Remember, if he tries to resist arrest that's a different subject."

Within minutes, Jaxon saw him coming with four others. After Matt viewed the situation inside the cottage, Jaxon and Matt devised a plan. Matt went around to the front door with Dylan and Kip. Gary and Kenny stayed with him. Once in place, they texted their countdown. One kick broke open the front door, and the other well-placed kick sent the back door against the wall. Jaxon flew through the door in enough time to see Peyton do a fancy kick sending the gun flying out of George's hand as Jessie took his legs right out from under him. She hadn't needed him at all.

If he hadn't seen it with his own eyes he wouldn't have believed. "Damn, ladies, that was something to watch." Matt cuffed George as he hurled insults at the two women.

Jaxon got in his face, his hand clenching at his side. "George, I'd keep my mouth shut if I were you. As much as I would love to punch you for hitting my girl. Oh, I can see I shocked you. You left the curtains open and I watched you, man. It might be perfect justice to leave you alone for a few minutes with the women. I think they could curb your tongue. What do you think, chief? Should we let Peyton and Jessie teach this scumbag some manners?"

"It's worth thinking about. Truth is, I'd rather let Gary and Kip book him and not waste any more time with him than I need to. I'd rather be spending it with my fiancée." Matt hugged Jessie, making sure she was all right.

Jaxon grinned at Peyton. "Remind me not to get in the way of that high kick of yours. It's lethal." He touched her red cheek. "Does it hurt?"

"It smarts. Why is it that a man feels the need to slap a woman's face?" The familiar burning sting filled her eyes. "I'm not going to cry."

"It's okay if you do. Did you hurt your wound with that move?" Jaxon asked her quietly.

"No, but now I have to redo my makeup." She pulled away from him and walked into the bedroom.

"Is she okay?" Matt asked as they waited for both

women.

"I think so." Jaxon looked at the closed bedroom door. "Did you see them in action? I broke through the door in time to see her kick, send the gun flying out his hand, and damn if Jessie didn't take his legs right out from under him. It was one beautiful sight."

"Jessie never fails to surprise me. They're a lot stronger than we give them credit for. I learned it the hard way. Jessie can take care of herself. We've saved each other more than a few times." Matt stood when Jessie walked out. "Hey, Kincaid, I think the wait was worth it, don't you?"

He couldn't stop looking at Peyton as she also entered the room. The dress and the girl in it—what more could a man ask for? "You're beautiful," he said in her ear.

She patted his cheek. "Did you sleep well?"

"What do you think?" He grinned.

"I'm only guessing, but I'd say you didn't get much. You sound a bit grouchy." She chuckled.

"Who me, not at all. I'm dreaming of how to get even with you."

"I was hoping you'd say that." Peyton took his hand and closed the door behind them.

They strolled toward the inn. "Not a great beginning to our second first date." He laced his fingers through hers.

"What is it about us and dates? Maybe fate is trying to tell us something." She sighed.

"The message I'm getting is we're perfect together. I mean I can't kick like that. I'd fall flat on my face. I'm good at diversion tactics though and you played your part with precision. I also think that you might fit perfectly in my arms. I've only had you there a few times, but it felt right to me. With your permission I would like to practice a lot tonight and test my theory."

"I'm okay with that." She stopped on the path. "Life is short."

"Yes, it is." He had no idea where she was going with her statement.

"I've learned that recently and was reminded of it again tonight." She started walking and pulled his hand.

"What are you saying?" he asked.

"Thinking out loud, is all." They walked up the stairs to the inn and the night was off.

****

Peyton had one too many run-ins with potential disasters the last few weeks not to enjoy every moment of the evening. Her body tired more quickly than before she was shot, but she wasn't about to go home and sleep. Jaxon had to go back tomorrow, and she planned on staying with him for as long as she could. She danced, flirted, and had a wonderful time. The last dance of the evening she reserved for him alone.

If she had to remember the song, she couldn't. It was nice enough to feel his arms around her. Leaning her head against his chest, she relaxed and felt safe for the first time in weeks

"Do you see what I mean?" he whispered in her ear.

"What?" She gazed into his dreamy eyes. The message was there in his eyes, whispering how he felt about her.

"How perfect you are in my arms. We fit together." Jaxon held her gaze.

"I guess we're good." She turned her face to hide

her smile. To her way of thinking, he was perfect.

"We're better than good, sweetheart, we're great." He grinned at her. "You haven't seen the last of me."

"I should hope not. You can't hold a girl like this and walk away."

"I'm not going anywhere."

"That's nice to know." She pulled his head down close and shocked him again.

A word from the author…

I am a multi-published Amazon best-selling author who writes romantic suspense with a touch of the paranormal. I enjoy writing fiction. The character development, their stories, and the twists and turns in the plot intrigue me. Once I let the characters loose, I can't wait to see where they take me. I'm hooked from the first words on the paper, and I have to keep writing to see how the story ends. Layer by layer I build it until I come to the happy conclusion.

I live in Colorado with my husband and family. I am a member of the RMFWPAL (Rocky Mountain Fiction Writers Published Authors League) and have enjoyed becoming involved in my community as one of the many authors living in Colorado.

I invite you to read one of my Blue Cove Mysteries and see for yourself why Blue Cove is a special and unusual place.

http://www.ionamorrison.com